THE UNKNOWN PAULINE SMITH

Pauline Smith

THE UNKNOWN
PAULINE SMITH

Unpublished and Out of Print Stories, Diaries
and Other Prose Writings
(including her Arnold Bennett Memoir)

Edited and introduced by
ERNEST PEREIRA

Associate editors
SHEILA SCHOLTEN and HAROLD SCHEUB

UNIVERSITY OF NATAL PRESS
PIETERMARITZBURG
1993

ISBN 0 86980 885 0

Cover designed, drawn and lettered by B.J. Heath

Typeset in the University of Natal Press
Printed by Kohler Carton and Print
Box 955, Pinetown 3600
South Africa

CONTENTS

PUBLISHER'S NOTE

The typesetting from which this book has been printed was prepared by A. A. Balkema several years ago. Although it has suffered slightly from excessive handling and long delays the present publishers have decided, in the interests of economy, not to re-originate the work.

PREFACE

This volume of Pauline Smith's miscellaneous prose comprises, in the main, writings which are out of print, have never before been published, or have appeared only in fugitive form. Apart from making accessible to the general reader selections from relatively unknown areas of the author's work, the present volume spans the full range of Pauline Smith's creative life, from the early 'Platkops Children' stories and 'Scottish' sketches to her last, uncompleted novel. What gives the wide diversity of pieces presented here a measure of coherence (and added interest) is their marked autobiographical bent. The scope and the place of these writings in relation to Pauline Smith's life and development as an author are discussed in the Introduction; editorial practices and procedures – as well as the selection and presentation of material – are also explained in the Introduction.

This volume would not have been possible but for the encouragement and assistance of a great number of individuals, and the co-operation of various libraries, museums and other research institutions. In the first place I wish to pay tribute to the well-known Cape Town publisher, Mr A. A. Balkema, who was primarily responsible, over many years, for keeping Pauline Smith's two major works, *The Little Karoo* and *The Beadle*, in print and before the public eye. The present volume was originally prepared for publication as part of a series to mark the centenary of Pauline Smith's birth in 1982; unfortunately Mr Balkema, who initiated the project, could not see it through to completion. Thanks to his associate, Mr J. Kaleveld, and the University of Natal Press, readers will now have the opportunity of becoming acquainted with a much more representative selection of Pauline Smith's work than has been available to date.

We are extremely grateful to the University of Cape Town and the Jagger Library for allowing us to use the Pauline Smith texts reproduced here. I should like also to express my thanks personally to Mrs Pam Stevens, former Chief Librarian, and – as custodians of the valuable Pauline Smith Collection – to Miss Etaine Eberhart and Miss Leonie Twentyman-Jones, whose unfailing kindness and helpfulness made my task very much easier, and much more pleasant.

I wish to thank Mrs Sheila Scholten of Durban, not only for her work on the texts of the 1905 *Diary* and 1934 'Wagon Trip', but for her constant advice, support and encouragement. It was largely owing to her enthusiasm that a new edition of *Platkops Children* has appeared; her contribution to the present volume is acknowledged only in part by the entry on the title-page. She has been colleague, friend, and a tower of strength, throughout.

Professor Harold Scheub of the University of Wisconsin deserves special thanks for focusing attention on two relatively unknown Pauline Smith stories, 'Horse Thieves' and 'The Cart', which he has also edited and introduced for this volume, together with the opening chapters of *Winter Sacrament* – Pauline Smith's last major undertaking.

I wish to express my gratitude to Mrs Olga Hann of Oudtshoorn and her daughter Mary, for providing the extremely useful sketch-map of Pauline Smith's real – and fictional – world of the Little Karoo (adapted for publication by Grant Christison), and to Mrs Jeanne Heywood of the University of Cape Town, who supplied the excellent photograph of the author. Mrs Hann has assisted me greatly by her detailed knowledge of persons and places associated with Pauline Smith.

The former Curator of the C.P. Nel Museum in Oudtshoorn, Mr Naas Ferreira, was most helpful in tracing information, establishing place-names and supplying copies of newspaper cuttings, and his assistance was much appreciated. The Museum now houses a permanent Pauline Smith exhibition.

Numerous other persons have assisted me, Mrs Scholten and Professor Scheub in researching material for this volume. The important work on Pauline Smith by Professor Geoffrey Haresnape of the University of Cape Town is gratefully acknowledged, and to Professor Dorothy Driver, in particular, my thanks for drawing attention to Pauline Smith's almost-forgotten 'Mrs Obbinson's Story'. I regret that it has not been possible to incorporate, in our commentaries and notes, the results of Professor Driver's recent research on Pauline Smith. The late Miss

Babette Taute of Mill River in the Long Kloof; the late Miss Marie Stegmann of Oudtshoorn; the late Mrs R. Morton (née Krausz) of Somerset West; the late Mrs Ethel Hooper (née Morris) of Sedgefield, who accompanied Pauline Smith and Kathleen Taute on the wagon trip of 1934; the Revd Arthur Beddy of Oudtshoorn; Mrs M. Curtis and Mr Charles Sayer of George; Mrs Nan du Plessis (née Coaton) of Rondebosch; the late Mrs J. Attwell of Betty's Bay; Mrs Barbara Thorburn of Johannesburg and Mrs Vanessa Pauline Thorrold of Amanzimtoti (both direct descendants of the Hicks family); the late Dr Arthur Ravenscroft of Leeds University; and Professor Barrie Goedhals of the University of South Africa have all assisted one or more of us with advice, material aid and patient good-humour. Finally, our thanks are due to Ms B.J. Heath, who designed the cover.

In so far as the present volume succeeds in evoking wider interest in the work of Pauline Smith and a truer sense of her achievement as an author, it will have served its purpose. It will also, I trust, give some satisfaction and pleasure to those who have helped bring it into being and to those who, over the years, have worked to gain for Pauline Smith the recognition she deserves. For the faults and failings of this particular endeavour, the editor alone must bear the responsibility.

Ernest Pereira

1982/1992

INTRODUCTION

Born in Oudtshoorn on 2nd April 1882, Pauline Smith spent a happy childhood in the Little Karoo and among people she grew to know and love. She was particularly close to her father, a doctor, who, despite his 'English' background, endeared himself to the predominantly Afrikaans-speaking community and at one time served as mayor. At the age of 13, Pauline was sent to boarding school in England; soon after, and quite unexpectedly, her father died – a blow from which the sensitive, withdrawn girl never fully recovered. To console herself, she began writing the imaginative childhood sketches, stories, and verses which, many years later, were to be published as *Platkops Children*.

In 1905 Pauline returned to South Africa with her mother for a visit of five months, recording in her diary the friends and places they visited. In December 1908, while staying at an hotel in Switzerland, she met the novelist Arnold Bennett, then in the full tide of success with the publication of *The Old Wives' Tale*. He took an interest in the shy, unhappy girl who 'wrote a little', and was struck by the potential of the Platkops sketches. With his constant encouragement and support, Pauline Smith began consciously to work at her craft, though she was always to find writing a slow and painful process. (A constant sufferer from neuralgia, she was not physically strong, and her diaries and letters contain frequent references to headaches and illness.) On a return visit to South Africa in 1913-14, she kept a journal in which she recorded her impressions and made copious notes of the homes, customs, speech, anecdotes, and attitudes of the Little Karoo farmers. When she returned to England, these became the raw material for the eight stories which, with Bennett's support, were published under the title of *The Little Karoo* in 1925. A year later came her novel, *The Beadle,* and more stories and sketches were written in the next few years, during which she paid another visit (1926-27) to South Africa. In 1931, however, Arnold Bennett died, and with that the driving force behind Pauline Smith's authorship was lost. She produced a sensitive, 90-page memoir, *A.B. '. . . a minor marginal note'.* in 1933, but after this her only important publication was *Platkops Children,* issued in 1935.

There were frequent visits to the Cape throughout the 1930s, but then war intervened and Pauline Smith lacked the health, and the spirit, to undertake further trips. During all these years she lived in virtual seclusion with her widowed sister and one-time Platkops playmate, Dorothy Webster, in Dorset. A year before her death on 29 January 1959, she was presented with an illuminated address, a tribute to her art and vision by 25 South African writers. She bequeathed her surviving manuscripts, letters, and memorabilia to the University of Cape Town Library, which now has a fine collection of Pauline Smith material.

For those readers who know Pauline Smith only as the author of *The Little Karoo* and *The Beadle,* the present volume will come as a distinct and, I trust, pleasant surprise. The centenary of Pauline Smith's birth was celebrated in 1982: to mark the occasion the publisher, A.A.Balkema, decided to issue a special centenary edition of her two 'classics', as well as the long out-of-print *Platkops Children* and selections from the unpublished and fugitive writings. A facsimile reprint of *Platkops Children* came out in 1982, with an introduction by Sheila Scholten. Of the journals and diaries kept by Pauline Smith on her numerous return visits to South Africa, the most important is the 1913-14 *South African Journal,* which contains much of the material she subsequently worked into the Little Karoo stories and *The Beadle.* A substantial selection from the *Journal,* edited and introduced by Professor Harold Scheub, was intended as a companion volume to this one.

An author's 'miscellaneous prose' often amounts to little more than the gleanings or sweepings of the crop. In Pauline Smith's case, it soon became apparent that there was a wealth of writings, some unpublished, others lost to sight, which were not only of intrinsic value, but revealed excitingly new aspects of the author's craft. Long before she was encouraged by Arnold Bennett to keep a daily journal, Pauline Smith was recording, in her 1905 *Diary,* impressions and observations of people and places in the Little Karoo which she obviously intended to put to use later. By the time of her 1905 visit she had written many of the *Platkops Children* pieces and had even appeared in print, as the author of a number of amusing 'Scottish' sketches and stories, set among Lowland communities and featuring characters she had come to know in the years following her father's death. These early endeavours, most of which appeared in the *Evening Gazette* after the turn of the century (under the pen-name of 'Janet Tamson'), are now generally inaccessible; for this reason one such story, *Aunt Elizabeth in the Highlands,* has been included in my selection, together with a hitherto unpublished *Platkops Children* sketch, called 'Martinus in the Mountains'. Another tale which has obvious connections with the *Platkops* series is 'Mrs Obbinson's Story': this was first published in 1931, in the *Cape Times Annual.* Professor Harold Scheub, editor of the 1913-14 *South African Journal,* was responsible for drawing attention to two other half-forgotten stories, 'Horse Thieves' and 'The Cart', which appeared in the *Cape Argus* in the period 1925-27. These stories, with an introduction by Professor Scheub, were reprinted in *English in Africa,* in March 1981. They reappear here, together with an abridged version of the introduction, because they conclusively demonstrate what few readers of *The Little Karoo* and *The Beadle* would suspect: that Pauline Smith has a great gift for humour, for perceiving and exploiting the comic potential of character and situation. The two stories are in my opinion noteworthy also for their uncanny anticipation of the 'Oom Schalk Lourens' tales of Herman Charles Bosman, which are set in the Marico Bushveld and were written in the early 1930's. What the two authors have in common is a shrewd but sympathetic insight into the world of the backveld Afrikaner, and an ability to expose the limitations and incongruities of that world through the self-revelations – ranging from the ludicrous to the profoundly ironic – of their leading characters. The humour lies as much in the teller as in the tale, in the mastery of a deliberate, quasi-Afrikaans idiom and cadence, and of the dead-pan 'throw-away' line which undercuts – with hugely comic, or deadly satiric, effect – the seeming seriousness

of what has gone before. The last of the stories included in Part
One of this volume, 'The Doctor', is also Pauline Smith's longest
and one of her most remarkable achievements. The story is
clearly autobiographical and contains many allusions to persons
Pauline Smith knew: this may explain why she never published
it. 'The Doctor' did, however, appear in a selection of South
African short stories edited by A.D.Dodd, in 1970: it merits a
place here as a most complex, poignant, and self-revealing piece
of work.

What the seemingly unrelated writings brought together in
the present volume have in common is, in fact, a strong personal
element. In one sense, of course, all creative writing *is* autobiographical, for as the poet Keats said: 'A man's life of any worth
is a continual allegory – and very few eyes can see the Mystery
of his life . . . Shakespeare led a life of Allegory: his works are
the comments on it.' In Pauline Smith's case, everything she
wrote came out of her own observation and experience: as she
later remarked, 'In my work I could set down nothing which I
did not "see" or, often painfully, feel and know to be true'.
By this of course she did not mean literal truth or mere adherence
to fact; the more one studies her writings, letters and diaries, however, the clearer it becomes how much she relied on fact, on
actual observation, firsthand accounts of persons and events,
for the raw material of her stories – and this applies as much to
diction and character as it does to setting. Hence, I believe, the
potential usefulness of a volume such as this one, offering as it
does a cross-section of Pauline Smith's surprisingly varied –
though never prolific – oeuvre.

Section Two of this selection is indisputably autobiographical,
encompassing a substantial selection from the 1905 *Diary* as
well as Pauline Smith's account of her 1934 'Wagon Trip'. Sheila
Scholten, who has edited and introduced both of these docu-
ments, was the first to unlock the riches of the 1905 *Diary,*
which had to be typed from the author's notoriously cramped
handwriting. The 'Wagon Trip' is a fascinating – though somewhat hastily compiled – record of a trip by mule-wagon, under-
taken by the author and two friends at the beginning of 1934.
What is remarkable about it is that Pauline Smith, chronic

sufferer from neuralgia and already in her fifties, should have
found the energy and enthusiasm to embark on such a hazardous
and physically exhausting expedition (it was in the heat of
January) – and at a time, moreover, when she was still deeply
under the impression of Arnold Bennett's death. The 'Wagon
Trip' is noteworthy, too, in that this expatriate South African
author should have set out, several years before the symbolic
'ossewa-trek' of 1938, to recreate and experience for herself
the kind of life led by the Voortrekker women of a hundred
years earlier.

The two art-forms which Pauline Smith set herself to master
were the short story and the novel. Her 'Scottish' sketches and
the verses she wrote for *Platkops Children* were relatively early
efforts; her only other venture was in the field of drama – a
one-act play entitled 'The Last Voyage', written in the late
1920's. It was such a palpable failure that she never repeated the
experiment. 'The Last Voyage' has been published in a selection
of one-act plays edited by A.D.Dodd and F.O.Quinn (Juta, 1970);
it does not bear reprinting here. After the success of *The Little
Karoo,* Pauline Smith did, however, continue to produce some
very fine short stories: some of them found a place in a later,
enlarged edition of her first collection, others are featured here.
She also started work on a second novel, tentatively called
Winter Sacrament. As Professor Scheub points out in his introduction to this never-to-be-completed saga, the task occupied
her, on and off, for some 25 years. What emerges is a sad story
of futile endeavour in the face of failing powers – spiritual as
much as physical – and especially in her letters to Frank Swinnerton, with whom she frequently corresponded during the last
decades of her life, the pathos of her efforts to 'get down to'
the writing of her novel becomes painfully apparent. There are
in the University of Cape Town's Pauline Smith Collection
numerous typed and ms drafts of the opening chapters of *Winter
Sacrament*; there is also an introductory piece headed 'Background to Platkops' which was obviously intended to provide a
historical as well as physical setting for the novel. What we have
of Pauline Smith's text provides abundant evidence of the care

with which she pruned and polished her work; there are hints of
the tensions and conflicts of character to come, but little to
suggest that the novel, if completed, would have risen above the
level of a 'historical romance', despite its undeniable poetic force.
Whatever one's impression of it, *Winter Sacrament* has intrinsic
interest as Pauline Smith's last major undertaking. It completes
the cycle of her creative life, which begins with such 'apprentice-
work' as the stories of her Platkops childhood and Scottish
adolescence, progresses to the maturity of vision and power
evidenced in her work of the mid-'twenties and 'thirties, and
lapses slowly – though not without a struggle – into a sterile
and premature old age.

The death in 1931 of Arnold Bennett, who had nurtured –
and nagged – the budding talent into full flower over a period
of some 15 to 20 years, must have been almost as grievous a
blow to Pauline Smith as had been the sudden death of her
father, just before the turn of the century. Then, the trauma
had been lessened – though never altogether overcome, as 'The
Doctor' makes plain – by having recourse to the memory of
her childhood years in Oudtshoorn. One of the most noteworthy
features of the *Platkops Children* stories is that they are entirely
unsentimental in their evocation of the child's-eye view of the
world – a world that must still have been painfully close to the
surface of the young author's consciousness, at the time of
writing. If the death of Arnold Bennett brought about a similar
crisis in the life of Pauline Smith, it also showed her the way to
assuage her grief, by recalling the past – not in fictional form,
however, but by way of a memoir in which she could relate the
story of her long apprenticeship to 'the Master' and the friendship that they enjoyed over the years. Like *Platkops Children,
A.B.'. . . a minor marginal note'* succeeds admirably in avoiding
excess sentiment, giving us a delightfully humorous but by no
means uncritical view of Arnold Bennett. It is a notable achievement, not least because it shows us Pauline Smith writing with
wit, sophistication and confidence about a world entirely foreign
to that of the Little Karoo and its people. One of the surprises
in store for South African readers of *A.B.* is the discovery that

'their' Pauline Smith inhabited two very different worlds, that
she was a celebrity in Britain and America long before she was
recognized as an author of stature in the country of her birth,
and that she was far more widely read and widely travelled than
is generally realized. If the *A.B.* memoir does nothing else, it
should draw attention to these almost forgotten aspects of
Pauline Smith's life and work; it also makes delightful reading
and fully warrants republication here, for it has been out of
print for close on 50 years. A short essay entitled 'Why and
How I Became an Author' aptly introduces Pauline Smith's tribute to the man who turned her 'why' and 'how' into realities.

The widely divergent and markedly autobiographical character
of the pieces brought together in this volume, suggested the need
for a contextual framework – some means of relating the writings to Pauline Smith's life or of assessing them in in terms of
her development as an author. My introductory survey is intended
to supply the necessary perspective; more specific discussion is
provided by way of brief introductions to the individual stories
and other prose writings. Those introductory sections which
were not supplied by the present editor, will have the author's
name at the end. The commentaries are for the benefit of readers
who wish to learn more about the nature and quality of the
piece in question, or about the occasion which gave rise to it;
they are not essential to the reading and enjoyment of the texts.
The same holds true of the notes we have appended to the 1905
Diary: they are intended to elucidate obscure references and to
identify persons, places and events which may be of local as
well as more general historical interest. The notes have been
placed at the end of the text (together with an interesting supple-
mentary piece) in order not to clutter the printed page; for the
same reason explanatory glosses have been kept to a minimum.
Such glosses are given in square brackets in the text itself, so that
the reader does not have to cast about for meanings or English
equivalents.
   Pauline Smith's mss, and even her typescripts, are often idio-
syncratic and inconsistent in matters of punctuation and spelling.

Obvious slips of the pen have been silently corrected; all amper-
sands have been replaced by 'and'; spelling and punctuation have
been regularized wherever possible; and names of persons referred
to by initials only have been given in full. Only where significant
deviations in spelling and idiom occur have these been retained:
they are signalled in the usual way, or are followed by a gloss.
(Pauline Smith's 'Afrikanderisms' are explained only where the
meaning is obscure: her attempts at rendering Dutch-Afrikaans
terms and expressions in anglicized form sometimes result in
grotesque hybrids, such as 'forehaus' (Afr. 'voorhuis') for front
room, parlour, or sitting-room. In all such cases the English equivalents have been supplied.

All editorial emendations or interpolations, other than those
noted above, are clearly indicated; wherever words or passages
have been deleted – this applies mainly to the 1905 *Diary* –
the normal typographical practice (. . .) has been followed. The
texts themselves have been checked against the original mss and
typescripts, where these are available: there are consequently
slight but sometimes significant differences between the texts as
reproduced here, and the form in which they first appeared in
newspaper, journal or anthology. In the case of *A.B.'. . . a minor
marginal note'* the text is that of the published edition of 1933:
necessary explanations are supplied in the Introduction.

A useful adjunct to a volume of this nature is a map showing
places referred to and routes travelled. Readers of the 1905
Diary and 1934 'Wagon Trip' will want to locate the various
towns and places Pauline Smith visited, and gain some idea of
distance, direction and topography. The sketch-map reproduced
on pages 130–1 in Part Two makes no claim to absolute accuracy; it will, however, help the reader keep track of Pauline
Smith's movements during her visits and enable him to identify
many of the towns and geographical features alluded to, often
by approximation, in her more specifically creative writings.
Pauline Smith's understandable reluctance to limit the imaginative range of her work by using real names and adhering to historical and geographical fact, resulted in the adoption of thinly-
disguised codes, such as 'Princestown' for 'Georgetown' (now

George) and 'Teniquotas' for 'Outeniqua Mountains'. Sometimes, of course, she gets a name wrong, or refers to places which no longer exist or have been re-named. Many of these otherwise elusive or simply puzzling references will, I trust, be resolved if the reader has recourse to the map.

The purpose of this volume of miscellaneous prose writings will have been well served if it gives readers, both in South Africa and abroad, some idea of the range and variety of Pauline Smith's work, the new directions she explored, and her capacity for humour as well as pathos, for shrewd observation as well as sympathetic insight. That readers will find much here to interest and entertain them I have little doubt: besides examples of her finest and most carefully crafted work, there are pieces of a more personal nature, revealing the woman as well as the author and allowing us to see for ourselves the raw materials from which she fashioned the structure and wove the fabric of her stories. Insights into the creative processes of a writer's art can take us beyond immediate enjoyment to an understanding and appreciation of the nature, the strengths as well as the limits, of his or her genius: as author and artist, this above all is what Pauline Smith would have wanted.

E.P.

PART 1
STORIES

'AUNT ELIZABETH IN THE HIGHLANDS': AN INTRODUCTORY NOTE

In the years following the sudden death of her father in 1898, Pauline Smith found solace in the writing of stories and sketches based on her childhood recollections of their life in Oudtshoorn ('Platkops dorp'), as well as her experience of Scotland, where her mother settled and most of her family lived. The Scottish pieces − including some examples of verse − were published in the *Evening Gazette* and *Aberdeen Free Press,* under the pen-name of 'Janet Tamson' during the period 1902-1905. Of the 'Platkops Children' sketches only one, 'The B'loon Man' seems to have been published; this appeared in the *Evening Gazette* of 31 August 1910 under the name of 'Janet Urmson'.

It was the handful of 'Platkops Children' pieces which impressed Arnold Bennett when he met P.S. in Switzerland, in the winter of 1908-9; the Scottish material, he remarked, 'anybody could have written'. Nevertheless, these first efforts are of interest as they reveal an unusual grasp, in so young a writer, of character and situation and, in particular, the peculiarities of dialect and parochial ways of life. The humorous 'Eltra' tales and sketches published in the *Evening Gazette* in 1902-3, exhibit a strong local flavour, with 'my Aunt Elizabeth' prominent as precipitator of minor crises in the lives of the village tenantry. This regional focus was of course to be the dominant feature of P.S.'s later work; as an example of the author's concern with the character, speech and custom of a particular locality or community, 'Aunt Elizabeth in the Highlands' may well be worth rescuing from the limbo of newspaper archives. Its limitations become apparent (thus endorsing Arnold Bennett's judgment) if one compares it with any of its 'Platkops Children' counterparts − or even with the rather later 'Martinus in the Mountains'.

E.P.

3

AUNT ELIZABETH IN THE HIGHLANDS:
THE 'PIPERS'

My Aunt Elizabeth came "quite prepared for anything," she
said, with awful resignation in her tone, and much emphasis on
"anything". When a woman does a thing against her will she
puts herself through a sort of preparation for the worst; while,
in justification of her own presentiments, the worst is discovered
in every conceivable shape and form.

To my Aunt Elizabeth the Highlands meant Gaelic and
whisky, bagpipes and kilts, and beautiful scenery, and fleas.

When a tipsy mannie got into the train at Inverness and made
the compartment mournful with his maudlin, sing-song, wailing
Gaelic, Elizabeth nudged me vigorously, and informed me this
was "a Hieland custom". Then came the whisky. They drank it
freely and openly, to the amazement of my dear relation, who
thinks that if men drink at all they should do it in tunnels and
secret places, and behind their newspapers and things, like low-
landers and Christians. But that was not all. In a corner of the
carriage sat a woman nursing a baby. The whisky was handed to
her. "Hieland custom" moaned my aunt, with visions of her
own turn coming. The woman accepted the drink, and — "Mercy!"
was all Elizabeth could utter.

As for the kilts; the first we saw adorned the precious legs of
an infant of four.

Then came the bagpipes. Well! Have you ever heard bagpipes?
Do you know their piteous wail and squeak? Their peculiar
resemblance to pigs in dire distress!

Coming as we did from a land where india-rubber melts, my
sister Dorothy had had little opportunity of becoming acquainted
with that particular musical instrument, and when for the first
time in her life she heard the woeful strains she could think of
nothing less than the arrival of the Turks, of whose appearance
for the purpose of battle at Eltra she had lived in daily dread.
The vision of being dragged to Turkey, and there placed in a
harem took possession of her terrified imagination. With all the
firmness characteristic of the least of her actions, she determined

4

to save herself from that awful fate, and knowing that drowning is supposed to be the easiest death, she fled to the mill dam. It was not till she reached the water's edge that curiosity got the better of her. She turned and looked back. Over the hill came a brake full of picnickers, and on the box sat a man in petticoats hugging a pig under his arm.

To my Aunt Elizabeth, after the singing of Shonat (which comes so near heaven that it somehow doesn't count), the sweetest music on earth is "There is a Happy Land" played on an old harmonium with one hesitating little finger by William John. But then my Aunt Elizabeth is not at all musical. Indeed if a body be "doon i' the mou'" we get her to sing, and the result is far, far beyond any that even Patti could hope to produce. So perhaps it is no wonder that, to Shonat's great sorrow, Elizabeth has never been able to see any beauty in bagpipes. How some people (mostly the senseless English they are to be sure) can rave about bagpipe music is "beyond her a' thegither". Even Shonat's singing of "Wi' a hundred pipers an' a', an' a'," though it left her dim eyed, left her also firmly contesting that the music of most pipers is just like that of squeaking shoon, which may be heard in any kirk on any Sabbath of the year.

I do not know if she is right, but Shonat has since declared that all we suffered afterwards was merely sent as a judgment upon Elizabeth for daring to lower the pipes to the level of "squeaking shoon." Certain, however, it is that we suffered much from both during our visit to the Highlands.

I think I explained that my Aunt Elizabeth started on her travels in her Sabbath coat and skirt, her second Sabbath hat, and her grand new Sabbath shoon. Well, no sooner had she stepped on the famous Hielan' platform, clutching the little yellow tin box of provisions, than there arose a mournful and unmistakable wailing squeak. I looked at my Aunt, usually the quietest of women, in amazement. But there was no denying it. She was clearly in possession of the pair of "pipers" whose music had startled me. "Elizabeth," I cried, "what shall we do? Everybody will be staring at us."

Elizabeth tightened her grasp on the little yellow tin box

while she held her breath. "I aye kent we'd create a sensation in these heathenish pairts," she said, and started for the luggage van in a determined manner. Immediately the "pipers" struck up what must have been a "march of a Forbes woman," what little there is of Elizabeth not Elizabeth, being Forbes.

Through the long tiresome struggle for our luggage the music sank to a wail — "a lament" I suppose Shonat would have called it. But when at last a man came up and, touching his cap, took possession of our goods and chattels, the music regained its dignity. Elizabeth had never been met by a man in her life before, at least not that kind of a man you know, she informed me in a breathless whisper as she rescued the little yellow tin box from his precarious hold. The man marched us to a carriage; not a governess cart, or a gig, mind you, but a carriage. And Elizabeth had never been met by a carriage before, either, I learned in another breathless whisper. She stepped into it, however, in her very best everyday manner, and as she did so the squeak of her "pipers" became almost triumphant.

With the little yellow tin box safe once more upon the seat opposite to us, Elizabeth and I were driven up to an old-fashioned, white-washed farm-house, and "piped" to a long low-roofed room, through the open windows of which clambered a wild white rose. That was the beginning, but by no means the end.

After tea a great loneliness took possession of my Aunt Elizabeth. Visions of her dear, cement-floored kitchen rose before her. There was Shonat in that kitchen singing "Robin Adair," which is Elizabeth's favourite, and "A wonderful musician" which is William John's, and "stopping a' the wark" as only she knows how. Elizabeth sighed. "Aye me," she said, "if only she were here to make us laugh. And infected by Elizabeth's mood, visions of home-sickness, of which disease I have had lamentable experience, rose before me.

"Let's go for a walk," I suggested in desperation.

"Well," said Elizabeth, slowly, "we'll go to the station and see an Aberdeen train come in, and maybe a kent face."

We set off. In the square as we passed through two drummers and four pipers stood drumming and piping as for dear life; but

Elizabeth and I were too unhappy to heed them. It seemed to us that the air was filled with nothing but squeaking shoon.

We returned from the station lonelier than ever, our souls filled with a melancholy equalling the most lamenting of pipers.

As soon as the privacy of our bedroom was reached, Elizabeth took off her shoes. She wasn't going out again, she said. She did not want to hear those "pipers" any more. So after we had cleaned all the boots we could lay hands on, to the utter amazement of the maid, we wrote a graphic description of our reception at the station, and the "sensation we were creating" to our people at Eltra.

I do not know if the sensation we created next day was of the kind Elizabeth had hoped for, but a sensation it certainly was. She determined that I should accompany her to the kirk in my "pretty dress and rosy hat." But trying to make one "look bonny" took longer than she calculated, and we arrived at the church door to find the service already begun. The beadle, either because our gardener impressed him, or because he deemed us in need of a lesson, marched us up to the very front pew. The minister, standing silent in the pulpit, watched us till we became safely seated, while through the expectant church rose the continued wail of Elizabeth's "pipers!"

Nor was this the only occasion on which we were put to shame by our musical attendants, for never during our stay in the Highlands did we take the air without the painful accompaniment of wails and squeaks, laments and triumphs.

This constant attendance upon us alarmed my mother. When letter after letter reached her containing fresh proof of the humiliation our "pipers" wrought us, she wrote saying she knew they were not "piping for nothing," and that the sooner we got rid of them the better. Should they prove too much for us the aid of the landlady must be called in.

The wisdom of my mother struck us so forcibly that we determined to get rid of our musical attendants without further ado. The way hit upon by my Aunt Elizabeth was, if not an original, yet a somewhat peculiar one. She led those "pipers" of hers through and over all the ditches, pools, and puddles which came her way. Every afternoon she took long walks in the regions of mill dams, burns, and marshy places, and bespattered those pipers with mud, tramping through it as if mud were her natural element, quite regardless of the fact that the shoon she wore were her Sabbath ones. Whenever it rained we were out and away doing for those tiresome wailers. And this treatment did at last do for them, for before we left the Highlands my aunt was, to her great satisfaction, able to take the air in a quiet and lady-like manner "without anybody kennin' she was doing it."

"But, whatever," cried my guileless mother, "led you to creating such an impression in the place as to cause those pipers to pipe you wherever you went?"

"Well," began my Aunt Elizabeth, the burden of what Uncle Alexander-in-law calls my great sin of exaggeration lying heavy on her conscience, "it was my Sabbath shoon."

"Your Sabbath shoon!" cried my mother, wondering why on earth that part of Elizabeth's apparel should play such an important part in the sensation we created. My aunt groaned softly. Unlike most people, she found it more difficult to confess my faults than her own. She looked at her feet and then at me; desperation was in her eye, and a twinkle in the wrinkle round it.

"Aye," she began again, "my Sabbath shoon, they costit—"

This was too much for mother. "It's the pipers," she cried, "the pipers I am asking about."

"Twal-an-sax the pair," finished Elizabeth triumphantly, thinking that now all would be understood.

"Twal-an-sax for the pair of pipers! Did you pay that for them?" cried that economical lady, my mother, aghast.

"At Aiberdeen," nodded Elizabeth, complete satisfaction writ large over her countenance. "Calf-skin the soutar ca'ed them and good for the money. But they squeakit awfa'."

'MRS OBBINSON'S STORY' AND 'MARTINUS IN THE MOUNTAINS': AN INTRODUCTORY NOTE

These two pieces are referred to in the 1913-14 *South African Journal,* as part of the 'Platkops Children' series: concluding the entries headed 'North Station' (24 February - 10 March 1914), Pauline Smith remarked: 'I finished Mrs Obbinson and Martinus-in-the-mountains in case they should be needed but have no particular hope now of hearing from M.M.'. The Cape Town publisher, Maskew Miller, had been approached by P.S. early in February, with an eye to publication of the 'Platkops' stories (they had been highly commended by Arnold Bennett). Maskew Miller had expressed great interest and the question of an illustrator was discussed, but in the event the publisher allowed the matter to lapse and *Platkops Children* appeared only in 1935, under the imprint of Jonathan Cape.

Although it has a 'Platkops Children' frame of reference, 'Mrs Obbinson's Story' is rather different in character from the series of sketches and stories included in the 1935 volume, and this probably accounts for its appearing separately in the *Cape Times Annual* for December, 1931. 'Martinus in the Mountains', on the other hand, is very much in the narrative style of *Platkops Children,* but was originally written as an introductory sketch to the story 'Horse Thieves', based on anecdotes related to P.S. by Thys Taute of Mill River, and recorded in her 1913-14 *South African Journal* (the typescript is headed: 'Martinus in the Mountains, and the Horse Thieves'). P.S. apparently realized that 'Horse Thieves' was an essentially adult-orientated story, with a very different brand of humour: she abandoned the introductory sketch (which is now printed for the first time) and published 'Horse Thieves' separately, in the *Cape Argus* for 8 January, 1927. By then she had written another story, 'The Cart', in much the same vein as 'Horse Thieves': this appeared in the *Cape Argus* a year earlier, on 19 December 1925. These two tales, with their remarkable anticipation of the 'Schalk Lourens' stories of Herman Charles Bosman (conceived and written in the early 1930's), are reprinted below, following on 'Mrs Obbinson's Story' and 'Martinus in the Mountains'.

E.P.

MRS OBBINSON'S STORY

All Platkops children loved Mrs Obbinson — the gentle round-faced little old Englishwoman who, when the rains came, tied up her house in tarpaulin. Her story, which ended with the tarpaulin, began for them always with "getting married in England to Mr Obbinson in a muslin dress and bonnet." Mr Obbinson was a Hertfordshire carpenter who, soon after his marriage, came suddenly to think that he would make his fortune in South Africa. So to South Africa he came, and Mrs Obbinson came too, bringing her muslin dress in a little hairy trunk and her bonnet in a hand-box. What Mr Obbinson brought was a carpet bag, his tools in a straw basket, and a firm belief in fortunes.

They came in a sailing-ship, the *John Dixon* of London, and it took them ninety days to reach Cape Town. "Didn't you get tired sitting ninety days in a ship like that?" the doctor's little daughters, her most particular friends, would ask her. And Mrs Obbinson would answer: "Why, no, my loves! The ladies sewed and washed and ironed, just like in a house, you know, and sometimes helped the cook to cook. And the gentlemen shot." What the gentlemen, so surprisingly, shot was not themselves or one another, but the sea birds which from time to time as they neared land, came circling round the ship. And it was with the feathers of these birds, collected carefully in a pillowslip with the feathers of the poultry killed on board by the cook, that Mrs Obbinson had begun the making of the feather bed upon which she still slept.

Of Cape Town Mrs Obbinson had strangely little to tell, though she could never forget, she said, how the land rocked when first she stepped out on it. In those days passengers were rowed ashore in ships' boats and landed on the beach. And on the beach, sitting on the beginnings of her feather bed on top of the hairy trunk, with her bandbox on her lap and Mr Obbinson's carpet bag by her side, Mrs Obbinson had been left alone, praying to herself and wondering if she would ever get accustomed to the strange black faces around her, while Mr Obbinson went into the town in search of the work which was to bring him his fortune.

10

"Did you *like* it," the little girls would ask, "sitting all alone on the beach like that?" And Mrs Obbinson would answer in her clear placid voice: "Why, no, my loves – I don't think I *liked* it. But Mr Obbinson had often to leave me alone when he went looking for his fortune, you know."

When at last, on that first day of his hunt, Mr Obbinson returned to his wife it was to tell her that he had been engaged to go to Platkops dorp as one of the carpenters wanted for the building of a new church there. And to Mrs Obbinson's question "Where was Platkops?" he had replied that he didn't know – a state of ignorance which never failed to impress all Platkops children when they heard of it! Who in these days, with them all living in it, could fail to know where Platkops was? All, however, that Mr Obbinson could then tell his wife was that a wagon was leaving for Platkops in half an hour and they were to travel by it. So to the Market Square they went, Mr Obbinson carrying his tools and the beginning of the feather-bed, Mrs Obbinson carrying the bandbox, and a "black man," as Mrs Obbinson called him, following with the hairy trunk and the carpet bag.

In the Market Square, under the shadow of Table Mountain, which Mrs Obbinson remembered but vaguely, so great was her preoccupation with the affairs of the moment, they found their wagon – one with a span of sixteen oxen and belonging to old Hendrick Cornelis, who, with his wife Betje, had brought some of the produce of his farm to Cape Town and was now returning to his home in the Platkops district. And no sooner had Mr and Mrs Obbinson climbed into the wagon than, at the crack of Oom Hendrick's long bamboo whip, the oxen began to move slowly out of the square on their homeward journey.

This journey took ten days and still marked for Mrs Obbinson the great adventure of her life. The month was September and the veld gay with spring flowers. "Like a carpet it was," she would say, and like a carpet the little girls would see it, with their dear Mrs Obbinson journeying across it. For ten days this journey lasted, and for ten days neither Oom Hendrick nor his wife Tan'

11

Betje, who could speak no English, nor Mr and Mrs Obbinson, who could speak no Dutch, took off their clothing. Yet strange as it was to be so long without undressing, and strange as it was to sleep in a wagon at night with Oom Hendrick and Tan' Betje on one side of her, and Mr Obbinson on the other, Mrs Obbinson was happy. And so, she would add, would Mr Obbinson have been had he only been able to forget his fortune. But this, neither then nor after, did he manage to do.

So, day after day, they went steadily on, trekking, outspanning and trekking again, building fires in the day time to make coffee and roast their salt ribbetjes, and building fires at night to keep the jackals and leopards and wild beasts away. Now and then they passed through a village, and of these it was Princestown, at the foot of the Teniquota mountains, that Mrs Obbinson remembered most clearly. When she came to that most English of settlements, with its low white-washed, thatched houses standing far back from the wide grass-grown oak-lined streets on the edge of the great forest lands she had cried, "Oh, couldn't we stop here?" And Mr Obbinson had answered "No." Platkops for fortunes – and on to Platkops they had journeyed.

Their way now lay across the great Teniquota mountains by a pass of such steepness that many oxen had met their death here, leaving their bones to whiten on the mountain side. And though Oom Hendrick took his wagon, his oxen and his passengers all safely across, Mrs Obbinson could never speak of this part of the journey without regret for the sufferings of the span, whose names she had come to learn and could still repeat – Spielman, Hartman, Koopman, and the rest . . . . Because of the terrors of this precipitous pass she never re-crossed the Teniquota mountains, and it was from the top of the pass that, for the last time in her life, she looked down upon the far blue line of the sea. Having looked her last upon it, down into the wide Platkops plain she went, and in this plain all the rest of her days were spent.

At this time Platkops dorp, in the heart of the plain, was but a long straggle of white-washed mud-walled houses on the left bank of the Ghamka River, with the Coffee-house and old Dutch

12

church at one end of the only street, and the new stone gaol at the other. Mid-way between the gaol and the Coffee-house came the half-built walls of the new stone church, in which Mr Obbinson hoped to find the road to fortune. But it seemed to Mrs Obbinson, when Oom Hendrick and his wife left her at the Coffee-house and went on to their farm, a strange place for fortunes.

Of Oom Hendrick and Tan' Betje Mrs Obbinson never spoke without affection. Though the old Dutch woman never learned any English, and Mrs Obbinson never learned any Dutch, the friendship begun in the wagon was broken only by death. "You don't need any particular language to be kind in," Mrs Obbinson would say, "and from the moment I climbed into her wagon Tan' Betje was kind to me." Never, indeed, did Tan' Betje come into the dorp without visiting Mrs Obbinson, and never did she come empty handed . . . .

On the kindness of all Platkops people in those early days Mrs Obbinson would often dwell. All then were poor alike, and all were dependent on their neighbours. Very little money was in circulation, and of fortunes such as Mr Obbinson dreamed of there was no sign. If a man bought land he paid for it in labour, not gold, and for his land by the river, as it always thrilled the little girls to hear, Mr Obbinson paid with a table and a coffin. In his labour as a carpenter he paid for the help that was given him in the building of his house, and in their labours others paid him. Only for luxuries was money brought into use – and one of the luxuries of those simple days was the hiring by Platkops brides of the wax orange-blossom wreath which had once adorned Mrs Obbinson's wedding bonnet.

It was drought which brought the bonnet and its wreath again into Mrs Obbinson's story. The drought was the "great" one of which all Platkops children knew tales, and during which the building of the church had been brought to a standstill through lack of funds. With his work gone and his fortune not yet made, Mr Obbinson earned what he could by the making of coffins, and Mrs Obbinson, like many another Platkops housewife, opened a small "winkel" in her living-room. Here she sold waffles, most-bolletjes and tamelaitjes; black tatted

13

hair-nets which she made for old ladies, and little print frocks
which she made for their grandchildren. Soap and water-candles
also she sold, made of the precious supply of fat which Tan'
Betje never failed to bring in to her. And here one day she added
to her "stock" the orange-blossom wreath of her wedding-bonnet
fixed to a veil for Platkops brides. For long had these wax
blossoms been the admiration and envy of those in whose gardens real orange trees flourished and flowered — and for long
did Platkops' brides proudly continue to hire them . . . .

While coffins were still the chief source of his fortune, Mr
Obbinson, in the Coffee-house one day, heard a stranger talking
of the diamond-fields which had just been discovered and to
which he was now on his way up-country. This was the first news
of diamonds which Platkops had heard, and giving him time
only to bid Mrs Obbinson good-bye and pack up his carpet bag,
it swept Mr Obbinson up-country with the Coffee-house stranger,
convinced that at last he was about to find fortune.

For many months after this Mrs Obbinson neither saw nor heard
from him. "Weren't you frightened?" the little girls would ask,
"left all alone in your house like that with jackals and things
coming right down into your yard?" And Mrs Obbinson would
answer: "Oh, no, my loves! Tan' Betje sent one of her orphan
grandsons to stay with me while Mr Obbinson was away, and I
never felt frightened with *him* in the house."

At first the little girls had supposed that the grandson had
brought with him a gun for Mrs Obbinson's protection. But
"Oh, no!" Mrs Obbinson had cried, "not a gun! Only a rattle.
He was just a year old when he came to me then, you know."
And she would say, when they asked her, as they invariably did,
"What made you feel so safe with a rattle?" "I don't know, my
dears, but nothing ever made me feel so safe while Mr Obbinson
was away as having that baby to look after."

The baby remained with her until Mr Obbinson returned —
without a fortune and with little in his carpet bag but emptiness.
Poverty drove him back to coffin-making, and to coffin-making
he stuck until Platkops was swept by the craze for ostrich farm-

ing. Every family in the dorp invested then in a pair of birds and started breeding; the chicks, when hatched, being sold to farmers in the district. And Mr Obbinson, with fresh hope of fortune, did likewise.

For some time Mr Obbinson kept his ostriches in the yard, and though Mrs Obbinson "couldn't bear the nasty creatures dancing around and booming out in the night like lions in a forest" she endured this new phase of fortune-hunting until the cock attacked Mr Obbinson and nearly killed him. Then she sent for Oom Hendrick, who took all the birds out to his farm and returned next day with a "liniment olie" from Tan' Betje for Mr Obbinson's bruises . . . .

For long after this Mr Obbinson "couldn't abide the sight of a bird" and went back, with something that was almost content, to coffin-making. But a day came when down in the Coffee-house he heard talk of the newly-found gold-fields — and returned to Mrs Obbinson "all wild and strange" to pack up his carpet bag and join in the rush to the north. By this rush he was carried out of Mrs Obbinson's life for four or five years, and once again Tan' Betje's grandson, now a growing boy, was lent to her for company.

It was while Tan' Betje's grandson, young Andries, was with her, and partly for his sake, that Mrs Obbinson, clearing out the lower half of her winkel, began "teaching school". Her school, the little girls thought, with cookies and tamelaitjes at one end of it, must have been the nicest in all the world, and certainly none of her old pupils ever returned to Platkops dorp without going down the lane to visit her. But tragedy came to her here, for it was into the school that there stumbled one hot still day the wreck of all that had once been Mr Obbinson — a wild-eyed but strangely gentle old man carrying in his hand a little medicine bottle half filled with small gold nuggets. Here at last was his fortune . . . .

In the next part of her story Mrs Obbinson would dwell again on the kindness of Platkops people, for all were kind to her and

Mr Obbinson then, she said. "It wasn't that Mr Obbinson was ill, you know," she would say, "but just that he was strange. He never spoke, and I never knew what had happened to him. He just sat still wherever I put him, rattling his nuggets in his bottle like a baby, and holding them up to the sun . . . ."

So, in that strange silence, for several years had Mr Obbinson lived content, playing in the sun with his fortune, while Mrs Obbinson "taught school" to Platkops children. Then had come the year of drought which had ended in the greatest of Platkops floods. Andries had gone back by then to old Tan' Betje at the farm, and Mr and Mrs Obbinson were alone in the little house when, at dawn on the second day of torrential rain, the rising waters of the Ghamka swept suddenly across the lands and through the yard towards them. Somehow, though she could never tell how, Mrs Obbinson had roused her husband and made him follow her up an outside ladder on to the roof. Here, while below them the waters swept into the house and out of it, bearing much of the lighter furniture away, Mr Obbinson had sat content in the rain, rattling the nuggets in his bottle. He was rattling them so when there came a sudden up-lifting of the waters against the gable end of the house, a shuddering of collapsing wall and thatch, and a fall which left Mrs Obbinson clinging to the roof alone . . . .

Over this part of her story the little girls, drawing close to her side for comfort, would beg Mrs Obbinson always to hurry. "Hurry and get to the nice bit," they would say, for with "a nice bit," they held, all good stories should end. And the nice bit for them of Mrs Obbinson's was the arrival a few days after the flood of Tan' Betje's grandson, bringing with him all his belongings in a wagon-box and crying that if she dared to send him away again he'd go and be a horse-thief. Mrs Obbinson had never sent him away again. He was, as the little girls knew, the nice, long, thin man who let them play in his workshop in Mrs Obbinson's yard, and who was getting to be, so everybody said, the richest carpenter in Platkops. And he it was who, to make Mrs Obbinson feel safe when the rains came, always tied up their house in tarpaulin.

16

MARTINUS IN THE MOUNTAINS

The instrornery thing was none of us knew there *was* a Martinus in the mountains, or how nice he'd be, till one day our Mother came to the schoolroom door an' said Would Miss Merrington please give us our lessons in the dinin'-room this morning?

An' before Miss Merrington could say Yes, very perlite, Six [playmate of the Smith children] said Oh, schoolroom table again, I serpose, — because, you know sometimes w'en people are ill they bring them to the schoolroom table an' our Father does something there to make them better.

But our Mother didn' take any notice of sich a imperint little boy, an' Miss Merrington said Would we please not talk so much, but come along quickly and quietly to our places?

So we went: Pato [P.S.'s sister, Dorothy] saying all the way how funny it was going to have your lessons in the dinin'-room, an' w'ere had she left her sewing could we think? An' jes' w'en we got ther, saying we couldn't, but wasn't it in the dolls'-house perhaps? a waggin came driving round the stoep an' into the yard in front of us. An' nobody had ever seen a waggin in our yard before, an' everybody ran to the window to look. An' there it was in front of us — a mule waggin, with fourteen mules an' red roses like cabbidges on the green sides, an' a cartel [hammock-bed] an' a water-cask an' veldt stooljes [fold-up camp stools] swingin' down below, an' a tent with the flaps down up above. An' an O'Baas [old man] like Moses in a temper in O'Ma's Bijbel, drove it. He drove it right up to the school-room steps an' said 'Staan', an' the mules stood. An' he climbed off his seat with his cullid boy, an' went to the back of the waggin an' lifted somebody out rolled up in a rug, an' carried him in to the schoolroom. An' altho' we didn' know it then, or how nice he'd be, it was Martinus from the mountains that they carried in. An' presently they came out again, an' the O'Baas climbed up on his seat an' said "Loop" — An' those mules looped [got going] right out of our yard an' back to the mountains where they came from, like a cirkus!

It took us a dreadful long time after that to go back to the

17

Kings of Englan' an' or'nery things like that, an' Miss Merrington said Was there ever such children as us, and how glad she was that the winter holidays were nearly here.

An' all that day the house was very still, ev'rybody goin' about in whispers an' askin' us to be good children, an' sayin' what a queer old man the O'Baas was, an' what a wonderful escape his son Martinus had had in the mountains. And it's too dreadful to think of, goin' about in whispers w'en you've left your sewing in the schoolroom somewhere an' can't tell anybody w'ere to find it. Inspechully w'en you're Pato an' wanting to make a new jackit an' trowsis for Kerblunk the frog.

An' it went on like that, us having lessons in the dinin'-room, an' Pato askin' everybody w'ere could she have left it, did we think? till it came to the winter holidays. An' that day Ellen said Was there ever sich a child as Pato, an' for goodness sake to stop worryin' her about it. Martinus from the mountains was goin' to be moved to the spare room soon an' then she would see for herself her sewing wasn' in the dolls' house or anyw'ere else. An' she went out very cross, leaving us in the bedroom thinkin' like always W'ere could it be? An' w'ile we were sittin' there thinkin' Martinus began speaking to hisself, and we heard him thro' the schoolroom door. An' wot he said was, Al-le-wereldt! Mar what ['Good grief! But what . . .'] is it then that sticks so out from the clock on the wall?

An' w'en he said that Pato rolled right off the bed an' ran to the door, an' turned the knob with both her hands an' went straight in to the schoolroom an' climbed on a chair without stopping an' got down her sewing from behin' the clock where we'd all forgotten she had put it. An' w'en she got it down, an' turned on her chair, there was Martinus, lying very serprised, lookin' at her.

An' she told him it was her jackit an' trowsis for Kerblunk, and held them up for him to see.

An' Martinus was mos' instremely intrusted, an' said, But Al-le-wêreldt, who was Kerblunk?

An' Pato insplained that it was our frog, an' called to the Paoli one [Pauline] to bring him. So we brought him. An' he hopped all over Martinus' bed, us talking to him all the time, an' thinkin' What a nice man he was, till Ellen came an' found us an' said was there ever sich children as us, an' What would our Father say now, did we think?

An' we told her we didn' know, but Martinus wasn' a sick man now — only a bullet in his body, an' a broken leg, an' very fond of frogs an' little girls comin' to see him.

An' Ellen said, Was he indeed? Well, a good thing he was goin' to be moved to the spare room tomorrow, where we'd not be allowed to go bothering him like this.

An' Martinus asked, What is it like, this spare room, and why mustn't we come bothering him there?

An' we tole him we didn' know, but it was jes' a wardrobe that was half a dressing-table an' a bed, an' a sort of smell like Sunday nex the droinin'-room.

An' Martinus looked at us, an' said Al-le-wereldt! Nothing else?

An' Six said, Oh well, a washing-stand, an' a chair an' a rug to get out on.

An' Martinus looked all round the schoolroom he was lying in — at the dolls' house an' Paoli's perambulator full of dolls, an' the little flat-irons-for-a-farthings, an' the blackboard an' the maps, an' the globe that opened an' shut like a umberella. An' then he looked at Ellen an' said, Nay vat ['No, what']. I shall stay here.

And he stayed there, Ellen very cross about it, but our Father saying the schoolroom was the brightest winter room for an invalid, and if we didn't tire him we'd do him good — (because you know a bullet in your body and a broken leg isn't anything dreadful like a headache. Martinus says he's known lots of men that could laugh with a bullet in their bodies, but he's never met a man that could laugh with a pain in his head).

And after that we went to Martinus in the schoolroom every day, telling him all about the Queen an' the B'loon man [stories from *Platkops Children*] an' intrusting things like that an' getting him to talk to us. An' what Pato an' the Paoli one liked him to talk about best was the O'Baas' farm in the mountains, an' the

19

old man called Allison who worked for them there. And Allison was an old old man from Scotland that had come to South Africa to make his fortune like Mrs Obbinson's husband. But instead of gettin' to Platkops [Oudtshoorn] like Mrs Obbinson's husband, he got to Martinus' Father's farm in the mountains an' stopped there, making tables an' chairs an' doors an' things for the new farmhouse they were building. An' nobody had ever seen sich things as Allison made before, but he never talked about them or who he was, or why he had come to South Africa to make his fortune. An' people got to know about him, an' came asking him, Wouldn't he like to go with them to work for a store in Cape Town? That's where fortunes were made!

But Allison always said No: His fortune was here. An' he would look all round him, at the mountains, Martinus said, an' at the little mountain sluit [ditch, furrow] running past the house to the big stone dam, an' at the mill-wheel he had built for Martinus' Father, an' back to the mountains again an' say Yes: It was here. And go back to his sawin' in the poplar bush. And Pato an' the Paoli one were never tired hearing about him, and always so glad he never went to Cape Town. It was too dreadful to think of, making your fortune in Cape Town when you might have been living with Martinus in the mountains — ·

But what Six and Nickum [another of the 'Platkops' children] liked to hear about best was the Sheep Inkspeckter and the Horse Thieves. And how we got to know about them first was this —

One day Pato asked Martinus Did his Father always look like Moses in a temper, like the day he came in the waggin?

An' Martinus laughed an' said No: not always. But when you've got a son who plays the fool and gets a bullet in his body an' a broken leg perhaps you get to feel like Moses in a temper.

An' we looked at him very serprised, an' Nickum said, What were you playing at then when you played the fool?

An' Martinus laughed again an' said Horse Thieves.

'HORSE THIEVES'*: AN INTRODUCTORY NOTE

In the 8 January 1927 edition of the *Cape Argus,* one of Pauline Smith's humorous tales based on stories told her by Thys Taute at Mill River in 1913, and recorded in her journal on Friday, October 17, 1913, was published. It was called "Horse Thieves". Pauline Smith exploited the dualistic possibilities in Taute's anecdote about the horse stealers, Buckley and Brown, introducing her own parallels to shape the anecdotal imagery into her short story. In the anecdote, the boys pretend to be the horse thieves; they whitewash the horse, and exchange it for the visitor's animal. Then, when the shout goes up that Buckley and Brown have stolen the creature, the visitor gives chase on his own horse, "remarking that the grey he rode trotted exactly like the horse he had lost".

Pauline Smith emphasized aspects of the Taute anecdote necessary to any trickster tale: the role played by the trickster, and the credulity of the dupe. She altered the narrative in several important respects. First, she brought into the story, as the dupe, the detested sheep inspector, characterizing him as an inveterate braggart; this would provide the parallel that she required: "forever boasting of the great things he had done and the fine horse he had owned . . .". Second, the boys in Taute's narrative were worked into full tricksters in Pauline Smith's story: "whenever the Platköps' sheep inspector came along, my brother Hans and I must play the fool". Third, instead of having the dupe recognize the qualities of his own horse in the disguised creature, as happens in Taute's tale, she has him pompously insist that the disguised horse is any but his own. "She's an elephant," the sheep inspector groans, "I'll never get anywhere near my Lady on this!"

In the reshaping of the anecdotal material, Pauline Smith created the set of images that would parallel the images of Taute's tale: first, the sheep inspector's puffery; second, the shallowness of the inspector's heroics. That is the model: the sheep inspector's

---

* From "Pauline Smith and the Oral Tradition: The Koenraad Tales", *English in Africa,* VIII, 1 (March, 1981), 1-11.

story; its duplication is to be the Thys Taute anecdote. The emptiness of the boast will make possible the bridging of the two.

The trickster will reorder reality to parallel the sheep inspector's yarn. In the reshaping process, Pauline Smith reveals the threads that unite the boast and the illusion, the two sets of images. The Taute anecdote, the disguising of the horses, is thereby brought into correspondence with the Smith contribution, the boasting sheep inspector. While Hans keeps the sheep inspector talking (the Smith contribution), Koenraad does the disguising and switching of horses (the Taute anecdotal material). Koenraad then enlists the assistance of a hired hand, who will play the role of horse thief (the Taute anecdote). The trickster returns to the sheep inspector to begin the game (the Smith contribution). Koenraad is establishing the environment for the duplication of the model as created in the inspector's yarn. This is the form of the story.

As Pauline Smith shapes her narrative, awareness of its several segments must be carefully distributed to characters and audience. The dupe must not know the dimensions of the illusion; the trickster and the audience must know all the details. This is where much of the effect of the trickster narrative lies, as Trickster sets about to convert illusion into reality. While the audience knows that what Trickster is doing is not reality, the dupe does not: he acts on the illusion as if it were reality.

Koenraad first tells the inspector that the horse thieves are in the neighbourhood this night — not true, of course; it is part of the illusion. And the dupe moves readily into the illusory world — when the hired man rides the horse by at a gallop, "Man, I tell you, for a moment there was not a sound in our voorhuis but the sound of the sheep inspector's hair rising on his head". When they rush out to the stable and find the inspector's horse is gone, the illusion gains credibility. As they give chase, and the tricksters give "our father's grey mare", actually the inspector's horse, to the dupe, illusion has now become reality.

Role-playing is another part of the illusion. Far from home, Koenraad plays the role of Kavanagh, Hans the part of Mitchell. The inspector, still snared in the web of fantasy, finds himself surrounded by thieves; they are in cloaks, they carry guns, his yarn is coming to life. "I tell you it was a sick man whom we had, sitting on his own horse and not knowing it, between us that night!" They make the dupe get down from his horse and remove his clothing, and the illusion created by the tricksters harmonizes with the tale told earlier by the inspector: "I'll leave you with another story about a shirt to tell," says Koenraad, "and this time it will be a true one." By means of illusion, the tricksters have recreated the world of the inspector's tedious gasconade. The inspector establishes the model by means of his tall tale; it is duplicated by the trickster-boys, manipulating the inspector's experience of the real world until it duplicates the tale he enjoyed telling — with certain significant modifications. As always, the replication of the model depends on the obscuring of the line separating reality and fantasy.

Harold Scheub

HORSE THIEVES

"I don't know how it is," said Koenraad as the sheep-inspector rode off from the farm, "but there is that about a sheep-inspector that puts the devil into a man. There was now the little man that used to come out from Platkops to poke among my father's sheep at Eseljacht when my brother Hans and I were still young men. Whenever that little man, who was forever boasting of the great things he had done and the fine horses he had owned, came riding among us, it was as if the devil himself came riding too, to drive my brother Hans and me into mischief against him. Yes. My father was a hard man, and if we played the fool he left us always to pay for it. Yet, whenever the Platkops' sheep-inspector came along, my brother Hans and I must play the fool. Yes, youth is like that, and age can never teach it.

"The sheep-inspector, I must tell you, for all his boasting, knew so little about horses that my brother Hans would often say he was sure if we put him on his own horse in the dark he'd ride it through the night and never know it to be his own. And the last time that that little man came out to us we made a plan together to prove it.

"In those days, you must understand, there was still much talk in our districts about Mitchell and Kavanagh, the horse-thieves, and one of the sheep-inspector's great yarns was how, riding alone from one farm to another, he had once come across Kavanagh down in a river bed doctoring a horse that was ill. You would have thought, being the man that he was, that Kavanagh would at once have swopped horses and gone off on the sheep-inspector's Beauty. But no. The sheep-inspector's story was that Kavanagh refused to leave his sick horse, and that he, the sheep-inspector, making him strip to his shirt, rode off in haste to the nearest farm for help to take him prisoner. When he got back with the men from the farm, there, in the river bed, was nothing but Kavanagh's shirt. Yes, Kavanagh gone, and the sick horse gone, and just the shirt left hanging on a branch for a sign.

"Well, if there was a man in our district who believed that yarn it was perhaps the sheep-inspector himself. Yet every time

24

he came to us he would sicken my brother Hans and me by telling it all over again. And the last time that he came we made a plan to cure him. But we did not work out our plan till all his inspecting was over. Then, his last night on the farm, when my father was already in bed, brother Hans kept the sheep-inspector talking late in the voorhuis [parlour] while I went out to the stables.

"In one of the stables that night, with the sheep-inspector's new brown mare, Lady, was my father's grey, and a grey that my brother Hans was then riding, and my own Starlight with the white star on its forehead. This was how my brother Hans and I planned it, and how the sheep-inspector had seen it when he stabled his horse there for the night. But now I took my father's grey quietly to another stable, and painted the sheep-inspector's new brown mare a nice grey with whiting. Then I moved her into my father's stall and called to our old coloured boy, Abram. In half an hour, I told him, he must take the old Baas's horse out of the far stable and ride past the house and down the road to the poplar bush, and hide there until he heard my brother Hans and me and the sheep-inspector go by. Then he must go as quickly and as quietly as he could back to the farm place, and put the old Baas's grey back into its own stall in the near stable. All this Abram promised to do. No matter how my father might afterwards thrash him for it, he would always join us in our mischief, whatever it might be.

"Well, presently I went back to the house, and there was the sheep-inspector laying it off to Hans about Kavanagh and his shirt, and praising his new brown mare, Lady, up to the skies.

" 'Man,' I said, 'it's strange that you should be talking now about Kavanagh, and I hope it's not your horse that he's after to pay you back for making him strip to his shirt, but I heard to-night that he's again in our mountains, and it was to make all safe in the stables that I've been out there so long in the yard.'

"And I went on to talk about Mitchell and Kavanagh, with Hans joining in, and keeping the little man hard at it until suddenly we heard a horse rush by at the gallop . . . .

"Man, I tell you, for a moment there was not a sound in our voorhuis but the sound of the sheep-inspector's hair rising on his head. Then brother Hans said:

25

"'Al-le-wêreld! That's him!' And out we dashed into the yard and down to the stable with the little sheep-inspector trailing behind us. When we got to the stable there was the door standing open with its lock wrenched away, and there was Lady's stall empty. This we saw by the smoking stable-lantern Hans was carrying, and he gave us no time to see more.

"'Quick,' he said to me. 'Op-saddle our father's grey mare for the sheep-inspector and we'll get him yet! If there's a horse in the district that can beat your new brown mare it's my father's grey,' says he to the sheep-inspector. 'You ride her and see,' says he.

"So we mounted the sheep-inspector on his own Lady that I had done up so nicely in whiting, and Hans got on his own grey, and I on Starlight, and off the three of us rode into the night after Kavanagh, the horse-thief.

"'Man,' I said to the sheep-inspector when I made up to him, 'she goes well, eh, my father's grey mare?'

"'She's an elephant,' groans the sheep-inspector, 'I'll never get anywhere near my Lady on this!'

"'Keep up your heart,' I shouted to him. 'You don't know the horse you're riding yet! Go on with Hans to the cross-roads and then divide. I'll take the kloof here and meet you as you come down, and if he's in the kloof we'll get him. That is if Mitchell isn't with him,' I said.

"And I turned quickly into the kloof while Hans and the sheep-inspector rode on. Presently I heard in the distance old Abram taking my father's grey mare quietly home from the poplar grove to the farm. Then I covered the star on Starlight's forehead to make it as brown as the sheep-inspector's Lady, and undid my saddle-roll and put on the long black cloak and the soft-brimmed hat that I carried there, and waited.

"Well, for all that he had boasted in the old days it was a long time, I must tell you, before the sheep-inspector came creeping down the kloof towards me. There was but a very little moon that night, hidden every now and then by drifting heavy black clouds, and as he came along the sheep-inspector was for ever bringing his horse to a halt until the moon should come out again.

26

He did this as he came near me, and just as the moon came out again from the clouds I rode out into the path and held up my revolver. The sheep-inspector gave one look and swung round on his horse — to find my brother Hans, also in a cloak and a wide-brimmed hat, pointing a revolver at him from above.

"I tell you it was a sick man whom we had, sitting on his own horse and not knowing it, between us that night! It wasn't much that his boasting could do for him now, with Kavanagh before him and Mitchell behind! There he sat with his mouth open and never a word coming out of it.

" 'Get down off your horse,' said I at last, speaking sharp and high like Kavanagh.

"And off he tumbled.

" 'Take off your coat now,' said I. And off it came.

" 'Your trousers, also,' said I. And off came his trousers.

" 'Now tie them on to your saddle, please, and drive your horse forward. I'll leave you with another story about a shirt to tell,' I said, as he sent his horse towards me, 'and this time it will be a true one.'

"And I caught the horse as it trotted up, and quick as a flash brother Hans and I were off, leaving the little man alone in the dark with the wind flapping his shirt round his bare legs . . . .

"Well, this surely ought to have been the end of the story for here we had proved very nicely to ourselves that the sheep-inspector could ride his own horse in the dark and never know it to be his own. And if he ever told his yarn about Kavanagh and his shirt again we knew well it would not be to us. But it wasn't the end. However a man may finish a story for himself, be sure that fate has another ending to it. And so it was with brother Hans and me that night.

"My father, I must tell you, was very proud of his horses, and a horse-thief was like a red rag to a bull to him. He had jumped out of bed when he heard us all three ride off, and when Abram got back with his mare from the poplar bush he was raging mad. The Lord knows how Abram explained things to him, but somehow he made him understand that the young baases were off after Kavanagh, the horse-thief. And when he had done cursing

Abram for giving up the chase so soon, on to his grey mare he gets himself with his gun, and off he rides.

"It was just as we were coming out of the kloof together, Hans and I, leading the sheep-inspector's Lady, that the old man came upon us, and man, I tell you, I was proud of the old boy that night.

" 'Kavanagh,' he shouts, 'I shoot!' And with that he shot. Yes, without giving us time to say a word the old man, in his passion, ups with his gun and shoots. And it was me, his youngest son, that he put a bullet into the leg of . . . .

"Yes, that was how the story ended for me, but that was not how it ended for my brother Hans. Many times afterwards did Hans tell me how he envied me my bullet that night.

" 'Man,' he would say, 'but surely you had the best of it, lying there groaning like a bull! I tell you it took me now all my time to explain to my father how he came to shoot his own son, and how the sheep-inspector came to be wandering through the kloof in his shirt, and how the sheep-inspector's new brown mare came to be painted so nicely with whiting. Yes, it wasn't easy for me to satisfy the old man about these things. And when at last I had done talking to him, the only thing he said to me was that if he himself was not mad then surely his sons were.'

"Yes, for a long time after that my father would say that if he was not mad then surely his sons were. But afterwards he also came to smile a little when he thought of the sheep-inspector riding through the night on his own brown mare and not knowing it."

'THE CART'*: AN INTRODUCTORY NOTE

"The Cart" is a humorous tale based on a story told to Pauline Smith in 1913 by Thys Taute of Mill River, and recorded in her 1913-1914 South African journal; the story was published in the Cape Town newspaper, the *Cape Argus,* on December 19, 1925.

In this narrative, Pauline Smith combines two of Taute's tales, that of de Wet and his desire for a cart, and that of the illness of a despised sheep inspector. The two main characters, James the Englishman and the sheep inspector, are the intended dupes; they are also the chief characters in the respective Thys Taute anecdotes. Standing against them are the tricksters, Koenraad and Arnoud Ferreira. Pauline Smith retains and emphasizes certain aspects of the original tales, the Bible/black book of vengeance, for example, and the convincing of the sheep inspector that he is dying. These depend on the intense dislike of the inspector, an attitude stressed in both of the tellings. The naivety of James, however, crucial in Taute's tale, is only a bit of deceit in Pauline Smith's story, a major alteration, for James's cunning adds another level to the action and to the experience of the reader.

In addition to elements retained with, perhaps, shifts of emphasis, the author has her own contribution to make. She reshapes and reorganizes the two Taute tales to bring them into parallel alignment. The cart is the important link, unifying the separate orally told tales. The sheep inspector owns a cart, the Englishman wants one. Pauline Smith adds a marriage quest to motivate the cart incident: the tricksters, also matchmakers, have selected a wife for the Englishman. She adds the cart to the anecdote about the dying sheep inspector, and the theme of marriage to the cart tale. With the cart the principal image in each of the two parts, the animating activity centres on the marriage motif: James will not go courting without a cart, inciting the tricksters to extort it

* From "Pauline Smith and the Oral Tradition: The Koenraad Tales", *English in Africa,* VIII, 1 (March, 1981), 1-11. The Thys Taute anecdotes referred to can be found in the October 17, 1913, entry in the 1913-1914 *South African Journal.*

from the inspector, and bringing the two characters, James and the inspector, as well as their separate stories, into correspondence.

The extortion of the cart from the dupe by the tricksters, and the analogous extortion of the cart from the tricksters by the intended dupe, are Pauline Smith's formal contributions to the unifying process. This dual swindle also represents the parallelism of the story, and has to do with the filching of the cart, in the first part (Taute's dying inspector tale), by the boy-tricksters from the inspector; in the second (Taute's cart tale), by the dupe-turned-trickster from the sometime tricksters, now the dupes.

The two boys deceive the inspector with ease, playing the role of grand manipulator, even to the point of apparently granting or denying life itself. There is a predictable parallelism evident in the early part of the story which proves to be erroneous: the boys seem on their way to using the Englishman in the same way that they have hoaxed the inspector. But in this narrative, the audience and the tricksters do not know all, and a sense of irony is generated by the slow growth of awareness that the tricksters are also the dupes.

In this story, as in "Horse Thieves", Pauline Smith reveals her sense of humour, and wields her rapier of irony in less tragic circumstances than in the tales of *The Little Karoo*. But the basic formal composition is identical. In converting anecdotal material to written narrative, she begins by emphasizing certain aspects of the original tale. She thus reshapes the original material to correspond to images and movements in the narrative segments that she will be adding as parallels. She will either invent correspondences (which she does in "Horse Thieves"), or bring two anecdotes into parallel relationship, as in "The Cart". In either case, she must as writer make these correspondences manifest. She does this by exaggerating or otherwise underscoring aspects of the original, altering details found in the original tale, and adding her own material. The crucial storytelling techniques are (a) finding potentially parallel imagery, and (b) establishing the parallels so that the audience fully experiences them. Formally, Pauline Smith's challenge was to place the anecdotal material that she found in South Africa into this mould, and to add what she was unable to collect from her informants.

Harold Scheub

30

THE CART

From the stoep of the farm could be seen the long grey trail of the Buitenkant-road, down which there lurched and swayed a white-tented cart. The cart was the only visible moving thing in all that stretch of the valley which lay below the farmhouse. Koenraad watched it lazily as he filled his pipe, then turned to his guest and said:

"Seeing old Dirk Grobelaar ride by on his courting like that makes me think of a time I once had with a cart. Yes, I was a young man then, you must understand, trading up-country in the Caroline district with Arnoud Ferreira. Arnoud Ferreira was a wild sort of chap, but with all his wildness he was always humble where a woman was concerned, and he was also the best friend a man could ever wish to have. We had a store together out in the Caroline district and we had also sheep. All Caroline was sheep-farming then, and I tell you there was a man we all hated, and that was the sheep inspector. The sheep inspector was such a man that if you had wet your finger and run it down his coat out of the trail there would have come a regulation about sheep. Yes, because he was the Government sheep inspector, he thought himself surely the Governor-General of all the sheep in the Caroline district. He carried always in his pocket a little black book the Government had given him. Whatever was in this book we must do and whatever was not in this book we must not do. The book was his ten commandments. And next to the sheep inspector, the thing that we all hated most was this little black book. Yes, sheep-farming was all very well when the sheep inspector was in some other district. But I tell you, when we heard he was coming, and always the news spread through the country like a veld fire, we would run about among our sheep as if the jackals were after them.

"Well, one day there came the word that the sheep inspector was on his way, riding in a Cape tent-cart. Always before this he had come on a horse, with April, his coloured boy, riding on another horse. But now he was coming in a cart. And as soon as he heard about the cart, Arnoud Ferreira sat up. But first I must tell you that there was in Caroline at this time a queer little Englishman, who was farming for his health. He was a man that you could not help liking, but surely there was never a man who took so long to make up his mind. Even about the women he wanted to marry he could not make up his mind, and he would come to Arnoud Ferreira and me to help him decide.

"Arnoud would say to him: 'It's a great pity they named you James. A man that's named James is bound to be a weak man. He can't help it. If they'd named you now Jimmy or Jim, you might have been able to choose a wife for yourself. But surely as you're named James, you do right to come to Koenraad and me to choose her for you.

"And we would choose him a very suitable sort of girl and send him off to court her. But Lord, no sooner had we got him all fixed up than back he would come again, asking if this other one wouldn't perhaps suit him better. I tell you, there wasn't a man in all the Caroline district that gave us so much trouble in his affairs as that little Englishman, and yet there wasn't a man among us that didn't like him. I can't explain it, but it was so. Even Arnoud Ferreira, who was always playing jokes on him, did more for the Englishman than he did for any other man in Caroline.

"Well, for long now the Englishman had been asking us to get him a cart. He said it was no use choosing a wife for him until we got him a good Cape cart with one of the new fixed tents (they were new in those days) to drive her out to the farm in. So Arnoud, who had found a very nice girl for the Englishman, was looking about for a cart. The girl was Alida Lategan, and she lived with her father and little sister out Nortje's River way. We had not told the Englishman her name. 'No what!' said Arnoud, 'this time we must say nothing about the wife we have found for him till we get him a cart. When we get him the cart, we must drive him out to Lategan's farm and take him nicely by the hand and ask the girl to marry him. Yes,' says Arnoud, 'surely that is the only way we'll ever get him a wife.'

So Arnoud was looking about for a cart, when along came the

sheep inspector in his. The sheep inspector didn't come very far, for up at old Rijk Raubenheimer's farm he grew ill, and old Rijk Raubenheimer sent in to the store for me. The nearest doctor and the nearest predikant in those days were at the dorp, six hours away. When a Caroline man grew ill, he would send to the store for me, and I would give him some droppels out of a big box of medicines that my grandmother down in Platkops had made up for me. Afterwards, if he didn't feel well, we'd bury him. But it was wonderful how often he got well. Yes, my grandmother's droppeltjes had a great reputation. Well, out I went to old Rijk Raubenheimer's with my grandmother's droppels and Arnoud Ferreira came with me. He said to me, 'No what! With the Englishman wanting a cart so badly and the sheep inspector having one, we must now see what we can do.'

"When we came to the farm, there was the cart out in the yard. It was a good cart, with a white fixed tent, and Arnoud thought, with a new coat of paint, it would do very well for the Englishman to drive his wife out to the farm in. And, feeling now quite pleased about the cart, we went into the house, where the sheep inspector lay on old Rijk Raubenheimer's bed groaning like a bull. I tell you, it was pleasant to hear him. The noise that he made was like music in our ears and, having him helpless there in our hands, for all the world like one of our sheep, made us forget at first about the Englishman and his cart. I saw quickly that it was colic that was wrong with him and gave him some of my grandmother's droppels. And presently Arnoud said to me:

" 'How looks he to you, Koenraad?'

" 'No, man,' I said, 'he looks to me very bad. He looks to me dying.'

" 'Man,' said Arnoud, 'that's how he looks now to me also . . . a dying man . . . and the ground so hard that we can never get it dug . . . .'

"And we stood there looking at the sheep inspector, whose eyes were starting out of his head.

"Says Arnoud again, 'I wonder now if old Rijk Raubenheimer has a good strong pick . . .?'

" 'Man,' said I, 'wait about the pick. Whether the ground is hard or not, we can't let a sheep inspector die like a sheep. Bring me a Bible and let us read to him.'

" 'Man,' says Arnoud, 'a Bible is a thing there is not in this house.'

" 'Well,' I said, 'read to him we must. Let us read to him out of the little black book he was for ever reading to us. Surely it was his Bible.'

"So we got the book and read to him. Yes, an hour we read to him. And I tell you, though I hated that little black book, it was a pleasant hour to me. And presently, when I saw that my grandmother's colic droppels were curing him and that we could not for long go on making him think he was dying, I said to Arnoud:

" 'No, man. It seems to me he is a little better!'

" 'It seems to me so also,' says Arnoud.

" 'It seems to me now is the time to save him,' I said. 'And surely I can save him with this other little bottle of my grandmother's droppels. But it's a very expensive little bottle,' I said. 'And if, after all, he dies and I lose my grandmother's droppels, what then?'

" 'Yes,' says Arnoud, 'what then?'

"When he saw us hesitating like that, the sheep inspector stopped in his groans and asked us in a whisper to save him. Surely now, when he groaned so loud, he could have spoken aloud. But no. All the time that he thought he was dying, he whispered.

" 'But man,' I said, holding up the little bottle, 'it's worth its weight in gold!'

" 'It is that,' says Arnoud. 'And also diamonds.'

" 'I will surely pay you,' says the sheep inspector in his dying whisper.

" 'But, man,' I said, 'there is always this . . . . If, after all, you die and I lose my grandmother's droppels?'

" 'Yes,' says Arnoud, 'there is always that.'

" 'I will give you anything you like,' says the sheep inspector with tears in his eyes.

" 'Man,' says Arnoud to me, 'there is now one thing we might

34

make a bargain over . . . But no . . . It's too valuable, that little
bottle of your grandmother's . . . .'

" 'Anything you like,' says the sheep inspector, beginning to
speak louder. And I tell you, when we found he was beginning
to get back his voice we thought it time to finish our bargain.

" 'Well, then,' says Arnoud, 'sell us the old cart of yours out
in the yard (and surely it's a disreputable old cart for a Government man like you to ride about the country in) and Koenraad's
grandmother's droppels shall be part of the payment.'

" 'Take now the cart,' says the sheep inspector, 'but give me
his grandmother's droppels.'

"So we gave him the droppels. And I tell you, it was a good
thing we came so quickly to the end of our bargain, for no sooner
did he drink the cinder water that I had put into my grandmother's
bottle, than he sat up in bed and began to talk again like the
Governor-General. Yes, that was a thing we could never stand.
So we left him there with old Rijk Raubenheimer and inspanned
the cart and drove back to the store. We put the cart in the workshop, which was a little way away from the store and kept quiet
about it till the sheep inspector had left the district. Then we
told the Englishman that we had found him a cart to drive his
wife out to the farm in.

"The Englishman seemed really pleased we had found him a
cart, and yet when Arnoud took him down to the workshop to
show it him, it took him just half-an-hour to make up the Englishman's mind that it was a good cart. And then the Englishman
said:

" 'Even if it is a good cart, I'd like to hear what Koenraad
thinks of it.'

"Arnoud said to him, 'Man, look how it is! I've made up your
mind for you that it's a good cart and your mind's got to stay
made up. Don't you go disturbing your mind by asking Koenraad
about the cart. You've got a weak mind, being named James,
and you need a man like me to take care of it for you.'

" 'Well,' said the Englishman, 'you've been a good friend to
me and I'll take the cart. But I'd like it painted.'

" 'Painted it shall be,' says Arnoud. 'What colour would you like it?'

"But the Englishman couldn't make up his mind about the colour. No, that was beyond him altogether.

"Said Arnoud at last, 'Well, how would a yellow body with red wheels suit you? That's what I advise.'

" 'Well,' says the Englishman, 'that sounds all right, but I'd like to know what Koenraad thinks about it.'

" 'See here now,' says Arnoud. 'If you promise to keep your mind made up that it's a good cart, I'll let you ask Koenraad what he thinks about a yellow body and red wheels. But, man! I warn you, Koenraad will disturb your mind for you, and you'd much better let me start painting it right away.'

" 'No,' said the Englishman. 'No, not right away, Ferreira. There's something, I don't know what exactly, a little familiar about a yellow body and red wheels, and I think I'd like to consult Koenraad first.'

"Well, back he came to the store alone. 'Koenraad,' he said, 'we've made up my mind that I'll take the cart.' (Yes, he said 'we' with a queer sort of twist to his mouth that might have been a smile and might not. And I tell you there were times when I saw that twist that I would wonder if the Englishman were playing with us just as we were playing with him.)

" 'I'm glad you're taking the cart,' I said. 'It's a good cart. Your wife will like it.'

" 'Yes,' said the Englishman, 'but I think it ought to be painted.'

" 'Yes,' I said, 'surely it ought to be painted.'

" 'The question is, what colour?' said the Englishman.

" 'Yes, surely that is the question,' I said.

" 'Ferreira suggested a yellow body on red wheels,' said the Englishman.

" 'What!' I said. 'A yellow body on red wheels? Man! It's a post-cart he'd be giving you. You don't want to drive your wife out to the farm in a post-cart, do you?'

" 'No,' said the Englishman, 'not a post-cart. A yellow body on red wheels did seem familiar but I never thought of a post-cart. Of course, it would be a post-cart. Ferreira must have forgotten that. Well, what do you suggest, Koenraad?'

" 'Well now,' I said, 'how would a blue body and red wheels do? I think your wife would like to drive out to the farm in a blue body on red wheels, don't you?'

" 'Perhaps she would,' said the Englishman.

" 'Why don't you ask her?' I said.

" 'You forget, Koenraad,' he said, 'that you haven't told me my wife's name yet.'

" 'Lord, yes,' I said, 'surely I forgot.' And I tell you, he spoke now in such a gentle way about his wife that I got somehow a little anxious about the girl we had chosen for him. 'She'll be a nice wife.' I said. 'Fair hair and blue eyes and all that. Just the kind of wife for a blue body on red wheels.'

" 'Well, then,' said the Englishman, 'you tell Ferreira that.'

" 'Man!' I said, 'I will not! Al-le-wêreld! If it was a yellow body on red wheels he fixed on for you, you must now tell him about the blue body yourself. It's a thing I would not take in hand to do for any man in Caroline! But you can't have a post-cart, you know.'

" 'No,' said the Englishman, 'I can't have a post-cart. But I haven't time to go back to the workshop now. I'll come again.'

"And before I could stop him, he had left the store and for three weeks we did not see him. I tell you, it must have been a bad three weeks for the Englishman, for he had come in for his month's provisions and he went off without them. It was matches and tobacco that brought him back at last. For two days he had had no tobacco and matches when back he came to us, sucking his dry pipe.

"We were both in the store when he came. Ferreira gave him his matches and said: 'It's a great pity you had to leave in such a hurry last time you were here, but surely, being named James, you were bound to forget your provisions. But what now about the cart? I've got here a very nice pot of yellow for the body and red for the wheels.'

" 'Well,' said the Englishman, puffing away at his pipe. 'Koenraad tells me that would make it a post-cart.'

" 'Oh,' says Arnoud, 'Koenraad told you that, did he? And

37

didn't I tell you that if you came and consulted Koenraad, Koenraad would disturb your mind for you?'

" 'Well, man,' I said, 'he can't drive his wife out to the farm in a post-cart.'

" 'And what would you have him paint it then?' asked Arnoud.

" 'Well, now,' I said, 'a blue body on red wheels is what I'd have.'

" 'A blue body on red wheels!' cried Arnoud. 'Man! That's a Cape Town butcher's cart. You can't have the Englishman driving his wife out to the farm in a butcher's cart!'

" 'Well,' I said, 'he can't drive her out in a post-cart!'

" 'Well,' he said, 'he shan't drive her out in a butcher's cart!'

"And with that, he took up the pot of yellow paint and I took up a pot of blue, and off we went, quarrelling about it, to the workshop, with the little Englishman puffing away behind.

"When we got to the yard, down sat Arnoud on one side of the cart and began painting it yellow, and down I sat on the other and began painting it blue.

" 'Man,' says Arnoud in a rage, poking his head round the back of the cart, 'leave now the cart!'

" 'Man,' I said to Arnoud, 'it is still half of it my cart, bought with my grandmother's droppeltjes, and my half of it shall surely be blue.'

" 'No, what, man!' says Arnoud, 'but my half of it shall surely be yellow.'

" 'But, man,' I said, 'think now a minute, for surely a blue body is the kind of body that will suit the Englishman's wife best. It will go with her eyes. If she had yellow eyes I could understand you wanting a post-cart for her. But her eyes are surely blue.'

" 'They are that,' says Arnoud very slow, holding back his brush. 'Yes,' he says to the Englishman, 'your wife's eyes are surely blue. And as it was Koenraad's grandmother's droppels that helped us to get the cart, perhaps it is only right that Koenraad should make up your mind for you about the colour of it.'

" 'Very well then,' says the Englishman, 'as my wife's eyes are blue, let the cart be blue. But are you quite sure they are blue?'

38

" 'I am that,' says Arnoud. 'Such a blue as there is not in the eyes of any other woman in Caroline.'

"The Englishman looked at Arnoud a second or two, with that queer twist about his mouth that made me always so anxious, and then he said, in his gentle way:

" 'Why don't you marry her yourself?'

"Man! I tell you, at that Arnoud flared up like a jubilee rocket. 'See here,' he says to the Englishman, 'I've chosen her for you because with all your weak mind you are still a decent sort of chap, and she will be able to keep it made up for you. But I tell you, if you ask me such a question again, I'll paint your cart yellow and you also.'

"Yes, he said that. It was all up and over in a minute, but believe me, for that minute I kept very quiet round my side of the cart. And I saw then for the first time how it was with Arnoud. Several times now he had been out to old Lategan's farm, preparing the girl for the Englishman's visit, and always he had come back very quiet and thoughtful. But only now did I see how it was with him. Yes . . . .

"Well, we had the cart all nicely painted blue for the Englishman, and when it was ready he brought his horses in from the farm. The horses were inspanned, and Arnoud and the Englishman drove up and down the road in the cart like a circus. And presently Arnoud says, 'No, what, man! We must now go and visit your wife.'

"And he turned the cart and set off for old Lategan's farm before the Englishman could say a word. Afterwards, when he told me all that happened at the farm, Arnoud said that surely he ought to have thought it strange that the Englishman kept so quiet about it. But at the time he didn't think it strange. He just sat there, with the reins in his hands, thinking of Alida Lategan. Even when the Englishman opened so quickly the camp gates on Lategan's farm, that were fastened in a way that it took a man a long time to learn, Arnoud did not notice it. Yes . . . .

"Well, they came at last to the house, where Alida and her little sister, Lenitje, were sitting on the stoep. Arnoud left the cart in the yard and took the Englishman up on the stoep.

" 'Alida,' he says, 'this is the Englishman I have long been telling you about. A good farm he has out Kraaibosch way, and his sheep are surely the only sheep in Caroline that the sheep inspector does not swear at. But, being a weak sort of man, having the name of James, he needs now such a woman as you to be his wife and to make up his mind for him. Will you marry him, Alida?'

" 'I will not,' says Alida very straight, but looking all the same at the Englishman with a very pleasant smile on her face.

" 'But alle-wêreld, Alida!' cried Arnoud, staring at her. 'If you will not marry the Englishman, what is then to become of him?'

" 'The Englishman,' says Alida, 'can take care of himself.'

" 'Now surely,' says Arnoud, 'that he can not.'

" 'Well then,' says Alida, 'Lenitje must take care of him.'

" 'Lenitje!' cried Arnoud. 'Lord, what has Lenitje to do with him?'

" 'I have everything to do with him,' cries Lenitje, clinging to the Englishman's arm like a child. 'It has long been settled between us! We were but waiting for the cart!' And down she went off the stoep with the Englishman to look at the cart.

" 'Alida,' says Arnoud, staring at them, 'think now what you are doing!'

" 'What am I doing?' asks Alida.

" 'You are marrying the Englishman to a child,' says Arnoud. 'It will be now two children with not one mind between them! Think how it will be, and for the Lord's sake marry him yourself!'

" 'Arnoud,' cries Alida in a rage, 'neither for the Lord's sake nor for your sake will I marry him. I have said that I will not. And I will not.'

" 'But, Alida,' says Arnoud, 'why will you not?'

" 'Because,' says Alida, 'the man I will marry must have a mind of his own, and even so I must make it up for him. Yes! That is the kind of woman that I am, and that is the kind of man that I will marry!'

"Arnoud stood for a little, looking down on the cart, and presently he said: 'And have you now found such a man?'

" 'Surely I have,' says Alida.

40

" 'Did he come to you this day riding in a blue tent-cart with an Englishman?' asks Arnoud.

" 'Surely he did,' says Alida.

" 'Man,' says Arnoud at last, holding Alida very close by his side, 'he thought he was bringing you a husband in the blue tent-cart, but he didn't know it was *this* husband!' "

'THE DOCTOR': AN INTRODUCTORY ESSAY

'The Doctor' is Pauline Smith's longest Little Karoo story and in some ways one of her most remarkable productions. The University of Cape Town Library possesses the only known typescript (with manuscript revisions) of 'The Doctor'; it has also been published – in somewhat arbitrarily edited form – by A.D. Dodd in *More South African Short Stories* (Cape Town, 1970). Apart from the intrinsic value of this flawed but complex tale with its profound ironies of character and fate, 'The Doctor' reveals a strong autobiographical strain which justifies its inclusion in the present volume.

One of the few critical references to 'The Doctor' comes from an unpublished M.A. dissertation by Marion D. Baraitser, in which she criticizes it as 'a sentimental fantasy of an ideal relationship between [Pauline Smith] and her father . . . undisciplined by the artistic technique of objectivity'*. The patently autobiographical parallel between the main character, Petchell, and the author herself, in the portrayal of a father-daughter relationship may account for P.S.'s failure to publish the story, though she obviously spent a great deal of time on it. There are undoubted elements of 'sentimentalized fantasy' in the depiction of the relationship between father and daughter which one cannot imagine the author countenancing if she had got so far as to prepare the MS for publication. These are limited to the first two sections; thereafter, despite a tendency to dwell on the details of Petchell's thoughts and feelings, the thematic deployment of the plot and the complex ironies of fate and human nature exert their own pressure. Whether Pauline Smith's own being is successfully submerged in the character of Petchell is a moot point; in this story as in other, more completely finished tales, the author's own life and experiences underlie – give authority and a sense of reality to – all she describes. She is Petchell in 'The Doctor' just as Olive Schreiner is Lyndall in *The Story of an African Farm*; she

* *Arnold Bennett and Pauline Smith: A Study in Affinities.* University of South Africa, Pretoria, 1976.

43

is the narrator who falls in love with Jan Boetje in 'The School-master' and 'the pastor's daughter' (in the story of that name) who finds fulfilment in the selflessness of a sacrificial love.

More explicit autobiographical elements can easily be traced to the *1905 Diary* and 1913-14 *South African Journal*. As usual, P.S. has given her story a semi-fictional setting, adapting names and places for her own purposes and transposing to the Ladismith-Calitzdorp-Ghamka River valley, characters, incidents and scenes associated with the Hazenjacht-De Rust-Meiringspoort region. Readers are referred to the following entries in the *1905 Diary*, for material used in the story; the close parallel between the author's friend Mimi Berg and her family at Kruis River, and the fictional 'Betti' of 'Vergelegen' may constitute another reason for P.S.'s failure to publish 'The Doctor':

i) 4 January 1905 (the topography of the region); ii) 31 January (the Roadman); iii) 13 April (the Bergs at Kruis River, and 'Justus in a gordon tartan dress'; the setting of the Berg's farm); iv) 14-15 April (the visit to O'Ma's; Mrs Delport; and Mimi's comment on her husband's bald head); v) 23 May (the visit by cart to Calitz-dorp, and the effect of the scenery on P.S.); and vi) 25 May (the trip through the Ghamka mountains; the narrow gorge and refe-rences to the work of the Devil).

Here are some relevant entries from the 1913-14 *South African Journal*:

Brother Hans's wife (first wife) died when her second child was born. She died of a typhoid fever. Mimi was here and her mother, ou'ma Piet. They sent into the dorp for Dokter (Father). [28 August, 1913]

De Rust a big village now, right under the Meirings Poort hills . . . The river a nasty one and dangerous when it comes down. The doctor drowned within sight of his wife a few years ago here . . . Mimi at great pains to show us the exact spot. [1 September, 1913]

[On a visit to Mimi Berg's mother, 'O'Ma Piet'] 'And presently

44

O'Ma came in . . . breathing very hoarsely and looking very
ill, with pale faded bleary blue eyes. She could say nothing
at first but al-la-wêreld! al-la-wêreld! and kissed me several
times as she said it, and laughed wheezingly when I spoke
Dutch . . . Mimi fussed around and got us real old Boer's
cookies like those [O'Ma] used to bring us at Nachtmaal.'
[11 September 1913]

Apart from such personal reminiscences, 'The Doctor' presents
a significant attempt by Pauline Smith to come to terms with a
central traumatic experience in her own life. It is concerned
with 'growing-up' and the recognition of suffering and death as
a reality in the life of every individual. The keynote is struck
early in the story: Petchell's concern that somehow the transition
from adolescence to adulthood has eluded her ('Would it ever
happen? Did it ever happen?') is counterbalanced by her sense
of participation in the rhythms of life pulsing beneath the seemingly immutable surface of the vast Karoo landscape. The elevated
notion she has of the veld as investing even the cruelties of
drought and death with 'a certain beauty, a certain sublime fitness' elicits an ironic authorial comment: 'But of death, either
on veld or in dorp, Petchell knew nothing'. This central idea is
developed in a complex structuring of events, an ironic juxtapos-
ing of ideas and attitudes, which makes 'The Doctor' *potentially*
one of Pauline Smith's most comprehensive and profound explo-
rations of character in the grip of circumstance — in sharp contrast to the singleness of purpose and austerity of treatment that
distinguish her other 'Little Karoo' stories.

One soon becomes conscious of the complexities of theme
and structure, the subtle balancing and ironic echoing of incidents,
ideas and observations. Some of these are in a minor key, such as
the fleeting sense of satisfaction shared, significantly, by Petchell
and the Roadman, in the rhythms of colour and movement;
others point to more insistent ironies, such as Petchell's annoyance at the 'impertinence' of the new pass through the Ghamka
River gorge — and 'the Dokter's' percipient (but fatefully ironic)
rejoinder: 'Some day the simple accident of its existence will
make that new pass of Frew's necessary to you'. There are other,

thematic as well as structural, parallels. The incident involving young Ludovic, who looks forward to the pig-killing with childish eagerness and ignorance — only to realize at the last moment, with shattering horror, what 'the trestle, the rimpjes, and the knife all meant to his old friend the pig' — anticipates Petchell's own stunned experience of death. It is she who carries the screaming child away from the slaughtering and, with the sympathetic aid of the Roadman (ironically, it is his pig that is being slaughtered to provide meat for his men) succeeds in calming him down. And at the close it is the Roadman who has to offer what comfort he can to Petchell when, with the same terrifying suddenness, death bursts the doors of *her* secure existence.

If *Platkops Children* reveals Pauline Smith's ability to project, with delightful humour, a child's-eye view of the adult world, 'The Doctor' presents a more serious and sustained exploration of child psychology — without, however, sacrificing the humour and imaginative insight which characterize the earlier sketches. (It is worth remarking that her only other story which focusses on the world of the child is 'Ludovitje', in *The Little Karoo* — a story which comes perilously close to 'sentimentalized fantasy', though based on reality.) Apart from the 'pig-killing' and its effect on Ludovic, there is the mysterious illness of Virginie and her aggrieved sense of neglect. Again it is Petchell who has to provide comfort and understanding, but this time the minor crisis in the child's life takes on very different dimensions in the adult world. The serio-comic bedroom scene, in which Virginie's 'sore throat' rapidly escalates into 'diphtheria', reveals strong elements of absurdist drama, as Petchell finds herself locked in a silent conflict of wills:

Betti, Piet and the O'Ma all turned to Petchell in silence. In the flickering candle-light their heavy anxious faces seemed to grow more and more unreal — the appeal in their troubled eyes more and more urgent and childish. And still, unaccountably even to herself, it seemed, the girl resisted.

The scene is managed with superb skill, and the oppressiveness indoors is reflected in the brooding silence outside, the prelude

46

to a violent thunderstorm. The resolution of the crisis within-doors, when Petchell agrees to her father being summoned, coincides with the breaking of the drought outside as the rain brings welcome relief — yet, with profound irony, these two seemingly unrelated events lead directly, inevitably, to the tragic climax of the story.

In the absence of external evidence, dating of 'The Doctor' remains a matter for conjecture. There are — perhaps for obvious personal reasons — no references by P.S. to the writing of this story, and its length, as well as its autobiographical character, may well have caused her to withhold it from publication. The inclusion of material from the 1913-14 *South African Journal* provides at least a tentative point of departure; and the creative energy evidenced in 'The Doctor' points to its belonging to the most productive period of her life: the decade spanning the Twenties. It may well have been written following on the impetus of the 1913-14 visit, when Bennett's sobering insistence on 'objectivity' was less pronounced; it may equally have been a product of the late 1920s, a reflection of her new-found confidence in herself and, perhaps, an attempt to explore, in her own way, the more subjective and introspective modes which writers such as D.H.Lawrence, James Joyce and Virginia Woolf had already successfully exploited.

In editing the typescript I have retained her tentative title, 'The Doctor', but have followed her throughout in using the term 'Dokter' as consonant with Dutch-Afrikaans idiom. I have discarded the subheadings which she pencilled in above each section as these add nothing, structurally or otherwise, to the story: however, all other additions and deletions — where clearly indicated in ink — have been reflected in the text. As usual, punctuation has been regularized and obvious errors ('Zekoegatt' for 'Zeekoegat') corrected. Certain 'Afrikanerisms' which P.S. clearly intended for purposes of authenticity or 'local colour' have been retained (e.g. 'buggy disselboom') but hybrids such as 'forehaus', have been replaced by more acceptable equivalents (in this case, 'voorhuis'). All editorial explanations and interpolations are given in square brackets.

E.P.

THE DOCTOR

I

Across the veldt came the Dokter's white-hooded two-horse buggy — the only sign of life on that dreary stretch of the Plat-kops-Princestown road which lies to the north of the Rooi Kranz hills.

From his tent on the Kranz the Roadman watched it idly. As it swayed and lurched, rose and dipped across the kopjed plain the buggy reminded him of a weather-beaten ship at sea. There was a rhythm in its progress which satisfied him vaguely. He watched it pass the camp trail which leads to the four Rooi Kranz farms — Zeekoegat, Vergelegen, De Rust and De Dam — then turned with directions to his men.

On the dusty drought-rutted Princestown road the buggy jolted steadily forward. The horses were good and well-paired, but the buggy itself was a disgrace to its owner. The paint of the woodwork was blistered and peeling. The once glossy leather splashboard was a spreading maze of cracked rings. Here and there the horse-hair stuffing of the padded seat protruded in little tufts. From its wooden frame the green lining of the hood hung and fluttered in forlorn streamers. The luggage rack, on which were a carpet bag, an old portmanteau, and several bundles of forage, was held in place by two untanned and hairy leather rimpjes [thongs]. Below the rack swung the water cask.

As the buggy jolted heavily into and out of a rut the swinging cask hit the rack, and the Dokter groaned gently. The girl at his side laughed, and putting her free hand for a moment on his coat sleeve said firmly, "Father! It isn't fair. If you groan again you must take the reins yourself. Who could drive well on a road like this?"

The Dokter shrugged his shoulders, left her question unanswered, and continued his study of the Tactics of War.

The Dokter was an Englishman, well-known throughout the South Western Province for two things, his silence and his skill. The ill-health of his wife had driven him out to South Africa in

48

the early sixties, and he had settled first in Princestown, south
of the Patchwork hills, where his old friend Mary Campion had
lately started her now famous girls' school. Full of enthusiasm
for the welfare of the colony Miss Campion had urged him to
start a companion school for boys, and so make Princestown a
centre of education for the South West. The Dokter had refused
to turn schoolmaster for the good of the Colony, but before his
refusal had been accepted as final by Miss Campion his wife had
grown seriously ill, and he had been forced to move north to the
pure dry air of Platkops in the Little Karoo. Here for a time his
wife's health had improved, and he had bought the old Dutch
Drostdy at the head of the Hoog Straat. In the Drostdy his only
daughter Petchell was born. And here, three years later, his wife
died.

Mary Campion had never forgiven gentle Emily Carless for
breathing more freely in Dutch Platkops than in English Princestown. She had never forgiven the Dokter himself for buying the
Drostdy and so permanently attaching himself to Platkops dorp.
When, after his wife's death, he refused to give up his Dutch
patients and return to Princestown, the Drostdy became for her
the grave of a Princestown college and ever after she visited it
only under protest. So great indeed had been her disappointment
that against Petchell, the Drostdy baby who ought to have been
born in Princestown, she had nursed for several years an unreasonable grudge. Only when Petchell became her pupil had her interest
in the child softened into a real affection, tempered at times by
exasperation. When Petchell left school Miss Campion had discovered to her surprise that she missed her, but not once in the
year which had followed had she found time to visit her former
pupil.

Petchell was now nineteen and grown-up. Occasionally she
tried to impress this astonishing fact upon her Father. The Dokter
greeted it always with an ironic chuckle. Petchell did not insist.
She did not feel in the least grown-up. That mysterious something which she had expected to happen when she put up her
hair and lengthened her dresses had never happened. It had not
even happened when, after a struggle with Delia and Katisje, she

49

had gained possession of the pantry keys and so become the Drostdy Mies [Mistress] . . . . Would it ever happen? Did it ever happen? She asked these questions continually, but found no answer.

Today the problem was forgotten. Leaning forward in the buggy, answering the call of the veldt with her whole being, she was conscious only of an intense satisfaction in the endless [succession] of kopjes and stones and little brown bushes: in the hum of the telegraph poles: in the excited scurrying of the veldt mice: the never-ceasing buzz of thousands of unseen insects: the beat of the horses' hoofs: the clank of the buggy disselboom [shaft or cart-pole]. Even the pitiless realities of drought which the fading glamour of sunrise revealed, seemed just, and in tune with the sweep of the kopjes, the hum of the poles.

This sense of justice, of proportion, of equality, was to Petchell one of the marvels of the Karoo. In some mysterious way the Karoo extracted beauty, rhythm — the rhythm of prose rather than of verse — out of all that passed over its veldt.

Even in its cruelty there was a certain beauty, a certain sublime fitness, and simplicity. As they passed the skeleton of a dead mule on the roadside it seemed to her that death on the veldt was at once grander and simpler than death in the dorp. Death in the dorp meant pitiful fuss and commotion. Death on the veldt meant unbroken peace. But of death, either on veldt or in dorp, Petchell knew nothing. Her gaze wandered from the white skeleton to the Patchwork hills on her right.

Already the heat haze had begun to dance and shimmer above the flat-topped kopjes of the plain: already the pink of sunrise, with its attendant soft grey-blue, had faded from the Swartkops mountains leaving only the purple, deepening into black, which gave the range its name. But on the Patchwork hills great splashes of colour — vivid reds, purples, browns, golds, soft greys and softer pinks — came and went with a rapidity almost startling under a cloudless sky

As she watched a splash of gold slip swiftly into a splash of grey, the glorious triumphant red of the Rooi Kranz hills flashed suddenly before her. As suddenly, out of the red of the hills, flashed the white of the Roadman's tents. The white of the tents satisfied her as the rhythm of the buggy had satisfied the Roadman. But she rebelled at her satisfaction. Drawing up sharply under a mimosa tree, she pointed with her whip to the line of tents above the Roi Kranz farms.

"They've begun."

The Dokter paused in his study of the Peninsula war, and took up his field glasses.

"Yes," he said, focussing slowly. "Yes. Good man that nephew of the Archdeacon's – Frew. Difficult bit of engineering this new pass of his. Want to see?"

The girl shook her head impatiently, and drove on. "No. It makes me angry, that new pass. It's so – so impertinent!"

The Dokter chuckled. "Impertinent! Oh ho!"

"Well it is," persisted the girl. "It's unnecessary. Unnecessary things are always impertinent."

"Then – " began the Dokter slowly.

The girl interrupted him firmly. "No. You're not going to say it, Father. My existence is not impertinent. You need me. I need you. We can't get on without each other."

"Accident! Sheer accident! If we hadn't met nearly twenty years ago we should never have needed each other now. The demand came simply because of the existence of the supply. Nature never tolerates waste."

"Father!" the girl protested, sitting back in the buggy with an indignant jerk.

The Dokter proceeded calmly. "Some day the simple accident of its existence will make that new pass of Frew's necessary to you."

"Never!" cried the girl with a sudden tightening of the reins.

"Oh yes it will! In a year or two the old pass will be nothing but a mule track –"

"Then we'll go over the mountains on mules!"

"– and the old toll-house a ruin."

"Then we'll buy it and go there for our summers!" The Dokter stroked his beard thoughtfully. "Then my old age is to be spent on a mule," he said. "Let us hope the spectacle will impress him."

51

"Impress whom?"

"The builder of impertinent roads, little daughter."

"Nothing will impress him," laughed the girl. "He's fat. Fat. And lazy. I've seen him."

"And did you discuss the Science of Road-building?" asked the Dokter curiously.

"I didn't say I had spoken to him, Father. I said I had seen him. Saw him from Miss Campion's balcony. Asleep in the Archdeacon's garden. Pretending to be reading. Snoring."

"How far is it from the Archdeacon's garden to Miss Campion's balcony?" asked the Dokter mildly.

"Father! How annoying you are! I didn't say I had heard him —"

"No — your conversation at present consists mainly of things you have not said."

"I said I had seen him. And I don't see how a man who is fat and falls asleep like that —"

"And snores —"

"And snores, *can* build a road that is worth building. Why, he hasn't got any sense of beauty! His new pass doesn't come anywhere near the Ghamka River at all!"

"His reason for building it. To get to the old pass we cross the Ghamka twice. And it is the most treacherous river in the Karoo."

"But the most beautiful," cried the girl. "Look at it!"

The buggy came to a halt on the top of a long lemon-shaped kopje as she spoke. Behind them to the west, stretched the drought-parched veldt. To the north towered the Swartkops mountains. To the south lay the Patchwork hills. Before them, in the distance, Patchwork hill met Swartkop mountain. And through the valley of their meeting wound the Ghamka river.

The Ghamka was, as the Dokter said, a treacherous river. In rains it came down with a suddenness that was appalling. It continually changed its course. It seemed to delight in sweeping away the lucerne lands, the mealie lands, the orange groves and tobacco fields that adventurous Boers planted on its banks. Flood after flood it left the valley a wilderness. Flood after flood the valley farmers rebuilt their dams, reclaimed their lands and fought doggedly for what was recognized as one of the wealthiest parts of the Platkops district.

52

The valley was called the meeting place of the Swartkops and Patchwork mountains. But in reality the two ranges never met. For seven wildly zig-zagging miles they lay within less than half a mile of each other. For seven miles the Ghamka alone held them apart, passing triumphantly on its way out of the Lange-hoven district into the Platkops. Through this gorge a road had been built — now on the left bank of the river, now on the right, now in the bed itself. But the Poort, as the gorge was called, was seldom used. It was so awful, so overwhelming, and at times so dangerous, that the Devil himself was generally supposed to have been its creator. For the sole purpose of worrying the valley far-mer, so the valley farmer believed, the Devil had flung the moun-tains apart and made a pathway for that silver snake the Ghamka.

Once in the valley the river chose its own path and, now among Swartkops foothills, now among the Patchworks, worked its erratic and treacherous but fertile way to the open veldt be-yond.

If the Ghamka valley was the first to suffer from flood it was the last to suffer from drought, and to the girl in the buggy the green of the lucerne lands, the deeper green of the orange groves, the golden spires of the Lombardy poplars, and the glint of white-washed farmhouses through their rows of cypress trees, came like a sudden vision of an enchanted country.

Between them and this country, at the foot of the hill on which they had paused, lay the river. The drift here was half a mile wide. The three small streams into which it had shrunk trickled forlornly through stretches of white sand, and desolate clumps of mimosa and China rose [double oleanders]. On the valley side of the river the low kopjes of the open veldt gave place to rocky flat-topped hills overrun by prickly pears and aloes. Between these hills and the lucerne lands, tobacco lands, vineyards and ostrich camps of the various farms, wound the Princestown road. Within a mile of the old Princestown pass came the second Ghamka drift. Here and there the evenness of the cultivated lands was broken by a clump of mimosa, a waste of bamboo, a willow-hung dam, or an occasional mighty oak. The greatest of these oaks grew in front of the old Delaport houseplace [homestead] for which Petchell and the Dokter were bound. Petchell was to remain with the O'Ma while the Dokter went over the pass to join in a [Princestown] hunt. So they had planned, unknown to the O'Ma, but sure of their welcome.

II

Delaport's was a long low white-washed building, with green plank shutters, and a green half-door. At one end of the wide uneven stoep was a new red iron tank. At the other a high-backed brick seat. In front of the house grew six tall cypress trees. The garden, surrounded by a crumbling mud wall, lay across the farm road.

As the buggy drew up to the steps it disturbed a group of dejected moulting fowls, an enraged turkey, a yellow cat, a yellow dog, a goat, two pigs, an old ayah smoking a clay pipe, and three naked piccaninnies. The hysterical greeting of this company brought O'Ma Delaport hurrying out on to the stoep.

O'Ma Delaport was stout as all her family were, and looked forward to dying sooner or later of a heart disease. Her features were heavy and expansive, and, except when she smiled, expressionless. She smiled now, hurrying down the stoep steps as fast as the disease of her heart would allow.

"Al-le-wêreldt!" she said simply.

The Dokter climbed out of the buggy and shook hands. Petchell with a little gesture of affection leant forward and kissed the large sallow face held up to hers. O'Ma was wearing a tight black cashmere dress, a blue and white checked apron, a pair of elastic-sided boots, and a bonnet. The apron and the bonnet disturbed Petchell vaguely. The Dokter saw nothing peculiar in the O'Ma's appearance.

Alletta Delaport had been the Dokter's first Dutch patient, and in this lay the secret of their friendship. They disagreed totally on politics. They disagreed about the virtues of gunpowder, green paint, and red flannel. They disagreed about the Almighty. They did not even agree about the Devil. But nothing disturbed their friendship, and it was to the Dokter rather than to one of

54

her own family that the O'Ma turned in time of trouble.

When Betti, her favourite daughter, insisted upon marrying Piet Westhuisen, the store man, it was to the Dokter the O'Ma appealed to reason her husband, the O'Baas, into forgiveness. And the Dokter had gained not only forgiveness, but the settlement, before the O'Baas' death, of the farm of Vergelegen upon Betti and her children for ever. For this the O'Ma had never ceased to be grateful. Though outwardly she had disapproved Betti's runaway match, secretly she had admired it. There was a furtive tinge of romance in this heavy well-to-do Dutchwoman, the mother of twelve children, grandmother of forty, great-grandmother of ten. And it was perhaps to this that, in the early days of their friendship, the Dokter and his motherless little daughter had appealed so strongly. To Petchell she was devoted. She had watched the little girl grow up – all the O'Ma's experience at housekeeping lay at the service of the young Drostdy Mees [Mistress]. Her pride in Petchell's store-cupboards was intense.

It was of these cupboards she thought now, as she turned to the Dokter, and said eagerly in Dutch:

"You go over the pass to hunt, hey? Yes? You leave the Keinke ['Little One'] with me? That is well. She will come with me to the pig-killing. She shall learn with me how to make the sausages that did get for me the first prize at the Dank Feast."

"Where is the pig-killing," asked the Dokter as he helped Petchell out of the buggy. Already a Hottentot boy had begun to outspan.

"At Vergelegen. Betti she is a good woman. But her sausages! The Lord help her!" the O'Ma panted heavily.

She turned with sharp orders to the Hottentot boy, then suddenly raising her voice to a shrill "Loup!" scattered in a single instant the piccanninies, the ayah, the hens, the turkey and the yellow dog.

"Al-le-wereldt," she groaned, mounting the stoep steps. "Al-le-wereldt!" and plunged into the forehaus ['voorhuis': front room].

Petchell and the dokter followed. The forehaus was in darkness, the green plank shutters closed to keep out the heat. The O'Ma walked heavily across the bare floor to the kitchen with orders for coffee. The Dokter groped blindly forward and struck a chair. But for a moment Petchell stood still in the doorway, unable to move against the alternate black and white waves of light and darkness which surged towards her.

Gradually the waves subsided, and she made out dimly the rimpje chairs stuck stiffly round the room, the painted Dutch clock on its varnished bracket, the three brilliant almanacs in cork frames, the enlarged photograph of the O'Baas, the small painted sideboard, and the long table, covered with shiny brown American cloth which furnished the room. On this table were an old "receepie" [recipe] book, a jar of spices, a skin of dried fruits, four variegated mealies, a well-filled green cookie-canister, a salt bag, a small tin of gunpowder, a pair of spectacles, and a Bible. These were the O'Ma's preparations for her journey to Vergelegen. Petchell remembered the canister. It had red [? cabbages] on the lid, and four times a year at Nachtmaal the O'Ma had brought it filled with a particular kind of rooi koekie [red cookie] to the Dokter's little keinke [child] at the Drostdy. She had cried when she came, giving Petchell loud wet kisses, and answering all the questions about the old Dutch Landdrost who had once lived in the white walled house which was now the the little girl's home. What the O'Ma did not know from hearsay about the Landdrost she had made up for herself, asking the Lord, in deep gutteral asides, to forgive her for telling lies.

The Dokter tapped the tin of gunpowder. "To kill the pig?"

"But nay, Dokter: for Betti's Virginie. Betti's Virginie she has the cold. With but a thimbleful of gunpowder, and a little sugar, I will now make Betti's Virginie that she no longer has the cold. What think you?"

"Possible. Hardly probable."

The O'Ma turned sorrowfully to Petchell. "Your Father laughs at the gunpowder as he laughs at the Devil. Do not laugh at the Devil my child. Believe me in what I tell you. Gunpowder, it is good for the cold. (Have I not now given it to my children and my children's children for forty years?) And he lives in the

56

Ghamka valley — the Devil. You believe now that? Hey Dokter?"

"Possible," admitted the Dokter. "Hardly probable."

The O'Ma sighed, gazed at the Dokter in silence, and without changing her position by the table, shouted to some unseen being in the kitchen, "Al-le-wêreldt, Classina October, and must I then come and make the coffee with my own hands?"

"All the same," she added in sudden triumph, "is it not because of the Devil they build them now that new pass by the Rooi Kranz?"

"Poss—"

Petchell stopped him. "Oh, Father, don't," she laughed. "I'm quite sure it is because of the Devil," she nodded encouragingly to the O'Ma. "Only the Devil could have put it into their heads to want a new pass."

The O'Ma brightened. "It is also the will of the Lord, my child. That new pass, it will make for Piet and Betti a little more geld [money]. They did buy, you know, some of Betti's land," she explained to the Dokter. "Rik and Klaas Rademeyer did want the new pass to go up by their camp. But Mynheer Frew, he said Nay. And it goes up now close by Betti's house. That it has made them baie mad [very angry] — Rik and Klaas."

"I'm glad," said Petchell unexpectedly and emphatically.

The Dokter explained: "She hates Rik. He wants to buy the Drostdy."

"The Drostdy? Take care then Dokter. He is slim [clever], that Rik. But it is the will of the Lord that the new pass goes up now by Betti's — Al-le-wêreldt, Classina October, and must I then come and make the coffee with my own hands?"

A cart drove round the house, and drew up at the stoep steps as she spoke. A moment later Classina October burst into the room with the coffee tray. Classina October, a young Kaffir girl, wore a new and noisy pair of velskoen [rawhide shoes], and little else. She dashed the tray on to the table and seizing the cow-tail from the side-board, began waving it vigorously above the Dokter's head. She too was bound for the pig-killing. Had not the Mies roused her at sun-up to prepare? Not a moment's peace had she had since sun-up And now it had pleased the Lord to add the Dokter and Mies Petchell to that verdomde [damned] pig at Vergelegen. She cast wrathful glances at her mistress.

"The cart waits," she said.

The false calm which she had hitherto maintained suddenly deserted the O'Ma. She was seized by the restless energy of indecision. She straightened her bonnet, untied her apron, pushed aside her coffee, and hurriedly collected her dried fruits and spices, torn distressfully between her sense of hospitality, and her anxiety about Betti's sausages.

Under the spell of the O'Ma's movements, and Classina's angry glances, Petchell became oppressed by an atmosphere of unnecessary haste. She had no desire to hurry. Like the Dokter she never did hurry. But she found herself drinking her strong black coffee in scalding tasteless gulps.

The Dokter alone appeared totally unaffected by the approaching death of the Vergelegen pig. With the O'Ma's permission, and on condition she did not desert the pig he would remain at the farm till the cool of the afternoon, and then make for the mountain toll-house where next morning the hunt was to meet. And having set her mind at rest on this point he listened good-humouredly to her stream of apology.

The O'Ma decided that she and Petchell would return to Delaport's the following evening. That is, if the Lord were willing. On account of the disease of her heart, the O'Ma always referred her movements to the Lord, and travelled with her grave-clothes in a roll of black American oil-cloth. She hurried to her wardrobe for the roll now.

The Dokter rose from his chair and flicked his cigar ash into a saucer. Petchell suddenly, and without any desire to do so, hurriedly removed her hat, and as hurriedly replaced it.

"I hate pigs," she murmured. "And I hate pig-killing. I don't know what Betti will say when she sees me. I suppose she can put me up somewhere. And I loathe sausages and pork. But I'll have to eat them. Both. All. And I've burnt my tongue. Is my hat straight? Never mind. I feel as if I had been running for miles and miles. And still had miles and miles to run. I'm exhausted. You needn't laugh. You are out of the whirlwind, but I'm in it."

58

Suddenly, and unexpectedly, she began to plead. "I don't like whirlwinds, Father. They don't agree with me. I want to get out. Can't I stay behind with you here? Can you possibly get on without me do you think?"

The Dokter stroked his beard. "On the whole little daughter I think I shall get on without you remarkably well. In fact if you stayed your presence might become impertinent."

Petchell placed her last hat-pin and looked at the Dokter sadly. "I believe she is right," she said. "He does live in the Ghamka valley."

"Who does?"

"The Devil. I begin to believe in the Devil. Only the Devil could be sending me off like this. In a whirlwind." She kissed the Dokter with a sigh, and went reluctantly out on to the stoep.

The O'Ma had already climbed into the cart, shouting last injunctions for the Dokter's comfort to the old ayah in the kitchen. She leant forward and shook hands in a final flood of apology.

At the cart step Petchell paused, and appealed for the last time.

"Father —"

"Well —?"

"Don't you think there is a kind of daughterly impertinence that is refreshing?"

"Go tell that to the Roadman," chuckled the Dokter, pulling her ear.

Petchell climbed into the cart and took up the reins.

"I said *daughterly*," she said severely, and with a sharp click of the tongue drove off.

III

With the exception of the willows round the dam, and the Lombardy poplars at the end of the house, the fig trees were the only trees on the Vergelegen house-place [homestead]. They were too the largest fig-trees in the district. They grew in a line at the far end of the yard, close to the brandy vat, and to Petchell gave always a peculiar impression of detachment from, and toleration of, the Vergelegen farm. As far as she could discover they had never been planted. They had simply arisen out of the earth, and grown to their present magnitude in complete indifference to their surroundings. And under their out-spreading branches everything of outdoor importance in the Vergelegen farm life took place. Here, on ground beaten as flat and smooth as the mud floor of the kitchen, the pots were scoured, the mealies were stamped, the horses were harnessed, the carts inspanned. Here the brandy was made, the fruits peeled for drying. Here Piet's boys courted Betti's ayahs. And here, on a board between two trestles, the pig was to die.

Petchell, once again incapable of resistance to a commotion in which she had no desire to share, found herself dragged to the fig-trees by Betti's three small sons, Wilhelm, Justus, and Ludovic. Her arrival in time for the pig-killing had been hailed by all at Vergelegen as a coincidence especially arranged by the Almighty. That pig-killing and sausage-making might not interest their guest did not dawn upon O'Ma Delaport, or serious-minded kind-hearted Betti Westhuisen.

Petchell, though unwilling violently to disturb their faith in Providence, mentioned diffidently her readiness to spend the afternoon in the darkened slaap-kamer [bedroom] with Virginie. Even Piet, however, devoted as he was to his little daughter, would not hear of this sacrifice. The O'Ma had examined Virginie's throat with a metal spoon, he said. There was nothing wrong with Virginie's throat which gunpowder could not cure. O'Ma had also diagnosed Virginie's seer-kop [headache]. Sleep alone could cure Virginie's seer-kop. It was of course a calamity that the condition of Virginie's throat and Virginie's kop [head] prevented Virginie's personal attendance on the pig. But such was the will of the Lord. And Virginie had moreover the doll which the Roadman had given her.

Piet, having spoken, closed the only door of escape. And after coffee Petchell drifted naturally, with the rest of the family, to the fig-trees. Here, while Betti and the O'Ma superintended the preparations for the coming death, Petchell, on an overturned mealie stamper, tried to win the friendship of Ludovic.

Ludovic had not yet arrived at the dignity of trousers, but quite evidently thought himself superior to the Mies on the mealie stamper. He wore a red and black tartan dress, a blue and white checked pinafore, yellow velschoen and an old felt hat of Piet's with a hole in the crown. Into the band of this hat had been stuck a white ostrich feather of unusual length. With every movement of Ludovic's solid little body this feather swayed and trembled.

For the greater part of the day Ludovic had employed his valuable time in chanting monotonously, "The pig goes to die. The pig goes to die." In vain had exasperated members of his family tried to stop him. He had gazed at each in turn with that total lack of expression which Petchell now found so disconcerting to her friendly advances, and had calmly and indifferently continued to remark that the pig was about to die. There was a certain grandeur about Ludovic which attracted Petchell. He had, it seemed to her, inherited all his mother's persistence and strength of character.

The once romantic Betti was already inclining to an unromantic stoutness and solidity, but she had lost nothing of that persistence to which she now owed her man, and her farm, and to which as a girl she had owed her astonishing six months at Miss Campion's Boarding-school in Princestown. In each of these battles she had been aided by the Dokter. The Dokter alone had grasped what her struggle for freedom against the prejudices of her family meant to her. For two years Betti and the Dokter had fought the O'Baas for that six months at boarding-school without which, it seemed to her, life could mean nothing. Betti was nineteen, and according to Dutch ideas almost too old to marry, when the O'Baas, worn out by her importunity, wrathfully gave way. And Betti, already aware of the Storeman's existence, and determined to be able to accept him in English, packed up her yellow Nachtmaal [Communion Service] trunk that same evening, and next day, in a buggy driven by an old Hottentot boy, arrived at Miss Campion's and calmly announced herself as a new pupil.

Her eagerness to learn, her willingness to submit to rules made for girls of twelve and thirteen, her courage in overcoming,

61

or calmly ignoring, the difficulties of her position, won Mary Campion's heart. In that six months Betti suffered much, as was inevitable, but only Mary Campion guessed it. At the end of the six months, which in spite of the Dokter's entreaty the O'Baas refused to extend to twelve, Betti went back to Delaport's in the buggy as she had come. But she went back with enough English to accept the Storeman in that language, and enough courage to marry him quietly one morning from the Dokter's house in Platkops.

For several years after their marriage Piet had remained Storeman, and Betti had been ignored by every member of her family but her mother. Then came the painful reluctant forgiveness of the O'Baas and the slow and much discussed granting of the Vergelegen farm. The granting of the farm estranged her still further from her brothers and their wives. They said among themselves that they could not forgive her for throwing herself away on a Storeman, ten years older than herself, with a bald head. But in reality what they had no intention of forgiving was her gain of the Vergelegen farm. "Ingelse [English] Betti," as she was called after her six months at school, wife of a bald-headed Storeman, had no right to deprive the eleven Dutch members of her family of their just share of the twelfth farm.

Such was Betti's romance. Gradually, imperceptibly, it had faded into a continual struggle against drought, a continual struggle to make of her man a successful farmer, of her children good scholars.

In this struggle she had lost most of the English gained at Princestown, and most of the glamour which had once clothed her love affair. But she still retained an intensity of feeling which at times astonished Petchell and left her speechless. To the girl who, in emotion, grew absolutely silent there was something almost volcanic in Betti's outbursts. Like volcanic eruptions they came without warning, regardless of time or season. And such an outburst occurred now.

Betti, deserting the trestle came across to Petchell, and pushing Ludovic aside, said quickly in Dutch:

"Yesterday my brother Hans, his wife, she came to borrow my

62

sewing-machine. She has not been in my house now five years, but she came for my sewing machine. Yes. When Ludovic was born, and they thought I must die, did she come? Nay, Petchell, she stayed home-by [at home]. But for my sewing-machine she did come. Yes. She did go first to De Rust. Katerin Rademeyer she has also the sewing-machine. But they are ill at De Rust. (They did send for the Dokter? Nay? He is too snoep [stingy], that Klaas Rademeyer.) My brother Hans, his wife, she think it is wrachtag [really; truly] the fever. She fly from De Rust. She has no time to ask now the sewing-machine. So she come to me. Yes. She come to ask for my sewing machine and she speak lies about my man. And when she can think no more lies to speak about my man, she say to me, Petchell, "You fool you, what for did you then marry a man with a bald head?" And what do you think that I say to her Petchell? I say to her this: "I did marry my man with the bald head so that I might kiss his bald head. Go tell that to my brother Hans, and to all my brothers," I said. "Al-le-wêreldt!"

And abruptly as she had come, Betti, her pale eyes blazing under her kapje [sun-bonnet], left the mealie stamper and returned to the trestle.

The pig had already reached the yard, and was being driven wildly towards the fig-trees by Wilhelm, Justus, and a Hottentot boy. In spite of the shrill cries of Wilhelm and Justus, the hysterical squeals of the pig, the excited questions of the O'Ma, and the slow serious replies of Piet, a strange unearthly stillness held the air. Ludovic had ceased to remark that the pig was going to die. He stood at Petchell's side, intent, yet expressionless, his feather swaying gently.

Piet and the old Hottentot caught the pig, lifted it on to the trestle, bound it. Its squeals became shrieks, agonised, appalling. Petchell forgot her visit had been arranged by the Lord expressly for this, and putting her hands to her ears, closed her eyes. An instant later the cries of the pig were drowned in a human roar. Ludovic, suddenly realizing what the trestle, the rimpjes, and the knife all meant to his old friend the pig, rushed madly across the yard to its rescue. With his velschoen he kicked his Pa, he

kicked his O'Ma, and he kicked his mother. He flung himself
wildly against the trestle. He yelled, he stamped, he scratched,
he tore, his feather swaying and quivering with his agitation.
Petchell rescued him. And with a tightness in her throat escaped
with him to the willow-hung dam. But the cries followed them
to the dam. Hardly realizing what she did she struck a path to
the left of the dam, and half dragging, half carrying the still-sobbing
Ludovic, she began climbing the Kranz.

The path was new to her. It had been made by the Roadman,
who depended on the Vergelegen dam for his water, and the Rooi
Kranz farms for certain of his provisions. It was used by the Vergelegen children who already depended upon the Roadman for
lekkergoed [sweets]. In his zinc provision shed the Roadman, so
the children believed, kept an unlimited supply of lekkergoed.
Certainly he did his best, with leisurely good-nature, to ruin the
digestions of Wilhelm, Justus, Ludovic, and Virginie.

As he came down the path now, and saw Ludovic's feather
subsiding under a Karreeboom his hand went instinctively to his
pocket. Then he recognized Petchell — the little girl he had last
seen on Mary Campion's balcony. Her face was flushed with the
exertion of carrying Ludovic. Her wavy brown hair was escaping
wildly, as usual, from the coil in which, as Drostdy Mies, she en-
deavoured to wear it. Her large-pupilled grey-green eyes were
troubled and misty. As she raised them in the shadow of her
mealie-plait [straw] hat the Roadman thought suddenly of cool
moss-grown wells.

Their meeting surprised neither the girl nor the builder of
roads. The vastness and simplicity of the veldt by which they
were surrounded, made surprise almost an impossible emotion.
Petchell accepted the Roadman as she had been forced to accept
his tents. The Roadman accepted Petchell's presence as he had
accepted the presence of the buggy on the Princestown road.
Each became part of the scheme of the veldt, as kopjes, and
stones, and little brown bushes were part of that scheme.

The Roadman halted opposite the Karree tree and gazed medi-
tatively through the large round glasses of his spectacles at
Ludovic's agitated feather. Ludovic, suddenly grasping the situa-

64

tion and its possibilities, made the most of his opportunity. His sobs became roars, increasing in volume.

The Roadman turned slowly, enquiringly to Petchell.

"You see," said Petchell simply, "the pig was an old friend of Ludovic's. He didn't understand —"

"I see." The Roadman was gravely interested.

He probably thinks I'm a raving lunatic, Petchell thought wildly. Aloud she explained, "It was a pig-killing."

"Yes," said the Roadman. And added after a pause, "My pig."

"Yours!" gasped Petchell, horrified, she scarcely knew why.

"I had bought it. Provisions for my men." The Roadman spoke humbly, apologetically, and waited.

Petchell said nothing. Why, she wondered, did the Roadman get his sun-helmet and boots and gaiters from England, and his corduroys and flannel shirt from Platkops? She found herself unable to detach her thoughts from this unanswerable and impertinent question. Some day she would ask his uncle, the Archdeacon, to explain.

Ludovic continued to roar.

The Roadman's hand travelled slowly towards the pocket of his store-made corduroys. "Perhaps —" he suggested.

Ludovic's gaze travelled with his hand. Ludovic's roars became sobs. And as the Roadman produced a cardoesie [paper bag] these sobs became sheepish broken chuckles.

"That's better," sighed the Roadman, relieved. He turned to Petchell again. "I suppose Westhuisen is at home? The drought is breaking. They've had rain in the Langehoven. It's on its way here. Fast, too. To-morrow, perhaps. I want to warn Westhuisen about his dam." His statements came as suggestions rather than as declarations.

Petchell forgot he was the builder of impertinent roads. He seemed in need of encouragement. "You'll find Piet under the fig-trees," she said, smiling kindly over Ludovic's feather.

"Thanks." The Roadman raised his Piccadilly sun-helmet, and as he raised it, paused, troubled by some thought.

"I'm sorry it was . . . my pig," he said awkwardly.

"It doesn't matter, now," said Petchell gently, as gravely forgiving as she might have been to one of Betti's children.

"Thanks," repeated the Roadman, gravely too, and turning, he descended the hill and was lost among the willows.

The Roadman was right. The drought at last was breaking. Unnoticed in the excitement of pig-killing, clouds had rolled, and were still rolling solemnly, steadily up the Ghamka valley. The air had become breathless, oppressive. A warning hush was stealing slowly across the valley, across the veldt. It might last for several hours, or for several days. None could tell. But already, in the stillness, Petchell could feel — could almost hear — the strange movement of the veldt towards rain. Something stirred within her. She too moved — towards what? She did not know, nor did she care. With Ludovic asleep in her arms she was free to answer the call of coming rain. And she answered it. The whirlwind under the fig-trees was forgotten. Rain came nearer and nearer. And under the Karreeboom, forgetful of time, Petchell sat a-soaking and a-seasoning in the music of its coming.

IV

The short southern twilight was beginning when Ludovic awoke. His awaking was a process which took fifteen minutes, and left him repeating at frequent intervals a desire for coffee and cookies. His sentimental concern for the pig had given place now to a wholesome interest in the state of his stomach. In search of cookies and coffee Petchell and Ludovic descended to the house-place [homestead].

On the stoep Betti met them. "The Roadman told me you were on the Kranz. You know the Roadman, hey? Such a great fine pig we have killed, Petchell. Al-le-wêreldt! And I did quite forget Virginie was in bed — I go in now to see her. Will you come?"

Together they entered the voorhuis and passed from the voorhuis to the still darkened slaap-kamer [bedroom]. Here, on a green iron bedstead, Virginie lay lost among the bedclothes.

And Virginie had not only lost herself. She had lost also her new wax doll, and her faith in the Almighty. Her faith in the Almighty varied continually with those astonishing, incomprehen-

66

sible accidents which make the life of a child of five a life of
continual adventure. Her faith in the Devil however never varied.
It was firm and unshakeable. The Devil lived in the Ghamka
Poort and the Ghamka valley. Occasionally he visited Vergelegen
in the shape of a jackal, Virginie knew. She had seen him. Wilhelm, Justus and Ludovic, they also had seen him. But neither
Wilhelm nor Justus, neither Ludovic nor Virginie had ever seen
the Almighty. He lived in Heaven — a vague magnificent Being
more grown-up than the ordinary grown-up person, and even
more stupid.

There was no Reason in this Awful Being. He had made Virginie ill on the eve of the pig-killing. And having made her ill he
had shut her up in the darkened slaap-kamer; had lost her in the
bed-clothes; had lost her doll; had placed the entire household in
the yard out of reach of her voice; and had treated her prayers
for an angel with a fiery sword to show her the way to her pillows with a contemptuous darkness.

For miles and miles she had travelled in a circle in the middle
of the bed unable to reach the pillows. She was as hopelessly
lost in that waste of hot blanket and sheet as any bewildered
traveller on the veldt. Once her hand struck something firm,
round. Her heart beat wildly. But the firmness and roundness
belonged to the O'Ma's well-filled salt-bag. She gave up her search
in despair. Her head, in its vine-leaf bandage, sank heavily on to
the salt-bag. Under her crumpled calico night-dress her feverish
little body shook with sobs. A bitter hatred crept into her heart.
She hated the Almighty. She hated the O'Ma. She hated her Ma,
Wilhelm, Justus, and Ludovic. And in the throes of this awful
hatred Betti found her.

"Al-le-wêreldt! What is it then?" she cried sharply.

Petchell groped her way to the window, and flung open the
shutters. The sudden terror in Betti's voice struck her dully. She
felt stifled and overpowered. The oppressiveness of the air, which
on the veldt seemed right and natural, became in the slaap-kamer
unnatural and evil. Unrealized, it interfered with her sense of
proportion. It interfered with Betti's sense of proportion, with
Virginie's. Betti became unnaturally excited. Petchell became

unnaturally calm. Virginie, usually affectionate, full of life, and of feeling, became an enigma.

"Feel her," cried Betti. "She is hot. She burns. She shakes with the cold! Al-le-wêreldt, my child! What is it then?"

Petchell came towards the bed. Virginie continued to shake, to sob, to burn. Betti, distracted, suggested that her throat was worse. Virginie with a nod, agreed. Betti suggested that her head was worse. Virginie again agreed. Betti went through a list of possible aches and pains, and each of these Virginie claimed with a nod and a sob. She had no definite desire to alarm her Ma. But she had a very definite desire to impress upon a neglectful world her sufferings, and her importance. With a child's instinct she grasped the situation, and used it to her advantage. She continued desperately to shake, to sob, and to burn. Every suggested remedy she refused with vehemence. It appeared to Betti that Virginie desired only one thing — to die in her arms.

Over Virginie's bandaged head she cast terrified appealing glances at Petchell, telegraphing, "Shall we send for the Dokter?"

Petchell resisted the appeal in Betti's pale terrified eyes. She felt suddenly unaccountably annoyed that Betti should wish to deprive the Dokter of the toll-house hunt — the only hunt, as Betti knew, which he was likely to get that season.

"I don't think it's as bad as all that, Betti," she said. "She had lost herself, and was feeling neglected. Take her on to your knee and I'll smooth the bed."

The calmness of Petchell's voice re-assured Betti, but Virginie resented it. Her beloved Miss Petchell who always understood, was failing her for the first time in their friendship. Her symptoms became rapidly worse. She began to shiver and sob afresh. Petchell, straightening the pillows, suggested coffee and cookies with a calmness she was far from feeling. Virginie intimated violently that she desired neither coffee nor cookies. A fresh symptom was thus added to the list. Again Betti telegraphed wildly to Petchell. And again Petchell resisted her appeal. And into the midst of their silent conflict burst the O'Ma. The atmosphere of the slaap-kamer became more and more crowded, and, to Petchell, the action of each became more and more unreal.

The O'Ma, her bonnet awry, her apron stained with the blood of the pig, her large expressionless face streaming with perspiration, was loud in her exclamations of wonder at the failure of gunpowder to cure Virginie's throat. This failure could mean only one thing — the dreaded white spot [diptheria]. Had Betti or Petchell noticed a white spot in Virginie's throat? Neither Betti nor Petchell had examined Virginie's throat. The O'Ma seized a spoon, and tried to examine it now. But the light was bad. She fetched a farm-made candle, and Petchell held it close to Virginie's mouth while the O'Ma manipulated the spoon.

The O'Ma to her surprise was unable to discover a white spot. Petchell was unable to discover it. Betti hesitated — There was something — The O'Ma looked again. She too became undecided — there was surely something — The O'Ma's indecision strengthened Betti. Betti became positive. Petchell alone failed to discover anything resembling a white spot. She felt that Betti resented this failure. And she herself resented this resentment. For a moment they gazed at each other awkwardly, incapable of action. Then Piet was sent for.

Piet came in from his dam, troubled and anxious. Rain was coming, and he felt unsure of the dam lately opened for the Roadman's use. Piet had been a good storeman. But as a farmer he was still struggling towards success through the failures of experience. His one desire in life was to prove to Betti's relations that Betti had not married a fool. It was incomprehensible to him that any one who knew Betti could imagine she would marry a fool. In Betti's judgement upon all matters he had implicit faith. And as Petchell had expected, he too, through Betti's eyes, saw the white spot.

Betti, Piet, and the O'Ma all turned to Petchell in silence. In the flickering candle-light their heavy anxious faces seemed to grow more and more unreal — the appeal in their troubled eyes more and more urgent and childish. And still, unaccountably even to herself, it seemed, the girl resisted.

Then Betti spoke, fixing pale sorrowful eyes on Petchell. "They have the fever at De Rust. My brother Hans, his wife, she did tell me."

Petchell stared at the candle flame.

"If it is the white spot —" began Betti hoarsely.

The air became more and more oppressive. Virginie's sobs, the hard breathing of Betti, the stable-smell of Piet's velskoen, the faint disagreeable odour of freshly killed meat which clung to the O'Ma's apron, became a nightmare to Petchell. But worst of all was the appeal in the six bewildered, helpless eyes which stared at her fixedly.

The situation became intolerable to the girl. If Virginie were really ill she had resisted unreasonably. As unreasonably, if Virginie were merely hysterical, she now gave way.

"Perhaps you had better send for him," she said.

A look of relief passed quickly over Betti's face. "Send Hans, Piet," she said.

Petchell lifted Virginie back into bed and bathed the hot swollen little face. The O'Ma decided on a second dose of gunpowder. It could do no harm. And she carried the salt-bag through to the kitchen to be re-heated. Betti went out into the yard to give last injunctions to Hans, and once again Petchell peered into the depths of Virginie's throat. She could see no white spot. And as she searched a horse trotted quickly out of the yard, taking the farm road which led to the first Ghamka drift.

Petchell put down the spoon and listened, calculating quickly. If Hans did not overtake him on his way to the toll-house the Dokter could not reach the farm till between eleven and twelve. She saw before her the long wait, varied by anxiety and preparations for the next day's sausage-making. Everything seemed horrible — unnatural. A nightmare. She slipped out of the kamer into the voorhuis, out of the voorhuis on to the stoep.

On the stoep the power to breathe returned, and with it the power to feel, to hear, and to think unprejudiced by emotion. Standing silent she caught the faint rustle of the willows swaying uneasily round the dam, of the poplars at the end of the house stirring in little gusts and spasms, of the leaves of the fig-trees fluttering gently above the deserted trestle. A loosened stone rolled slowly down a kopje. A jackal called. From a neighbouring kloof came the weird cry of a babiaan [baboon]. The veldt seemed alive, expectant.

And as she listened darkness came out of the East, and with it, like a timid lover, crept the rain.

Petchell went back to the voorhuis.

At the head of the long table on which supper was set, and on which a blue glass lamp was burning, sat Betti. The glare of the lamp and the shadows on the wall behind her accentuated the white largeness of Betti's face. She blinked miserably at Petchell round the flowered lamp-shade. The anxiety in her pale weak eyes gave her an almost childish expression. For once she was suffering an emotion too deep for volcanic outburst. Petchell had failed her. Virginie was ill, and would probably die. And Petchell did not believe she was ill. Petchell did not want the Dokter's holiday to be spoilt to save her. Petchell would rather Virginie died of the white spot than that her Father missed his hunt. There was a cloud between them — a cloud which had arisen not out of spoken words, but out of unconcealed glances.

And suddenly this cloud vanished. Petchell came across to the older woman and said in the low sympathetic voice Betti loved, "Dear Betti. How tired you must be!"

And Betti, pushing the tea things aside, wept her relief on the edge of the table.

Supper was a quiet meal. The usually tumultuous Wilhelm and Justus and the ever persistent Ludovic were awed into silence by their Mother's tear-stained face. After supper they escaped thankfully with Petchell from the tragedy of the voorhuis to the comedy of their own slaap-kamer. Here, for Petchell's benefit, and in muffled silence, out of respect for Virginie, they stood on their heads, turned somersaults, and played trek with the bed for the waggon, and two rimpje chairs, two stoolies, four pillows, and eight velschoen for the regulation span of oxen.

On her part, with a knowledge which surprised herself, and completely satisfied the three small boys, Petchell, in halting Dutch, answered the astounding questions put to her concerning the personal habits of the Almighty and the Devil. It was by her supposed intimacy with the Devil that she at last gained the affection of Ludovic. She could tell the same tale of the Devil six times over without the slightest variation — a gift priceless in the eyes of all children. For the second time that day, but now of his own free will, Ludovic fell asleep in Petchell's arms, insisting that she should lie down beside him.

And in the silence which followed his gradual indifference to the Devil she too fell asleep to the first low murmur of the slowly coming storm.

V

A terrific peal of thunder, followed by the crash of a falling poplar, awoke Petchell. She sat up quickly, trying to realize her whereabouts. The candle had burnt out, and the vivid flashes of lightning bewildered her. Gradually she remembered the slaapkamer and the span of oxen with which she and Ludovic had set out on trek. It amazed her to think that the children slept, the crack of the thunder among the kopjes was so deafening, the swish of the heavy rain so insistent. Then suddenly from the next room came a child's voice crying wildly, "It is the Lord! It is the Lord!"

She slipped off the bed, and groped her way to the second kamer. As she reached it Betti entered from the voorhuis, carrying a candle. Cowering in a corner of the green iron bed sat Virginie screaming without cessation that it was the Lord. Her pale blue eyes were large with terror. Her little ratstail plaits of fair hair stuck out at odd angles from under her bandage of vine leaves.

"I did eat the Rooi cookie!" she shrieked. "It is the Lord! It is the Lord!"

"It is only thunder, Virginie," said Petchell soothingly. "It will stop soon."

"Nay, nay," wailed Virginie. "I did eat the cookies. It is the Lord!"

Betti, bewildered at first, suddenly understood. She turned to the washstand, on which had been left the O'Ma's cookie-tin. The tin was open and empty.

72

"Al-le-wêreldt," she muttered. "She was sick. I could not understand. To eat cookies like that with a white spot!"

She thrust the candle into Petchell's hand, and once again examined Virginie's throat. The white spot had gone.

Betti turned heavily, troubled, towards Petchell. And Petchell laughed.

"I expect she was hungry," she said. "And too proud to admit it. I quite understand. Poor Virginie!"

But if Petchell understood Virginie's mental sufferings Betti failed to do so. She grasped Virginie by the shoulders and shook her.

"Virginie, be still! Is your kop seer [head aching]?"

One by one Betti went over the long list of Virginie's recent ailments. Virginie suffered nothing now but extreme terror of the Lord, Whom she believed to be bent upon punishing her for telling lies and stealing cookies.

Petchell sat down on the bed, and drew the terrified child towards her. Betti gazed at them both with that unearthly heaviness of expression which Ludovic inherited. Her hair was twisted in a tight plait pinned with a single hair-pin. She wore a white cotton nightdress over which she had placed a black skirt. Her feet were bare. And her eyes were full of an anxiety she seemed unable to express.

"What is it, Betti," Petchell asked.

"Your Father. He is not yet come. Nor Hans."

"But Virginie is better."

"Yes."

"Then it doesn't matter if he is a little late."

"No," said Betti. But she said it without conviction. And Petchell wondered.

"What is the time now Betti?"

"It is near one," said Betti reluctantly. And the reason for her anxicty dawned slowly upon the girl.

"Has it rained like this long?" she asked quietly. And though Betti did not realize it her calmness was the calmness of terror.

"Four hours. Soft first. Then hard like now. You did sleep. I do not know how you did sleep. But I did thank the Lord."

Petchell did not answer. She was straining for the first beat of a horse's hoof — the first clank of a buggy disselboom.

"Perhaps," said Betti miserably, "perhaps he would stay at Delaport's till it stopped."

Petchell tried to say "Perhaps" — tried to think she believed it. But the word stuck in her throat — the thought driven from her mind by a vague dread.

"The Ghamka is a treacherous river," she whispered. "The Ghamka is a treacherous river."

"What do you say," asked Betti, whispering too.

"It rained in the Langehoven yesterday. The Roadman told me —"

Betti said nothing. The Ghamka came down with heavy rain in the Langehoven. With rain this side the mountains as well . . . .

"Will you not come to the voorhuis," asked Betti. "Piet is there. But he sleeps. My Mother she sleeps in the other kamer. It is light there, hey?"

Petchell shook her head. "Here," she said. "Here." And then, quickly, "Go to the other kamer too, Betti. You are tired. Go!"

Betti went.

The candle flickered and flared, and in the far corner of the wide bed Virginie sobbed herself to sleep unheeded. On the pale blue wardrobe strange shadows came and went. And stranger shadows still crept out of the corners to meet them. Petchell found herself gazing at them as if fascinated. They held her, and in holding her interfered in some peculiar way with her hearing. While she watched them a horse might trot almost unnoticed into the yard. She blew out the candle, listening.

Minutes passed. She felt she had listened, staring into the darkness, for hours. Half an hour passed, and listening had become a pain. Yet she dared not move. The slightest irregular sound — the very rustle of her print dress — would drown the beat of a hoof, the clank of a disselboom. An hour passed. She became numbed to every sense but that of hearing. Hearing was now an exquisite agony. But more exquisite still was the dread that she might not hear.

The storm had passed at last from the east of the Platkops

valley to the west. But the rain fell relentlessly — an avenger now, no lover. And in the house, it seemed, all slept but herself. In the darkened slaap-kamer she endured. suffered, lived, alone —

— Of course he might have been warned in time and stopped at Delaport's place. She tried to convince herself that this was the most reasonable explanation of his delay. But her ears would not — could not — obey her brain —

Once she flung herself down on the bed, and burying her face in her hands, cried "God! And I slept! I slept!" It seemed horrible to her that she had slept. This strangely, was her only regret.

Of Virginie she never thought. Virginie's supposed white spot had, for her, no connection with her present anxiety. The consultation which had led to the sending for the Dokter came back to her, if it came at all, like the faint memory of a half-forgotten dream. She lived only for the beat of a hoof — the clank of a disselboom — Her mind refused to grasp anything else. Twice Betti came to the kamer door, shading her candle with her hand. But Petchell made no sign that she saw or heard, and Betti went back to the voorhuis baffled and unhappy.

Between three and four the rain subsided and Betti awoke Piet. The low murmur of their voices annoyed Petchell. It interfered with her hearing. She longed to scream — to implore them to be silent. But she sat on the edge of the bed incapable of movement or of sound. And slowly there forced its way to her brain the dull roar of the Ghamka in flood.

[Piet]* opened the voorhuis door, and went out on to the stoep. Some one called to him from the yard in great good humour. It was the Roadman.

"Well, Westhuisen," he said, "your dam stood, but —"

Piet left the stoep, and joined him. They passed close to Petchell's window, on their way to the yard.

"The Dokter," she heard Piet say. "He has not yet come."

"You expected him?"

"Last night. At eleven."

* The typescript has 'Wilhelm' — an obvious error, as the context makes clear.

75

In silence they crossed the yard to the stable.

"Where shall I find a saddle," asked the Roadman.

"Daar by [Over there]," Piet nodded in the direction of the saddle-rest in the harness room.

Nothing further was said. A few moments later two horses trotted out of the yard. And Betti came into the room, with a cup of strong black coffee. Petchell drank it, not knowing what she drank, or that she drank at all. In the same way she ate the finely cut biltong brought her by the O'Ma. She became strangely passive in their hands, accepting their sympathy and attention with indifference. They gazed at her sorrowfully — then mercifully left her.

Out in the yard a dog barked sharply, and Petchell became suddenly roused. The O'Ma and Betti were in the kitchen. She could hear Betti waking Classina October who had slept under the kitchen table.

She rose from the bed, paused an instant, then slipped quickly out of the house, and across the yard to the farm road which led to the Ghamka drift. Once on the road she began to run, then halted.

From the far side of the next kopje came the beat of a horse's hoof. With a little cry she ran forward again, blindly —

The Roadman dismounted. He put out his hand instinctively, as to a running child. Mechanically Petchell grasped it, lifting her tired eyes to the kindly troubled face under the dripping helmet. Then a voice — her own voice — said dully, "I know. He is dead."

PART 2
DIARIES

THE 1905 DIARY: AN INTRODUCTORY NOTE

In January 1905 Pauline Smith and her mother returned to
Oudtshoorn after an absence of about ten years, for a visit of
six months. They stayed with Mr and Mrs George Wallis (Jean
Wallis was Mrs Smith's sister) for most of the time, but also
went on many excursions and short visits to friends in the sur-
rounding districts and George. During her stay Pauline kept a
hand-written diary in which she recorded impressions and events,
gossip and descriptions of people and places. The people we
meet most frequently are Aunt Jean and Uncle George (Wallis),
Aunt Maud and Uncle Tim (Smith) and Helena, a younger half-
sister of Jean.

Oudtshoorn, seen now through the eyes of a young woman
of 23, was something of a disappointment to Pauline Smith.
Gone was the idyllic little village of her childhood. The ostrich
feather industry which had flourished before the Boer War had
caused the village to grow into a small town, with an influx of
business people and many new buildings, so much so that when
the old Coloured driver Koos took her on an outing in the horse-
drawn cart along a route where, as he said, 'we use always to
come . . . for a drive', she did not recognise her surroundings at
all, much to his chagrin as well as her own. However, old friends
had not changed, and most of the pleasure of the visit was
derived from seeing them. It was now some seven years since the
death of her beloved father, and although there is little reference
to him in the diary it is certain that many poignant memories
were revived, as when she visited the local hospital and saw items
donated from their old home, in which the doctor's surgery had
been situated.

Apart from calling on old friends, the Smiths were invited to
croquet and tea parties, and in the evenings they nearly always
played bridge (which Pauline often referred to a 'broeg' in the
diary). She was sometimes an unwilling partner at this, especially
on the very hot evenings when it was preferable to sit on the
stoep, or — as she and Helena sometimes did — on the pavement
with their feet in the open furrow of water which still coursed
through the village as it had done in her childhood.

Pauline Smith had left Oudtshoorn as a delicate schoolgirl of 13 years: she was now a slim, pale, reserved young woman whose best features were her beautiful brown eyes and soft dark hair. Although she had outgrown the back ailment which had troubled her as a child she was not strong and already subject to the neuralgic headaches which were to plague her for the rest of her life. The extreme heat of the summer of 1905 aggravated the condition and spoilt some of the expeditions.

What of Pauline Smith the writer? By this time she had written while still at boarding school (and after the death of her father) several of the stories which later were published in *Platkops Children.* (One of these, 'The B'loon Man', was published in a Scottish newspaper in 1910.) She had also contributed sketches on Scottish life to *The Aberdeen Free Press.* The 1905 Diary in no way pretends to be a literary document, but there is much that is of interest to the student of Pauline Smith's work. There is strong evidence, in her detailed descriptions of places and people and her notation of dialogue and strange turns of phrase, that she was collecting material for further stories (see for instance the character sketches of Miss Blant, the Archdeacon and Miss Fogg; she had also set aside a page for South African idioms which unfortunately was left blank). The Diary was also intended for her sister, Dorothy, who would have known many of the persons and events sometimes rather cryptically referred to by Pauline.

Apart from throwing some light on Pauline Smith as a young woman, the diary also presents a vivid picture of life in a Little Karoo 'dorp' during the early years of the century. It opens without preamble on New Year's Day 1905, and ends almost as suddenly on June 10th. The extracts comprise only about a third of the original; the entries omitted include many references to the heat and to illness, and add little to our knowledge of the author or the persons and places visited.

In transcription obvious slips of the pen have been silently corrected, as have spelling variants (such as 'Reitvlei' for 'Rietvlei') which are of little or no significance. Pauline Smith often used abbreviations for persons and places: for ease of reference

the full names — where known — have been given (thus 'Mrs B.'
becomes 'Mrs Burns'). The ampersand, appropriate to the 'diary'
form, has been retained, but punctuation has been simplified
(e.g. by the deletion of full-stops after 'Dr', '4th', etc.). Apart
from these minor editorial procedures, the text remains unaltered.
All editorial interpolations are given in square brackets, as are
the usual deletion marks where an entry has been abbreviated.
Where Pauline Smith uses an Afrikaans/Dutch word or expression,
the English equivalent follows; often, however, her usage is in-
correct or approximate; in such cases, subsequent occurrences
of the term have been silently corrected or regularized. For items
requiring fuller explanations, as well as comments on persons or
events of topical significance, the reader is referred to the foot-
notes. The 1905 Diary has an entry — however short — for each
day, from 1st January to 10th June: dates and entries not featured in this selection must therefore be taken as having been
deleted *in toto*.

An attempt has been made to 'sign-post' the sometimes con-
fusing account of routes followed and excursions made, in the
course of the visit; the map on pages 130—1 will enable the reader
to locate most of the place-names referred to and gain some idea
of direction and distance, as well as topography.

Thanks are due to Miss E.K.Bird for typing from the extremely
difficult, often almost illegible handwriting of the original text.

Sheila Scholten

SELECTIONS FROM THE 1905 DIARY

UNCLE GEORGE'S, OUDTSHOORN, C.C.[1]

Sunday evening, Jan. 1st 1905

New Year's Day — Dreamt about a house, full of lovely old curios, including a beautiful carved cradle which a nice old man showed us . . . . Breakfast — Spent morning in looking over photo films . . . . Dinner — Goose — Lay down & read John of Gonsau — too full of Grand Duchesses etc. Tea . . . . Supper . . . . Uncle George & I went to church[2] — High — came back with Curate & wife — Talked to Haslett & Jean George about our trip to Switzerland — Bed.

Monday, Jan. 2nd

Very hot — Liza & old Mrs Burns called & brought some figs. Stood talking till I felt queer with the heat — Lay down. Coloured people always smile when speaking to a White person — Mrs Burns smiled when telling us of Nonna's death — Nervousness, I suppose — Also told us she lived "*in* the graveyard" now! At 5.30 went to Pococks'[3] for croquet — Lots of fruit — Couldn't get Mother away from mulberries. Back at 7.30 — Supper — Went down to Aunt Maud's[4] for eggs & store of canned stuffs for Meirings Poort. Leah and Rachel quarrelled last week — Uncle George thought they should make up on New Year's Day, so went to the kitchen to speak to them. "Leah, has the devil gone out of you yet?" — "Ja, Mas'r" — "And you Rachel?" "No, Mas'r, he not quite out of me yet" — Retreat of Uncle George — His Satanic Majesty not yet departed.

RIETVLEI [Le Roux: a siding on the way to Meiringspoort]

Tuesday, Jan. 3rd 05
We decided to come out here last night, so were driven down to
the station by Willem to catch the train at 9.30 — The station
is near the old Dutch Church with a colony of zinc houses
round it, & not at all like Oudtshoorn — A great crowd was at
the station owing to the 4 days holiday. With difficulty got a
carriage with Addleys & Alloe Anderson on her way to Port
Elizabeth to be married — stopped here & there on the veldt to
pick up passengers. Watered at Hazenjacht, where some naked
black boys sold figs, probably stolen, in beakerkies [small tins] —
one boy wore a soldier's cap, another a soldier's jacket, picked up
on the veld somewhere, I suppose.[5] Le Roux (Rietvlei) is a *proper*
station, with a platform, a station master & a refreshment table
— Walked to the "Hotel" — great heat, & terrible dust — Sat in
darkened sitting-room killing flies & time till lunch when Uncle
George, who had driven out, arrived — Lunch — Black damsel
waited, & *pinched* us before asking us whether we wanted
"Shoup?" or "Lobsterincole tonguein corn beef?" Also went
solemnly round the table saying to each separately — "Will you
take some more?" "No" — "Will you have some pineapple?"
Her wool was done up into numerous little plaits, &, with the
bare partings in between, looked for all the world like a map
of mountains divided by rivers — After lunch, the thermometer
being 102° on the stoep, which was the coolest & draughtiest
part of the house, we retired to bed. . . . At 6 we rose again &
walked down to the river gathering ostrich feathers from the
roadside, & diseased thorn branches in all sorts of queer shapes
from the Mimosa [flowering thorn] which are all in full bloom
at present — The river was quite dry, & everything very dusty.

Wednesday, Jan. 4th
Coffee this morning at 6 — Started for Meirings Poort at 6.30,
Willem driving Royal & [?] — So hot that we had to put up the
sunshade. Near De Rust, a new village that has sprung up, it
grew cool and cloudy — threatening rain — after all Helena's

[half-sister of Jean Wallis] boasts concerning the steadiness of Cape weather — De Rust has an elegant church, a most ecclesiastic looking school, & some nice homes — The farms along Leroux River are very pretty, & the great red hills around are grand — Kitty Leroux's[6] farm is one of the prettiest. Further on we passed the Rankin's old home, now in ruins. Helena says I was taken there at 9 months old, & again at 21 months — The latter I remember & was shown the pond in which I remember seeing mother bathing with a box under her head to keep her from sinking while trying to swim — They put dynamite into the water, & nearly scared me out of my wits, which probably impressed it on my memory — Just beyond Rankin's we saw two huge baboons as big as men, darting across in front of the cart — Uncle George told us that Mr Walton & a friend, after shooting one had been attacked by the whole troop & had to fly for their lives! Soon after Rankin's we got to the opening of the poort. On either side rose the Swartberg Mountains with just enough room between for the river & the road — Indeed there is not always room for *both* & the river having been there first the road has to give place to it & often we seemed to be driving along the river itself — The poort is 12 miles long, & about 7 to the waterfall — In those 7 miles we crossed over the zig-zagging river 23 times. It was a wonderful drive. The mountains seem to be piles of natural castles and arches firmly packed one on top of the other, & all of red stone — The whole poort is so narrow, & so zig-zagged that it gives one the idea of the mountain having been surprised & shaken apart.

We reached the waterfall at 8.30 — lit a fire, made coffee, & had breakfast — Then climbed up to the fall, accompanied by a kaffir woman, who was trekking with her husband & family & had camped out near us — The husband stayed below with the family & allowed his wife just time to get up to the fall & down again when the march was resumed — They carried their household goods upon their backs, all the small children even having packs & tin cans to manage — The waterfall is rather weak at present owing to want of rain but must be lovely when the rush is great — The great round pool at the foot of the fall is 40 ft

deep — The climb was a little stiff in parts — There are really 3
falls — The big one we climbed to, one above, which can't be
seen, & one below which is seen from the road & coming down
we all hunted for gold — except Helena, whose activity astounded
us, she being the first up, & the first down, & very vigorous in
her commands to follow her quickly — Got down & climbed
into the cart when the Wrensch family came up & outspanned
— Lovely cool, almost cold drive back — a little rain — saw lots
of dassies [Hyrax: rock rabbits], & at the waterfall heard the
mournful boohoohoo of the Babjan [baboon] (we suppose) &
the whoop a whoop of the whoop whoop [Hoopoe]. Saw lovely
birds too, especially a king-fisher perched on a rock above the
2nd. fall. Very few ferns or flowers, owing to heat & want of
water. Frogs croaked & the bisje [*sonbesie*: cicada] bissed
steadily — Back to hotel to lunch, & then down to train.
Crowds of folk here, mostly coloured & very excited — Met
Kitty Leroux. "Don' you fin' Oudtshoorn mich change?" "Yes"
"Do you like *him* so?" Got off at last, after the culled pussons
had been crammed into 1st class carriages & trucks amid much
laughter & shouting — Got back to Oudtshoorn, and found
Willem waiting for us with 2 carts — All went early to bed.

Saturday, Jan. 7th 05 Idioms
. . . Cape girls have some curious idioms — "Ach now, you
know what?" at the beginning of a sentence which is to convey
some astonishing or distressing fact — "Now well now" — another
is "Now well now, you know" "Ach wot, you know" "And oh,
you know? I've got a new dress" — "Ach but it's hot, come let
us go by the stoep so long? And fancy now, you know, her girl's
not going to stay with her any more — Have you got a good girl
now, hey? Yes? Ours is also a good girl — but so slow! Oh, you
know it's too awful! " Shall leave this page blank to fill in as I
come across more[7] — Also they begin with "You know wot?"
& use Now already — "He's now already got a store" — And I
used to take her once but "*now no more*". Will you have supper
"*by* us". . . .

85

Friday, Jan. 13th The Carriage Story

... Afternoon Dolly Bernhardt came for me with Amy [Kent]'s
phaeton, Willem & Sonny, & drove me over to hospital — Matron
did not make an appearance, tho' we saw her watching from the
window. Saw over the hospital — Father's instruments in the
theatre — our old bookcase side-board in the dining-room — &
our old sundial in the garden — Watched Dolly, Six,[8] Walter
Thorne, Uncle Harry & Nurse Stevens play tennis — Driven home
again — Dinner — Went with Aunt Jeanie to see Morrises[9] — Julia
at home (just returned from Port Elizabeth. She had seen our old
Emma[10] who is well married in Port Elizabeth). J.Morgan told
Julia that she had met such nice friends who had been so kind
to her & taken her for a drive in a pony carriage with such
spanking horses — Julia & Florrie went to visit Emma, & found
her husband an undertaker — J.Morgan having been driven about
in the mourning coach! ...

Thursday, Jan. 19th

... *Koos*[11] called & asked if he might take us for a drive that
afternoon, as he had got a cart. He came about 5, with Prince
Vintcent's cart, & took us out to Baakens Kraal. It was a very
nice drive, Koos and I sat in front, & talked a bit — Just as we
turned we met Mr Sidney Vintcent in Mrs Vintcent's "private
kerridge" with some friends! Enjoyed the drive very much. Lots
of changes all down there. Koos seemed sorry I did not remember that road better as "we use always to come out here for a
drive in the afternoon". Miss Polly had seen the train, & had not
been frightened, & Koos had promised to take her for a ride in
it some day. ...

Sunday, Jan. 22nd

Cold still miserable — Did not go to Church. Six came — In
evening we all felt so loff [*laf*: weak, feeble] & melancholy that
I suggested going up to the graveyard. Six, Aunt Jean, & I went
& wandered around it. Jack's grave & Dorothy's [Margaret's][12]
are two of the only things quite unchanged in all the 10 years
of our absence. The graveyard has a wall around it now, — no

dam. The Dutch graveyard is desolation itself, & a disgrace to
the Kerk.

Saturday, Jan. 28th Caves[13]
Cart came at 7. . . . Started at last for the caves, Mr Miller (the
clergyman from Mossel Bay, whose wife has just died), Mother,
myself, & Willem in one cart — Uncle George, Mr Porrill, Aileen
& Reg Miller with our "old" Hans in the next, Aunt Jean, Julia,
Miss Bunce, & Mr Taylor in No. 3. Reached the Caves about
10.30. On the way Mr Miller told us that an uncle of Scheepers
had spoken to him at the Boarding House. He had been up to
the Victoria Falls, but Mr Miller could get him to speak of
nothing but Oom Paul's funeral which he had also seen.[14] He
had the commemoration medal of which he was very proud, but
was filled with regret over the loss of the *programme.* He could
talk of nothing but the funeral, & his nephew Scheepers. Told
Mr Miller a strange story concerning Scheepers — Scheepers was
captured when ill, & was taken prisoner to Grahamstown, where
he was shot — His friends found out the grave & went to get the
body to bury it among his own people. On opening it nothing
could be discovered but a handkerchief & the badge off his hat-
band. Hence, it is believed among the Boers that Scheepers is
risen again. Indeed some swear to have seen him, & it is expected
by them that he will return to them & help them to win back
their own! Yet he was shot, & buried as a traitor. — Had breakfast under the willows at the Cango — Then walked up in *awful*
heat to the caves — Got candles stuck into bamboos, signed our
names (having changed into old clo'es in the natural dressing-
room) & started with our two guides — I was not very well, so
Aunt Jean & I did not go far. The caves are wonderful. The darkness intense, but when the guides lit them up by magnesia wire
the stalactites & stalagmites glistened beautifully. Here & there
we came across pools of water springing up from the ground —
the small guide brought us back while the others went on — We
went down to the willows again, & I rested while Willem & Hans
cooked the gridiron chops & potatoes. . . . On our way back we
stopped at the Deas' farm. Grace & Mrs Deas[15] not a bit changed.

87

We all went into the garden which is ablaze with all sorts of flowers still, tho' they say going off — Roses, holyoaks [hollyhocks], verbena, sunflowers, sweetwilliams, sweet peas etc. etc. — Along one side is a lovely walnut avenue. The house is very old — A forehouse [*voorhuis*: entrance hall] with an oilclothed mud floor & reed roof — They are building a new house higher up — Very glad to get home again, & soon to bed, where I was visited by Mimi Leroux[16] & her little daughter Joey, in tears. She thought she had lost Mimi for ever, & was brought down here by a small boy to be comforted! Mimi is just the same. They leave for the farm again to-morrow, & want us to go out to see them. . . .

Tuesday, Jan. 31st Eddie Edmeade's language[17]
Got up early & at 7.30 went for a drive with Uncle George & and Road man & his little daughter "Lucy May Williams" to see the dam by the reservoir. While George and Mr Williams examined the dam Lucy May & I entered into conversation. Said Lucy May (aged 8) "Are you goin' to have supper by us?" "No, I don't think so." "Oh, but *we* have *also* puddin' for supper, you know," said Lucy May coaxingly! . . . The town is growing very much out the dam way, & the Humphrey-Crockett house is now quite *in* the village, not out of it! Yesterday Eddie Edmeades called — His language is most amusing. He & his wife, both being "still young" had an awfully enjoyable time in England. They lived at St Margarets, from thence proceeded every day to Victoria (I think) by train, whence they took the tube into the city, from whence they *radiated*! He also wished he were in England at present to *avert*(!) the hot weather. Suppose we looked astonished for he hastened to *avoid* it. He had also conceived quite wrong conceptions of Paris! Puir mannie! . . .

Thursday, Feb. 9th
In morning Julia sent round to see if we'd care to drive out to Oliver's with her in Mrs Vintcent's carriage — It came for us, with Florrie, at 3.30. Had a lovely drive out, across the veldt — the view of the mountains all around is beautiful from the farm — When we arrived a coloured youth called Saamp ushered us

into the "best room" — a very narrow room clothed &
furnished by photographs of the family particularly Mrs Olivier
& Maggie looking like a duchess & her daughter — No other
furniture seemed worth noticing — Mrs Olivier at length
appeared — Talked 16 to the dozen in very broken & peculiar
English — Wonder what the *duse* it was Mr Pocock sending
papers when the Boers refuse to read them, etc. — & 'fraid
"livings on de Continen' is much more less expensive dan dey is
in Englan', hey?" Cames, & wents, & does most things in very
peculiar participles of her own. Didn't we not likes to went &
sees her new house? Gave us tea, & lots of fruit — When Florrie
made a move she called for Saamp — Saamp — Saampie & told
him to let the dames go into the vineyard & eat grapes, "We eat
noch [still]," said the emotionless Saamp — At length, after being
invited to come out with her from England (she sails this month)
to live "wids me in my new house", we were allowed to depart
with a huge basketful of grapes, & a basketful of peaches. . . .

Sunday, Feb. 12th
Headache & white mixture. In morning Grace Deas came — Did
not go to Kerk — Grace came again in afternoon to tea — Told
us how she had become a "Pro-Boer" thro' writing a letter
opened by the Censor, saying she thought Scheepers "good-
looking" — after which all her letters were opened — She told
me how she had once, as a child, overheard her parents discussing
business difficulties, & had come to the conclusion that they
were going *bankrupt*, which dreadful suspicion she confided in
me — I was so sorry for her that I got a huge basket & filled it
with green mealies, peaches, etc., especially green mealies, for
her to take home *as it would save them a supper*! I was to repeat
this performance, but don't think I did, as Mrs Deas could not
understand my kindness, & Grace, who had got her information
regarding their affairs by eavesdropping, could not explain it!
All Mrs Deas said was, "And what's all this for?" Irony!

In evening Six came & talked in my room, & I changed his
Italian coins for him — Poor boy — He tries to keep up bravely,
& not proud — I read him some of Us, Six etc.,[18] & he laughed
a good bit — Read Us, Six to Coolie.

GEORGETOWN[19]

Thursday, Feb. 16th

Packed, & went down to Mr Speedy for my camera — He lent
me a Brownie — At 11 the post driver's boy came to the hall
door — out of each of the 3 doors in the passage popped a
female, Jean, Helena, & myself. "Can I see Mrs Smith," said the
boy, "Yes" said the 3 of us in chorus — "please Mrs Smith," he
said, addressing us all "can I speak to you please!" "Oh" said
Helena, "You've no seats for us?" The boy explained that two
"post office generals" had come over from Calitzdorp & must
be taken on to George at any rate, — Could we put off going till
Friday. Helena doubtful as her daughter [a jocular reference to
P.S.] must have a day's rest before going on to Oakhurst — but
if no other cart can be had to-day will *have* to put off till Friday,
she supposes — Boy departed, & we sat down to tiffin much
amused, when he drove up again in the butcher's cart (the post-
cart man is a butcher too) & said "Oh, Mrs Smith, it's all right,
& you can go! (the kindness of the creature) We'll send you in a
private cart" — At 11.30 the "private cart" arrived. It turned
out to be the old post *coach* in which the "2 post office generals"
& the other passengers were to be packed with ourselves. It had
6 mules inspanned, & into it Helena & I scrambled, leaving Aunt
Jean behind, much amused — We were driven down to Post
Office with the horn blowing vigorously, & on the way picked
up passenger No. 1 — At Post Office the mails were piled on to
the coach rendering exit by back impossible. Uncle Tim came to
speak to us while at Post Office, & gave Helena some money.
Then we tooted down to Edmeades & picked up Pat, then on
round to Pickards, & down to Green's, where we picked up passenger No. 3 who said No. 4 had gone on ahead. Picked him up
at Bawden's garden, & there we were Passenger No. 1, the brake
wheel, & driver in front seat — In second seat Pat, & passengers
3 & 4, both foreigners, &, we supposed, the post office generals
— On back seats Helena & self. None of these seats had backs
to them, & if it had not been for the mail-bags we'd have been
toppled out! Started at last — grand, but very wobbly & swaying

style — Very hot, & very, very dusty, especially when we got into a whirlwind which was not infrequent. . . . For the last 12 miles of this stage we saw not a single living thing but a blue Karoo hawk. The desolation was awful, & the road fiendish. Even Helena never knew it to be so bad — At last we got to the outspan place & changed the slow mules for 4 horses — (Two of the horses we *ought* to have had, we had met on the road in-spanned to a cart going back to Oudtshoorn.) While this was going on passenger No. 4 gave us lovely pears, grapes, peaches, nectarines, & tomatoes. Helena took it into her head that passenger No. 3 was Mr Carlson, Laura's fiancé. He looked too un-kempt for a bridegroom, I thought, but Helena clung to his foreign accent, & his riding-breeches! On we went thro' greener cooler country now to North Station, where we halted for coffee which passenger No. 4 paid for — He was most kind and attentive, the poor man he had only the *middle* seat and no rest for his big back whatsoever — My head was getting very bad, & after we started I began to feel pretty cart-sick, but kept arguing with myself that it was impossible for me to get out without either sliding down the mail-bags, or disturbing the 5 men in front of me — so I sat still, and "wished I was dead" — The [Outeniqua] mountains were lovely, but I did not feel well enough to enjoy them as I hoped to, & took 2 photos on one film — we were stuck for 10 minutes by 3 wagons in one place [on the Montagu Pass], & at another very narrow one had to pass a cart by scraping along the rocks on our left — The men all leant over to the right to keep the coach from smashing into the rocks altogether, as the left wheel went down in a gully, but we managed all right and passenger No. 3 said even if we *did* fall over we couldn't fall far against a straight wall of rock! Very thankful to see George in the distance, & the green grass here is lovely, tho' no cattle can graze on it owing to its sourness. The coach drove up to the Post Office to deliver the mails. At 6.20 they brought us over to the hotel [the 'George Hotel'], where I went straight to my room leaving Helena to go to dinner alone — Helena discovered that passenger No. 4 is not a general in the Post Office but an Austrian, Mr Krausz[20] who is on his way to

91

Oakhurst to be Mr Carlson's best man, while the one she took for Mr Carlson himself, is, in spite of his breeches, a little Jewish jeweller whose shop is just opposite! Mr Carlson came in from Oakhurst [the Dumbleton Estate] to meet Mr Krausz and stayed here —

Friday, Feb. 17th

The bridegroom and best man departed while we were in bed — Got up for breakfast feeling much better and wandered down to the graveyard alone to see Charlie's grave[21] while Helena read the newspaper — Then we both went down to see Kathleen Snow, who is as nice as ever, & *very* happy. . . . In afternoon lay down, then dressed & wandered up across the veldt, & landed at the new graveyards there! Back again. Wonder why we always land in graveyards — It is a pleasure to see the green grass here, & the great cool green mountains almost at our doors, after the dry Oudtshoorn district — George has changed very little — The streets, which are red red roads, run thro' wide strips of green grass, lined with great oaks, sometimes gums & blackwoods — The houses are all white-washed, & mostly thatched, built in the old Dutch style — The gardens are failures, due to sheer laziness, I think, for with all the water and rain they have here things ought to grow well. . . .

Saturday, Feb. 18th Laura's wedding

Breakfast at 7, & at 7.30 cart & three horses arrived, with Mrs Moore — Helena too excited & flurried to sit down to breakfast, & too hurried to use her knife, so struggled with her fork alone. Started at last, & saw Kathleen on the balcony. A lovely 3 hours drive out, but all the rivers are bridged now, & that takes from the excitement of the journey — Heard baboons in the forest, & saw a dear little baby grass (?) buck, quite tame & not at all afraid of the cart — Mrs Moore told us a drove of 30 baboons had crossed the road in front of her cart once, the mothers carrying the young ones, & an old male, the chief of the clan, keeping cave behind, & bossing the whole show. It is 16 miles to Oakhurst, & there are "milestones on the Knysna road" now

— Saw lovely heaths on the grasslands, & Scotch heather too, which is not quite so purple in colour as it is in Scotland — Also the wild grape-vine & honey flower — A long way behind us we saw the Archdeacon's spider which had been done up especially for Laura's wedding, & was not allowed to be used until to-day by *anyone*, the Archdeacon[22] was walking in from his Pacaltsdorp service (4 miles)! to save it! Arrived at Oakhurst & found everyone in a great bustle — Mr Dumbleton, the bridegroom, the best man (Krausz), Dr Snow, Reg, Hilda, Helena [Helen Dumbleton], Violet, Esme, Bertram, Willie Robotti, Mrs Douglas Dumbleton & Cicely & Norris, Mrs Moore, Archdeacon, Miss Fogg [Anne, the Archdeacon's sister], Helena & self. . . . up to Laura's room (the one I shared with her 11 years ago) where she stood in her pretty wedding-dress having her veil pinned on by Helen [her sister], who was first bridesmaid — She looked so happy & pretty, with her cheeks still Englishy-pink & while we were talking to her, Miss Fogg came up, in her olive coloured silk dress, with her big gold earrings & brooch ("of foreign writings"). In her hand she carried a little brown hand-bag, & she, Helena & I drove off together in the spider to church — Here all the coloured people on the estate were collected, all in their Sunday best, bobbing & curtseying in a way that made me think of America in the good old days of respect for the white man — In the church we found the old Archdeacon bustling about in his surplice & golden wig, & soon the others joined us, & Mrs Moore began playing the old Harmonyam. The groom and best man sat together in a seat (the groom is a Swede, the best man an Austrian) & then the bridal procession came, Laura on her father's arm, followed by Cicely & Norris (the Kimberley siege baby)[23] carrying her train, & Helena [Helen], Violet & Esmé, as bridesmaids. The groom & best man seemed so surprised at this array that they sat in their seats till poked out by Dr Snow! It was a very pretty little wedding, & after they had been congratulated in the vestry, we stood outside the church with handfuls of confetti, & watched them drive off in the Archdeacon's spider, with the bridesmaids following in Reg's cart. . . . After the breakfast we sat in the drawing-room for a bit, & Miss Fogg said the Archdeacon & I were counting up, & we think he must have come out to Oakhurst at least 200 times. We were all very impressed, when she hurriedly added "But I don't mean to 200 *weddings* you know!" She and Helena & I sat on the stoep & talked while the bride changed her dress. She came down again in her "race" hat, & a red cotton dress with her trousseau in an old & hole-y pillow-case ready for Fairy Knowe,[24] where the honeymoon is to be spent — She asked me to write an account of the wedding for her, & I wonder if it is to go into the Family Bible! Reggie drove them off at last to the Fairy Knowe turn-out, amid showers of confetti — The best man, Esmé, & a coloured driver going down as far in a dog-cart to see the "scenery" — I don't think I've ever seen a bride whose new wedding-ring looked so thoroughly as if it "belonged there" as Laura's does, & Mr Carlson is the nicest man I've met for years — & his moustache is no longer waxed. . . .

Tuesday, Feb. 21st 05 The Archdeacon
Did nothing particular all morning, then went to Archdeacon's to lunch. . . . The lunch was most amusing, "When we have visitors we call it lunch," Miss Fogg explained — "otherwise it is just ordinary dinner" — Good many of us do that! Miss Fogg is like a delightful little lady out of Cranford, & strangely enough the Archdeacon's name is *Peter.*[25] They both speak very slowly deliberately & distinctly, never raising their voices when excited — Miss Fogg "Anne" — lived in a state of great terror during the [Anglo-Boer] war, & her tales seemed to amuse Mr Gibbs very much tho' she saw nothing in them but tragedy — wish I could write down their sentences as they spoke them — You felt almost as if you were living in a cathedral when Miss Anne said "Pe-ta," & Pe-ta said "Anne." Their conversation is most interesting — They lived in Australia for a good many years, & Archdeacon in St Helena too — Their mother had estates out there, & married a second time so that she might have someone to help her to manage them. But the second marriage, to Dumeresq, was not a success. Miss Anne told us of the first Commandant who was "such a nice man — Oh, just a delightful

man! A great favourite with the Boers. And a great favourite with the English – The Boers would bring him in presents. The English would invite him to dinner. Really he was a greatly sought after gentleman. You see he never hurt the feelings of either side – Indeed we could not tell *which* side he was on – The Boers felt sure he was on theirs. The English that he was on ours – And we never discovered which – For a new Commandant was appointed, & the old one left with the good wishes of both sides. And furthermore – new regulations, much stricter than the former, were issued just as the old Commandant was leaving – But he thought it would be better for them to come into force with a *new* Commandant – So he left as the friend of the Boers – But the new regulations would have been from their enemy – Ah yes, he was a delightful man!"

She told us too that a certain Major declared that every night he saw signalling from the Outeniqua mountains (he used to spend the night in a hut on the pass) which was answered either from the sea or from the village – Oh, the awe in dear Miss Anne's voice at this supposed treachery of one of the inhabitants of English George! Also that the organist of the Dutch Church, a lady, was suddenly & unaccountably dismissed, & a stranger from up-country, a man with a wife & (family?) appointed in her place – And this man was supposed to be no more – & no less – than a spy! Indeed, said Miss Anne, we lived in terror of our lives, with a spy in the town, & boers in the mountains, & our horses all commandeered. Oh, Miss Smith, it was a terrible time – a terrible time – Why, they had a *Battle* at Oudtshoorn! (The one in which Uncle George lost 3 men, I suppose)[26] – It seems that the men in the forts were simply spoiled by her – She made great tins of coffee & sent them up to them every evening etc. etc., & when Mr Gibbs said that was nonsense, took up arms strongly in defence of the men who risked their lives in defence of the village! It was terrible, she said, not to know what would happen in the night. . . .

The Archdeacon spoke of the "fuimi", I think, "the would have beens" – (pro-Boers) I think – "Fuimi" said Miss Anne – "Fuimi Pe-ta – and what are they?" (I think she thought "they"

95

were "*microbes*") Peta explained that "fugeo to flee" No, no, I beg your pardon Anne, esse, to be — Anne was satisfied — "It sounded Italian", she said — "When we were children we were given a half holiday for every Italian verb we learnt — I can remember some of them still. My mother was such a good linguist —" The archdeacon wanted to know if I crocheted — or did my hair, with great puffs on top of my head — Because I did neither seemed to think me a non-perfect being & chuckled over my lack of accomplishments mightily, while Helena, as usual, explained I had never been very strong! . . .

After tea went for a walk to extreme end of village, on Pacaltsdorp road. Then I went over to see Kathleen Snow — It seems that the Commandant who so delighted Miss Fogg by his thoroughness, was a great fidget, & the signalling on the mountains was possibly a man looking for a lost pig, while that from the sea, or village, the Mossel Bay lighthouse! Miss Fogg's staircase window looks out to the mountains, & Miss Fogg used to say she never passed it without thinking what a good shot she'd be for the Boers. She seemed sure they'd pick her out of all the rest — The "thorough" Commandant hearing the Boers were at Brak River sent out a company, commanding them to ride on the grass so that their hoofs would not be heard — Company, to his great distress, clattered off gaily on the road — English mail came.

Saturday, Feb. 25th Wet

. . . Wrote a little in morning. In afternoon (it had poured hard watter [sic] steadily all morning) went hunting about for a shop where we could get ink & nibs — Coming back Dr Snow met me & asked me to come for a drive with him and Kathleen — Went arrayed in mackintosh & tammy [tam-o-shanter] — We drove to Swart River on the Knysna Road which is in greater flood after this rain than it has been for many months — It was lovely. The water almost pitch black, & the foam a coffee colour with the trees on its edges being turned & kinked about as it rushed along — Everything looked so fresh & green and the way big trees grow out of the rocks here makes you wonder at the parable which

says the seed which fell on stony ground failed to bear fruit —
It was grand to feel *cold* again. . . .

Saturday, Mar. 11th [P.S.'s return to Oudtshoorn from George]
Called at 5.30 — Got up — Down to breakfast, & then post
coach came — Kathleen saw me off. Dr Snow in bed with bad
throat — Down to hotel for luggage of other passenger then to
Post Office for mails, & passenger No. 3, who was standing on
the stoep — Had arrived at 3 that morning with Riversdale Post,
I think. His luggage consisted of a tin box, a camera, two pillows
in soiled pillowslips, & a wooden box containing stones with
specimens of gold in them — Asked if I objected to smoke —
Said if continuous I did. With bad grace pocketed his pipe. At
hotel picked up the other man — Brewery man, he was, & his
letter case — Started — Big man began to talk. Talked sixteen
to the half dozen — Was a gold prospector — Had been out here
only 8 months & had already hit upon an extraordinarily rich
reef in the Robertson district, & was on his way post haste to
Johannesburg to float a company on said reef — Would point
out to Brewer's man a bit of reef or conglomerate on pass — Had
been lost in Harrod's store, & nearly gone demented trying to
get out. Had gone with Mr Harrod, after shop was shut & missed
him. After 2 hrs of banging into mirrors found a fire alarm,
smashed it, & was rescued by 17 firemen — Had lately been in
Lyttleton's[27] office when young under-secretaries were tumbling
over one another's feet & doing nothing but idle.
   I tied up my head in my handkie & he looked rather
astonished, while the Brewery man kept turning round to look
at me — He & the big man got out to walk up pass — I sat still.
Big man took photos — I tried to — On to North Station —
Brewery Man & big man drank beer & coffee — I felt too ill to
do so — On again — More talk, then reached Post Office near
Doorn River — Tried to buy fruit — On again — More talk —
Had hunted a lot in India, & rattled off Indian names by the
score — Every story the Brewery Man told was capped by one
such another of lengthy dimensions. Brewery Man told how
Mr Varkenvisser in the old days had gone up country & the

rivers were down — his brother had swum across one & been attacked by a crocodile. His leg was bitten clean off, but they got him ashore, & took him a day's journey to a doctor — He lived 10 days, then died — Crocodiles! The big man had shot them by the score. . . . Raubenheimers — Changed horses — Got out to stretch our legs. Big man spoke to me by wall — Not a "place in the world worth mentioning I've not been to" — Take photos of every place I go to. Helped in conversation (I thought he did not need anything to do that!) — On again — Began to feel pretty ill — Big Man & Brewery Man piled coats etc at my back as seats had no backs — Talked all the way — very very hot & miserable — In at last but had to go to Post Office & both hotels before I got up here where Mother, Six & Aunt Jean were waiting for me. Lay down — ill — Bed. . . .

Sunday, Mar. 12th
Lay a-bed recovering from yesterday's trials & afflictions — Had a reception there, Aunt Jean said, as she, Uncle George & Six arrived. After they left for kerk I had a bath, & dressed, then Grace Deas came — She is to try to get me a chair,[28] but seemed much amused at the idea of doing so, also at my Blanco cup & saucer & calabash — The latter will make a splendid shower bath when we have our caravan — There have been great ructions in the Dutch Reformed Kerk over the English Evening services, & it is on that account that Mr Deas came in, for as the English Presbyterians helped to build the Kerk they have the right to have one English Service a Sunday. . . . Grace came again in afternoon to tea — The big man, gold prospector is a detective on the hunt for Lazarus![29] £1000 worth of stolen feathers, Stewart says! Came thro' a week ago & passed there as a photographer but was found out, as he could not even hold a camera properly.

Wednesday, Mar. 22nd
In morning went down to Speedy with Six & films developed by self — decided to take camera — 15/- — But to astonishment & distress Speedy refused to be paid for films which he said

were "old" (they were), or for developing of same (which I think the great heat had spoiled) & for the photo of Meirings Poort — Also, to greater distress, said — "Are you going to the dance to-morrow?" I said "No" — You don't dance, I suppose, vigorously twirling his moustache — No, I did not dance, & made my exit hurriedly. Jean much amused at this, also Six.

Sunday, Apr. 2nd 05

My birthday [her twenty-third] — Aunt Jean came in to wish me many happy returns, armed with a silver button-hook, & shoe-horn, & told me there was a rimpje chair & a bag of walnuts in the back passage, from Grace. Dressed in a great hurry to see the chair & I know it is one of the nicest birthday presents I've had for a long time — Took it in to the drawing-room to Rachel's amusement. Mother gave me 4 little gold brooches to choose from. And after breakfast Uncle George put a dear wee gold chain & heart round my neck with strict injunction to "wear it always". "Even," says Aunt Jean, "to have my bath in it!". . .

Monday, Apr. 3rd

In morning while Helena was at Uncle Tim's Mr & Mrs Anderson[30] from Pacaltsdorp came. I trotted down for Helena. Mrs Anderson spent the day with us. After lunch she and Aunt Jean lay down together & had a *terrible* "news" — After tea Julia & Florrie [Morris] came. Then the buggy for Mrs Anderson — Then I went down to thank Miss Blant for my present. Sat & chatted with her a bit. She thinks, as I do, that Oudtshoorn society has sadly degenerated — Oh — While we were at tea Passon Attie [Parson Atkinson] brought in Passon Hughes, a terrible time of it we had — Puns steadily — Aunt Jean says I looked as if I wanted to put a knife into Parson Atkinson & indeed I felt my back getting stiffer & stiffer — Passon Atkinson asked me if I remembered much of Oudtshoorn — said "I remember enough to know it was much nicer in the old days than it is now" — "Oh dear me, dear me, thank you, thank you I'm sure — *Allow* me to pass the butter" said Parson Atkinson. Great roars of laughter

from both of them at this huge joke — Tried to patronise me as
a child of 3 — "poor thing, o yes delicate delicate, poor thing &
a weak back like Mr Hughes — Both of you half backs Ho! Ho
— No *full* backs I should say, Yes full backs — ha ha ha." Save
us from a punning parson! . . .

Thursday, April 13th Kruis River[31]
. . . All drove down to station together. Left Oudtshoorn at 9,
& reached Kruis River at about 11 —
. . . At the siding Mr Bergh met us with a coloured boy & Justus — Justus in a gordon tartan dress, turkey red pinnie & cap —
Walked up to the house along the line — I had bad head, so on
getting here went straight to my room & lay down till dinner
time — Our room is next the storeroom where waggon tents,
brandy casks, dried fruit, meal, etc is all kept, whereof we have
the conglomerated odours. There is no window in our bedroom,
only a half-door, so when we want light we have to open the top-
half. At lunch a little coloured girl (very ugly) waved a bamboo
with a bunch of feathers at the end of it instead of the ordinary
cow's-tail. All plates are put face downwards in each person's
place. Pudding not being the order of the day there was great
excitement among the children on the arrival of one — Vinny
[Vincent] is 12, Pieter is 8, Joey 5 (going in for 6, Mimi says) &
Jussie [Justus] going in for 3 — Joey is a dear little damsel —
Very quick & fond of helping with the housework — Vinny is
quiet & steady, Pieter, poor fellow, has a weakness, Mimi says[32] —
He is very fond of making pretty 'pretty tunes' — & so Mimi
hopes he is to be musical — He certainly *makes sounds*. Jussie
(Yussie as Mimi calls him) is a pickle, & very very sharp for a
Boerchild. They all have nice blue eyes, & all, but Pieter, are
well-favoured — After lunch (*dinner*) we lay down. Then coffee
— Then in the cool we walked up the valley with Mimi past the
pig-lily [arum lily] dam — The valley is very very pretty, just
underneath the gloomy Swartbergs[33] — It looks so cool & green,
with its poplar trees, & patches of lucerne lands, for all around
are great dry barren kopjes — The farm itself is very bare & dry
— In front of the house is no garden. Just 4 pepper trees which

Mimi does her best to keep alive with water from the sluit about ¼ of a mile away, from which *all* their water has to be carried up in buckets — Some distance away she has a garden which is wonderfully green — Aloes in front of the house & a little farm hut made of reeds, which is wonderfully green — A little way away is a dam surrounded by fig trees, & orange trees — beyond that the mealie land — To the north the Swartbergs — to the South the glorious Outeniquas[34] — The valley is very narrow, so we are very near the mountains, which are *always* changing — Especially the Outeniquas which go from dark blue in the morning to all sorts of wonderful colours in the afternoon — then pink in the evening, then red — Outeniqua is a splendid name for them, if it really means patchwork — There are a few houses near & one shop kept by a"Yew" as Mimi calls him — All thro' the walk Mimi talked of the war & her troubles — How she & her husband were cut by the other boers in this part on account of their loyalty long before the war began[35] — When the Transvaal Boers came down they had been told of Bergh's loyalty & came straight for this house — Bergh hid out on the veldt while Mimi was left here with the children alone, all the servants having fled to the mountains. After that commando had passed Mimi & the children went into the town where they stayed 4 months — On their return *nothing* was left in the house, the only food they had was a bucket of rice they had hidden in the land — There was no food for "my little vone's" as Mimi calls the children; & Pieter & Joey told me snake-stories — one in particular of 4 little "broderkies en sisterkies" [little brothers & sisters] who found a hen's nest & each put a finger in to feel the hen pecking them — The hen was a *snake*, & those 4 children all died — Dear little Joey told this tragic tale (which Mimi says is perfectly true) with such sorrow, & terror, & mystery in her big blue eyes — The children have also a dog called "Collie" a cross between a jackal & a collie, which they are much attached to — Little Pieter began telling me some wonderful tale in Dutch — I made him repeat it slowly & learnt that "This dog's Ma did die of worms" — In the evening, after these snake stories, I felt "real bang" [frightened] about leaving the top half of the door open, & was

guiltily relieved when Helena, as usual, discovered a distinct
draught, & insisted upon having it closed — Mr Bergh shot a
snake in the "Skellar" [cellar] below the children's bedroom. . . .

Saturday, April 15th

Vinny came back with word that he could not get thro' Olifants
river yesterday, but it is passable to-day — He had spent the
night with relations on this side. Joey was very anxious to take
me to "de pick lilies" but it was so hot that I begged to be
allowed to go to the "tein" [*tuin*: garden] instead, where the
children all ate tomatoes — After lunch we had coffee & then
started with Mimi & Vinny & the driver for O'ma Piet's[36]— The
other children had all been given "tickies" [threepenny pieces]
to keep them from crying — We went along *very* fast, the horses
seeming very fresh, but not excited. The road in parts was very
very bad, especially at Olifants river when we had to go down a
cliff as steep as the side of a house! However we managed safely
tho' we noticed the horses becoming more excited as we neared
O'Ma's — We passed Mimi's old house, now empty at the store
end, then up under the great oak, & at last O'Ma's house —
Schoemankie, now 16, a big awkward boy, very excited at seeing
us, especially me, who to his surprise, turned out to be *grown
up*! O'Ma delighted to see us. Sat in the sit-kamer [sitting-room]
& had coffee & cookies — O'Ma talked Dutch, & I tried to —
Then Mrs Delport came round — Afterwards we all went thro'
the house — Saw the old big feather bed which was covered with
bundles of freshly plucked ostrich feathers[37] — Then to the mud-
floored kitchen where a coloured girl was busy "smearing"
[spreading a mixture of mud and dung on the floor]! — She is
the daughter of the fine looking old kaffir woman who used to
be there in the old days — I admired a lustre bowl, & O'Ma took
me in to her china closet to choose something out of it for myself — I did not know what to do — afraid to choose something
she valued, or to break a set — Old Mrs Delport came in & found
me mounted on a chair (riempje) trying to make up my mind —
She strongly urged me to climb on to a high cupboard to look
at some big plates on the top shelf. I did this & found there

some lovely old ashets [meat dishes] — She strongly advised me
to take the largest which was blue and gold and had a gravy dip
— But I chose an old blue & red one much smaller, & older, I
think. Then she [O'Ma] took me to the spare room to choose
some feathers — She gave me a bundle of 9 lovely white ones, 2
of which are for Dolly [Dorothy] — She told me never to forget
her & O'Pa [*oupa*: grandfather] as she would never forget us, &
was very very "jammer" [sorry] that we could not spend a few
days with her — We had the cart inspanned & began but almost
as soon as we started the horses began to kick — In front of
Mimi's old house they pranced about so that the driver & another
man had to get down & quiet them — We went on again when
another runaway horse started ours off & they tore down to the
river bed where they began kicking so that we all got out & fled
while they careered round and round. The driver never once
used the whip, which was wonderful for a coloured man. He
drove them up the hill on the other side of the river at a gallop,
& we got across the stepping stones — We got in again then, all
feeling very unhappy & uncomfortable & with a strong presenti-
ment that we'd not get home before my beautiful ashet had been
broken — However we did, tho' every now and then they started
at a gallop — All this way we simply *flew* — Very very thankful
we were to land here in safety — supper, & sat outside watching
the train — Mimi has much trouble with her relations on account
of her husband's loyalty — She told us in the cart that she had
told them that they had only two things against her husband —
One was that he was for the English — The other that he had a
bald head! "And do you know why I marry a man with a bald
head I say? Jes' so's I can kiss it!"

Bed early. The story of Mr Bergh's baldness is rather amusing.
It began at 22, & he came to father [Dr Smith] about it, but
father, to his indignation, only laughed. Then a drunken painter
told him if he gave him 2/6 and half a bottle of brandy he'd make
a lotion which would cure him. The lotion was to be half brandy
and half camphor — But the painter *drank* the brandy, & gave
Mr Bergh camphor & water, with which he innocently soaked
his head every night. The camphor soaking in like that killed all

103

the roots of the hair & Mr Bergh finding his baldness was getting no better determined to go to Cape Town to see a hair specialist — He had then £150 to his credit, & spent most of it on this trip. The hair specialist said the camphor had killed all the roots & nothing could make it grow, & advised Mr Bergh to give his sweetheart a pair of tweezers to remove the rest! Mr Bergh much distressed & annoyed, & would gladly have given his £150 for a fresh crop of hair, but to-day he says I'd not give £150 for it. Still he holds a woman's chief glory is her hair, wherefore little Joey's is kept tightly plaited all round her head on week-days & let loose on Sundays, to the annoyance of the Leroux family.

Sunday, April 16th

In the morning Joey insisted upon my accompanying her to the pick-lilies. Vinny & Pieter came too — Vinny got me a lovely branch of castor oil seeds, which are a wonderful pink but not dry enough yet to be of any use taking to England. After we had examined the "pick-lilies" (there are no flowers yet) we went along the dam wall thro' the ostrich camp to the poplar bush for ferns — Then home again — Watched the train from the dam wall — In the afternoon the children went to Sunday school — A Miss Leroux came by train — She is governess of the school here & a daughter of Baakenskraal Leroux who was accidentally shot not long ago. . . . On our return a young far-mer called — Very smart, but very silent — He sat against the wall with a cup of coffee in his hand all the time we were at supper & made only *one* remark, tho' he can speak English all right — After we had finished supper he took his departure with much state & solemnity — A very curious but, I suppose a very common, specimen of Boer youth. . . . As I was going to bed Mimi came in & seeing Madam de Sévigné's letters [38] on my bed said Oh my goodness me, Pauline & do you also read novels? I said yes — "Oh my goodness me," said Mimi in great distress — I asked her if I looked very wicked. "No", she said "dats vot so serprise me — your face it don' look a bit vicked. And yet you read novels — I don't un'erstan' it at all" — neither do I — . . . .

Monday, April 17th

I wrote my English letters; Mimi, who thinks me very "long and thin" (long & narrow) says I spend my time writing. Little Pieter not being well did not go to school & amused himself by "making pretty tunes" — When at breakfast(ostrich biltong)[sun-dried meat] I told Jussie we were leaving he grew very indignant & in his vigorous stammering Dutch told us he'd lock up all the doors & get the "fleare mese" (rats) [*vlermuise*: bats] to keep us in the house — He is wonderfully fond of me & Mimi says when I'm not there goes hunting thro' the house for the "Tante" [aunt] — Little Pieter came & asked me to stay till his "Ma" went into the dorp to Nachtmaal [Dutch Reformed Church communion service], but Joey said "you must buy for me a kleine poppie [little doll] an' make for her a kleine rockie [little dress] — As a keepsake Pieter gave me a pear very large, but bad in one corner — Mimi a little calabash to darn my stockings on & a silk handkie for Dolly, a patch-lapje [patchwork] mat for Mother, & a kaffir bowl (baked of clay in Kaffirland by the natives) — After coffee we walked down the line with Mimi, Mr Bergh, Pieter (who was well enough to do so) & a black boy carrying our bags — I clung to O'Ma's ashet, my camera, my castor oil branch, & my keep-sake pear! When we got to the siding we squatted in the shade of the "Yew's store" & waited for the train — When it came little Joey rushed out of school to say good-bye once more — We clambered up, & found Amy Hudson & Perle Hitge in one of the carriages & sat talking to them for a bit till my head got so bad I went & lay down in the next — On the way we saw a swarm of Monkey-babies as Joey would call them [rock-rabbits] all clambering up the rocks near Middleplaas — about 70 or 100 I should think, & so like little kittens — Helena spoke in glowing terms about my plate, & Perle said Mrs Lind would be sure to want to see it as she knew something about old china — I began to feel uncomfortable as we have no idea that the plate *is* really "old china" — At the [Oudtshoorn] station (we had a pillow slip full of dried fruit, biltong, mealies, & a pumpkin which I had climbed up into the loft to get) Aunt Jean met us with Willem & the cart — Drove home, & my head got so bad that I retired

to bed with mustard plasters, etc. without seeing Uncle George
at all —

Tuesday, May 2nd

. . . In the evening Gerhardus took me down to the library
[Literary] & Debating Society — The opening meeting it was —
F.Muller Rex, Esq.![39] very much Esq.! gave the opening address
on South African Literature. I did not know there was any, but
he had managed to find several names of note — Pringle being
one, who wrote O why left I my home (*I think*).[40] Several
others were mentioned that I had never before heard of & have
already forgotten — But all the excitement surrounded the
name of Olive Schreiner.[41] Mr Rex tried to praise her writings,
& succeeded to a certain extent but the scorn with which she
was discussed afterwards as "*that* woman" was terribly vigorous
& very amusing — as men were as bitter against her as the
women, & that is saying a good deal. It struck me as rather
queer on the men's part for it seemed almost as if they were
jealous of the fact that the only writer of real note in South
Africa has been a woman, not a man — Booker Harle, immacu-
late in a white waistcoat which he was always straightening, was
one of the most vigorous denouncers of "*that* woman" — said
we all knew the disappointment that had enfiltered her life &
pen etc. — He "er-ed" so often & so graciously during his
lengthy speeches, that whenever he paused a youth at the back
began to "er" too, & at last Mr Harle noticing this, sat down
abruptly — He however found courage later to graciously
request us to "look upon this debating society as the garden of
future poets & novelists" & to go home & consider, each of us,
whether we were not one or other? Mr Langenhoven[42] spoke
too, & grinned & chuckled hugely — Also a Mr W.Thesen.[43] The
latter denounced the book most strongly, & Mr Langenhoven
got up and quite agreed with him. Said we must not think Mr W.
Thesen denounced it because he was an Englishman merely. He,
Mr Langhoven, "had lived on a farm" & found life quite different from what it is depicted in the Story of a S.A. Farm &
thought if Mr Rex found it true to life it must be from life in

106

another country not this. Finally Mr Pocock [editor of the *Oudtshoorn Courant*] jumped up at the end & spoke very fiercely about "*that* woman".

Wednesday, May 10th
In morning . . . Uncle George took me up to Grandstand, subscribers end,[44] where Mrs Just was — Talked to me, but I was glad when Hannah Hugo & Olive Hoole came along. The "ladies" were very smart — or imagined themselves so — They all suffered "agonies" from neuralgia & had great delight in comparing notes on the same. In spite of their all seeming to be in agony as they spoke they got along very happily, one lady proudly announcing that she had been as sick as a dog that very morning. Some of the garments were very elaborate, &, I've no doubt the wearers imagined themselves equal to the ladies of Ascot. Sweepstakes were arranged by Mrs Vintcent on "Aubrey" — One gentleman brought 2 ladies and we had tried to find out which of the two was his wife, but discovered at last that neither was — The Gorgon [unidentified] was there, & Olive Hoole's interest in her is tremendous — She certainly has not the expression of an angel — Olive Hoole won 9/-. I did not go in for any betting as I was staying only one race — When at last the race did come off it was a very good one — one of the best — Miss Commins, Warrington, & Bachelor all coming in close together etc. — (Behind me I heard one lady accusing another of looking before she did the stakes.) Objections were lodged, but over-ruled. After waiting about ¾ of an hour Uncle George came for me & we went off to hunt for old Willem who was not to be found, having kindly lent the cart to a Coloured man to drive about some "Coloured ladies" — We trudged about looking for him in dust over our ankles — all around the paddock where the carts were outspanned & families picknicking — At last he was got hold of & scolded & cart emptied of his friends, & it was driven over — He was most talkative as he always is when slightly intoxicated — Of course on these occasions "Royal" [the horse] is the subject of his muse — or news. . . .

107

Thursday, May 11th

The day of Mother's "Speech" [at the Girls' School], & presentation of prizes. . . .

In afternoon we had a great hunt for our "invites" as we could not remember the time of the break up — Helena refused to go & enquire at the Stegmanns for it, & as she was the Church personage, we thought she ought to be punctual — However she would not listen to reason & we all lay down, & were only saved from a terrible breach of good manners by Mrs Ken who arrived at 3.30 (the time the thing was beginning) to find us all sleeping! Helena dressed in great hurry but insisted on having tea first — Then started off with Mrs Ken — Aunt Jean & I following — Miss Jenner [the Principal] received me & was in state of great anxiety thinking Mother was not coming as she had not seen her arrive — However she was discovered somewhere at the back — sat in the square & had tea & listened to "Mossies"[45] as Ian calls it — Mother presented the prizes, but said never a word & looked very miserable & unhappy — Mrs Mataré made a speech in praise of school, teachers, & Father's work on the old school Board. Walked thro' to new buildings — Sadie Sarah Sally Valenski was there. On to Aunt Maud's. Aunt Maud in bed. Up with Amy Hudson, and walked up a bit with her after. English papers & were all shocked to read about Fay White's[46] suicide. In evening Broeg [*brug*: bridge] till Mrs Stegmann,[47] Murray & Daniel came in when Helena went off with them to dining room as cards would have shocked them. Uncle Tim came up for lemos drink for Aunt Maud. All very tired & a bit upset.

Monday, May 15th

. . . Aunt Maud told me a tremendous compliment paid me by the schoolgirls — After Thursday's ceremony (I went in my pale blue coat & skirt; & my sailor hat with Caldecote[48] badge) they told Miss Jenner they thought me "so pretty & ladylike, that I dressed so nicely, & was so *neat*" (the last astonished us all most). This thorough inspection is the result of me coming out from England — Miss Jenner quite agreed with them, & said she hoped they'd take me for an example as they needed one!

Never had so many compliments in my life! In the evening we dressed for Mr Attie's [Atkinson's] Broeg — I in my pale blue dress of 4 summers ago, & Aunt Jean in the white silk blouse Mother gave me against Mr Black's taking us to the theatre — which he never did! It fits her so well that, as I've only worn it once I gave it her. Down to the Rectory, where we found the Pococks, the Bank Manager, & the Morrises & Mr Daltry [the Curate] — I fled to a secluded chair which was propped up against the wall, & gave unmistakable signs of collapsing when I sat upon it. The rector & his wife thereupon rushed up to rescue me, but I very courageously remarked "Oh no thank you, I'll stick to it — I think its *settling*." However as it gave signs or sounds of doing no such thing they confessed it was not meant to be sat upon, & would I *please* take another. As Uncle George could not come, owing to English mail, there was no fourth for the 3rd set & Mr & Mrs Atkinson & I sat out — Mr Atkinson entertained me by showing me Cathedral books & Stratford-on-Avons — He was born & bred in S-on-A, & I began to be afraid I'd have a S-on-A nightmare!

Aunt Jean had begged me not to snub him too much, so I tried to behave nicely & he was wonderfully subdued & did not pun as much as usual but there is *nothing* too sacred for him to joke about — The festivities were concluded by refreshments of light wine or dark wine, sandwiches & rice cake. The light wine (or the dark) got to Mrs Pocock's head & made her reel, and sandwich got to Helena's digestion & made it suffer — Mr Pocock is very proud of his wife — even to her inability to take *half* a glass of light wine — or dark — without getting tipsy!

Tuesday, May 23rd Calitzdorp
O'Willem & Uncle George came up for us at 10.30, & we started for Calitzdorp — Helena says she is to be very busy paying calls, washing blouses etc. & we are not to think she will be lonely. Also she has promised to look after the cats & kittens (7) — It was a lovely morning, but the drive out is *so* long & for the greater part, very wearisome (34 miles) — For many miles the road stretches straight out thro' the veldt ahead of us, with farms

109

only in the far distance — The hills & mountains are always glorious, but one's immediate surroundings consist of dusty barren veldt & field mice by the thousands — I found myself relieving the monotony by making up stories about Pa & Ma & Kleinke [*kleintjie*: little or baby] field mice, as I used to as a child — once or twice we caught sight of a hawk hiding behind a bush to pounce on Pa or Ma — And that for a while was all the excitement — Then we got to a more interesting part, near to Varrm Waater [Warm Water, near Calitzdorp] , where the hot springs are — The farms looked so much greener & prettier, especially those with Lombardy poplars all golden in the sunshine — Of every farm Willem knows the history — He could tell us where each gets the water from — He showed us one stagnant pool, & explained to our horror that it was the drinking water of a farm a few miles off (the water is drained into dams dug in the dooibank[49]). When I exclaimed at this he explained that the people just skim back the green coat on the top of the water, & drink what is below! He could explain why some woman had pumpkins & watermelons at the side of her house; where those who were not at home had gone to — etc etc — And everyone knows him — We drove past several outspan places with the proprietors of which Uncle George has striven — But at last, when Aunt Jean & I were getting desperate for coffee we reached the house & winkel [shop] of a Russian Jew — While Uncle George went to see if we could get coffee Aunt Jean & I climbed up the shadow of a rock on the side of a kopje & lay down on the rug — It made me think of the Israelites — this dry & thirsty land — At last the coffee was ready, and we went down to the house & were ushered to the best kamer [room] by the Jew — he has a young wife, not long married, & the best kamer is furnished solely by wedding presents & photographs. . . . Coffee was brought, & we were thankful for it — Then his wife came & we talked a bit. The room was beautifully clean — We left at last & the man begged us to come back that way as he'd like to take us to Warm Water where he has a bathing house. He thinks it very 'infective' to bathe with others, & once saw such a dirty, sick man get out of the water, & another one go in to the same pool, wash his face, & drink of the water!

110

The drive after that was prettier, & the country began to remind me of Sierre [Switzerland, on the Rhone] — You come upon Calitzdorp suddenly, & it looked so peaceful & restful — so green & golden in the evening sun — We were glad to get tea — & soon after supper 'bedded'. The hotel is nice and clean, but "fleas" are rather more numerous than is comfortable & both Aunt Jean & I had very bad nights with them —

Wednesday, Queen's birthday, May 24th
To-day is Queen's birthday, & all the town is a-holidaying — Early in the morning carts & waggons & buggies began going out with picknickers. . . . After breakfast Aunt Jean & I went thro' the village, scarcely a home has a garden (except the Predikants) [D.R.C. minister] & the houses are stuck down any-how anywhere. It is very very Dutch & more like a foreign country than Oudtshoorn or George — but perhaps I think so because of its likeness to Sierre — for the Swartbergs are so like the Alps.

We walked on to the bridge & along the other side of the river — There we came across a small boy, & a slightly larger girl trotting along together — The boy was a chubby-faced lad with red cheeks, like Ogustus [Augustus?] had — He was carry-ing a coffee tin & was going to get sand he told us — I took a snapshot of them both with 2 other stray children, & as we went along heard them discussing it — He was very anxious to know what was going to happen. They did you affneem [took your picture] the girl told him in Dutch — "And what next" he wanted to know "Nix" [nothing] said the girl — This so disappointed him that I tried to find out his name so as to be able to send him one "if it comes out" — Neither of them could speak a word of English, so I had to make the best of my Dutch[50] — "Wat is jo naam?" — "Bart" — En vot ok? "Nix" — "Nix? Marje moot a anner naam hae" "Nay — mej naam is net Bart." Then a brilliant inspiration seized me — "Mar vot is yo Paa's naam?" — "Andries Van Wyck" — "Oh — dan je is Bart Van Wyck" — "Ney," with decision "Ik is nie Bart Van Wyck — Ek is net Bart" — a very determined 5-year-old! The little girl

111

who was with him looked *so* like a "tinkers lassie" — she did not know who he was, she told us, but all the same she was domineering over him, whipping him up and exhorting him to "Hastag" [hurry] as if she was his nurse! They went on ahead of us & evidently told some poor whites, living in huts on the edge of a kopje what had happened, for as we passed we heard the old women laughing & talking about the young niefie's affnemer [the young boy's photographer]. . . .

In the river bed we overtook a Coloured woman & begged her to step into the sun to be affneemed [snapped] — Affneemed! Goodness grayshus, in a patchlepje [patchwork] dress! Not she — (all this in Dutch) Nothing would drag her into the sun — If I'd come vermoorer [tomorrow] she would "optrick" [trick herself out] for me in her "grand rock [frock, dress] — No, said I, I want you so — you are more so, & I will take your "photographs" to England — Engelant — Moie [? That's a good one!] — Allamachtic! The storm of amazement, indignation & ridicule I raised — To-morrow she would come — to-day she had not time — & off she went shouting Engelant — Moie — We heard her afterwards relating it all amid shrieks of laughter to two old washerwomen in the river bed. I snapped those, but could not get near enough to get a good view — It will last as a topic of conversation among them for days! We were very tired when we got back, so rested till lunch time, & again afterwards till 3, when Willem inspanned & we drove up the Cango valley, along the banks of the Groenfontein — The road is terrible — very narrow, very rough & very "up & down" — This bit of the district is different from all others. The rivers are fresh, & the banks just lined with brambles & China roses[51]. . . . On the way Willem was very communicative — He is not only a geologist (he can point out all the likely [gold-bearing] "reefs" in the district, & pointed out several to-day) — he is also an encyclopaedia, a philosopher, & the most popular Coloured gentleman in the district — Every Coloured man we met greeted him. To the old he is O'Willem — to the young Oom Willem — we felt like royalty, with such a run of salutations! He could tell us all about the suits [law-suits re water rights] etc & proved himself

112

a philosopher when he made Aunt Jean hold the reins till he had
let down the tent [hood of the cart] "because," he explained,
"if we had to be drove out, den we can be drove out far away"
— but if de ten' is up we is drove done with an' can't get out"
— This he told us after we had been nearly capsized trying to
pass one of the picnic carts coming home — We met 13 of them!
It was very exciting, & Willem's earnest expectation of being
"drove out far away" did not reassure us — The first 2 carts we
met in the river bed, which was fortunate for a few yards
further we could not possibly have passed — Then a waggon &
another cart which we passed with great difficulty at a terrible
angle — Then 5 more carts, with one wheel high up on a rock
— it was after this cavalcade that Willem took down the tent &
prepared himself & us, very cheerfully, for the worst — Then 2
waggon loads full of children, all wearing little tabs of pink,
blue, or white, or green, ribbons (the Transvaal colours) (most
of them Boer orphans) — To pass them we had to go into
somebody's back yard — at least one wheel was down in the
yard, & the other was up on the road, while the mules of the
waggons careered about as they pleased, but were at length
hauled past — Each waggon had a banner — The first pale laven-
der, with the one word Emmanuel — The 2nd dark green — the
whole thing reminded us rather of the happy band of children
joyously chanting & waving pocket handkerchiefs, in the
Inquisition [ref. unknown] — The next waggon contained prickly
pear trees, & the next cart, small boys, who were commanded
by Willem to stick to their own side — i.e. the *precipice* side,
while we as usual were perched on a rock to let them pass — It
was really all very exciting, & tho' the harness had broken
going out, we managed to get home without being "drove out
far away" to our great relief. . . .

Thursday, May 25th
After dinner O'Willem drove us up thro' the Ghamka mountains into the Ladismith district — That part of the district is
very awe-ful & terrible & gave me the shrinking feeling that the
Devil had had a finger in the making of it — For a mile or two

113

it is flat veldt with here & there ragged clay washaways — Then for some miles we seemed to go down hill, between great rugged hills, which seem to have been tossed up "somer so" [any how] Then came the Ghamka river — very empty with its bushy borders of China roses — It passes thro' a very very narrow gorge between huge hills, & I wanted to snap-shot it from the river bed — But O'Willem seemed to have added photography to his many accomplishments & told me to wait till I got to the rise as the view from there was better — It really is a wonderful gorge — From Calitzdorp to there we had passed no house, but between the Ghamka & the next drift lies a little valley at the foot of the mountains, — all along it are tiny farms, with terribly poverty-stricken farmers, & such miserable houses — They are all poor whites, & there seems no school of any sort — They have vineyards & make their own brandy, tobacco, & make their own "twak" [tobacco],[52] make their own soap (we saw one family doing so as we passed), grow enough grain to make their own meal, & have mealies etc. & goats, & that is all — No cows, no milk, no butter — They belong to Ladismith — We went to the foot of the Ladismith pass [the Huis River Pass], & then turned & came home — On the way we picked up a Boer who had come back looking for a whip dropped from his waggon, & took him up to the waggon which had gone on slowly — He had in his pocket a packet of "stationery" — Coming back we passed several bush gatherers, & what we suppose was a runaway couple in a buggy with a man on a box in front driving them & a huge kist on the back — In the village a man on a very tired & spent horse stopped us, & questioned Willem in Dutch about a couple who had gone off in a buggy, having been married that morning — He looked so distressed that we came to the conclusion it had been an elopement. . . .

Saturday, May 27th [Return to Oudtshoorn from Calitzdorp] Cold & cloudy — Uncle George said he'd be ready to start at 10, & Aunt Jean & I wandered about disconsolately till then — However he did not turn up till 11, to our misery. We went up the village to meet him, waved back to Willem (also impatient to be off) to inspan, hurried back to hotel & got some milk & bread & butter, & started — The drive was very very cold, for there was a snow storm on the Outeniqua [mountains] thro' which the wind blew — And as most of the drive is thro' a "vlaakte" [plain] there is nothing to break the wind when it does blow. Very very few field-mice were out, & I suppose have retired for the winter — It is winter, Uncle George says "when there is snow on the mountains" — In between while I suppose it is summer! The cold & driving gave me neuralgia, altho' I took off my hat, & wrapped my head into the cape of my coat — Snow is called Kaapock [kapok] — the dust is terrible, for the drought has not broken yet — It came into the cart in clouds & covered O'Willem with a rich coat of reddish brown — We did not outspan till we got to Gavin's [farm] — O'Willem says the man who stopped us at Calitzdorp about the run-away couple was the father of the bridegroom, & was so distressed because he did not know whether the couple had been married or not, for they had certainly not been married in Calitzdorp. . . .

On the way we passed some Coloured persons flitting — They carried all their household goods & worldly possessions upon their heads — A tin box (yellow & battered), some pillow cases over which were strung a calabash & a pair of boots, blankets etc — Also lots of carts coming back from the Dank Feast [D.R.C. Thanksgiving celebration]. In Oudtshoorn it got suddenly colder, & it is colder than Calitzdorp on the whole in spite of the latter's nearness to the mountains. Found Mother very cold but full of news, having tea at the Dank feast with Florrie & Julia [Morris] and indulging in all sorts of good things, including Sout Ribitjes [salted rib of mutton]. The Dank Feast is one of the best there has been for years — It is the Dutch "Thanksgiving" — The men-folk give in money or forage or farm produce etc, the women-folk in work, & clothes of all kinds — Helena is sorry I missed it. So am I. Helena's been rather lonely at nights — One night thought she heard burglars, yet was too afraid to go & see till daylight when she went out courageously *with a candle*, & discovered — the cat! Aunt Jean on our arrival at once lit a fire which was nice & cheery after our cold journey. Bed early.

115

Sunday, May 28th

All very late & mooch [*moeg*: tired] — Helena the only Kerk goer in the morning — Grace [Deas] called, & told me they have made £11,000 at the Dank feast collected from those who did not give in kind. The greatest sum they have ever made. Grace says the Predikant is very pleased, & "Thanked the Lord" in his prayers, which Grace seems to think impertinence on his part, as, according to Grace it was the farmers, not the Almighty who made the money. Her ideas on this subject would horrify the Predikant, I'm afraid. . . .

Monday, May 29th

Father's birthday. In morning tried to write English letters, but Aunt Maud came up & we all sat on the garden stoep gossiping over 10 o'clock tea — The amount the people here know about one another's underclothes & private affairs is marvellous — as soon as the cool weather begins gossiping seems to get more & more personal — What it must be like when "the snow is on the mountains", goodness only knows! I heard all about Mrs Vintcent's toupée & the row over it with Mrs Schalk when, at the public dance these two ladies called one another "*liars*". . . . It is rumoured too that Julia & Florrie are contemplating a Book tea, & great is the excitement concerning it — We are all on the qui vive for invitations — In the afternoon I wrote, & as it grew dark went down to Uncle Tim's with some plates etc & my letters for post — On our return got Uncle George to come up from office with us — The lamps had not been lit & I stumbled into the drawingroom to find Aunt Jean & a strange man. I recognized the looks of the strange man as belonging to Six — Six it was, a pound & a half fatter (all in the face this 1½ lbs is, I think) lanky as ever, rather more moustache now than before & the faint outlines of a beard. Very brown, & his nose even redder than mine — A regular Boer, very happy, & very jolly, & *riding togt* [transport riding] with 2 Van Royens! I think Helena & Aunt Jean felt sad at hearing that Artie's [?Bertie's] boy was "riding togt", but I was so glad to see the creature that I hadn't time to be sorry about anything —

116

He had come up from Mill River[53] with these Van Royens to bring forage, potatoes, wood & 5 fowls to the market — They took 3 days & 2 nights, travelling with 10 mules — They travel about 2 hours & then outspan, but do not really outspan the mules unless they have to water & feed them for mules are such terrible things for running back to their farms at night — . . . . Uncle George says very few farmers outspan at night — The mules just have to sleep standing harnessed & yoked — He also knew one poor boy who was run over & killed while lying asleep under his waggon. He had got up & told them to inspan, then lain down again & fallen asleep — The others thought he had got on the waggon, & did not notice him till he had been run over — Six and the 2 Van Royens have a brush & comb between them, one towel, one spoon, a pocket-knife each — cooked sweet potatoes, some ribitjes, bread, jam, & coffee & a kettle, & I suppose one cup, & I envy them heartily! Six says he'd love to take me with them but it would kill me! Still he thrives on it, & it is making him manly. Poor boy. There is certainly *no* false pride about him & he is not ashamed of work — He speaks of trying to go farming up Vryburg way with the 2 young Taute's if he can manage to scrape together enough money — Aunt Jean & Mother were exercised about the thinness of his garments, & told him he ought to wear his thick blue one — "Oh Law, No" said Six, that's my Sunday suit, I wear it to dances." "Dances!" cried Helena & Jean — Goodness me yes, the jolliest dances I've ever been to. We dance about 6 dances without stopping, with the same girl" — The governess on the farm plays the banjo & the piano for them, one at a time I suppose, & the diningroom is cleared & they set to — He has shorn a sheep (half a one) ploughed, dug potatoes, tramped the woolsack ["treading" the wool in bales] & got up at 3 in the morning to kill a sheep by moonlight & a candle! His accomplishments are many! Before I went farming, he said, I used to believe it was true, what people always say in stories, about the Baas sitting drinking coffee on his stoep. But goodness me it is all lies — The Baas never has a minute to sit on his stoep — He just flies in for his coffee, & out again. . . .

117

Thursday, June 1st

Finished my patchwork dress,[54] & oh, but it is beautiful! Leah showed me how to put on the dook [scarf]. . . . After lunch Aunt Jean photographed me in my patchwork garments to the huge excitement of the damsels. . . .

Friday, June 9th

In morning Amy called with Wrensch's buggy & took me on a lovely drive — Out to Baakenskraal, & then to the left along the road on the red cliffs overhanging the river — Over the Karminiatie [Kamanassie] & Olifants drifts & home past the Station — Karminiatie drift was so deep that the water was *almost* in the buggy. Amy is as fond of "Royal" as O' Willem is & thinks him as perfect as he does. She used to ride him when he belonged to Pam Sanders — was thrown once & it took ¼ hour to quiet him down enough for her to re-mount — She is as tomboyish as ever, in spite of her delicacy. She told me of an experience of Hougham's on the Swartberg pass — The wheels of the waggon "burnt fast" & they discovered they had no cart oil or grease to free them — There they stuck until Hougham remembered that Mrs Hudson had packed up a tin of vaseline in the portmanteau — much against his wishes! They managed to free the wheels with this — Another time Laura & Amy went over with 18 other passengers, & the whole concern thundered down the pass — safely!
. . . .

In the evening Miss Spence & Mr Bank Manager came to dinner — Then Mrs Pocock & Mr *Speedy*(!) for bridge! I was very wroth, but Aunt Jean says "behaved very nicely" in spite of the great shock of "Oh ay's" arrival!

[The Diary ends with a short entry for 10th June.]

APPENDIX: Report published in the *Oudtshoorn Courant,*
3/5/1905 (see the Diary entry for 2nd May, 1905)

DEBATING AND LITERARY SOCIETY: SOUTH AFRICAN LITERATURE (Communicated)

There was a fairly good attendance at the Victoria Memorial
Hall last night, despite the wintry weather. It was decided to
hold the meeting in the Memorial Hall on the 2nd and 4th Tuesday instead of Thursdays. Mr E.J.Hart was appointed Editor of
the Magazine. It was suggested that the Magazine be issued at
the close of the session, and that it be printed. The matter was
left to the Committee.

The subject of the evening, the President's Inaugural address
followed. An interesting and able paper on 'South African
Literature' was read by Mr F.Muller Rex, the President, which
was listened to with great pleasure. Extracts from our early
writers, verse and prose, sandwiched into the text of the address
which must have proved to sceptics that we have, after all, the
germ of a South African Literature. Mr Langenhoven said that
he had come there expecting to be bored, as the subject did not
appear to him capable of much interesting treatment, he had
been agreeably surprised, and he proposed a hearty vote of
thanks to Mr Rex for the evening's instructive and entertaining
paper. Rev. Mr Withers in seconding the motion, expressed his
sense of indebtedness to the President for the able address.

At the hands of Mr Withers, Olive Schreiner came in for a
severe drubbing, to which many others present added their quota.
Messrs Pocock, Hart and Martin contributed to the discussion.
The resolution of thanks to the lecturer was carried by acclama-
tion, Mr Young occupying the chair. Mr Young said he had hoped
to hear more about the journalistic contribution to the South
African Literature.

Mr Rex in "brief" replying to the various speakers, said that
as a matter of fact the pamphlet literature was considerable and
of a quality comparing favourably with the like literature of the
old country. It is hoped that an interesting debate will be
arranged for the next meeting.

NOTES

1. George Wallis, husband of Jean, Pauline Smith's maternal aunt. He was an attorney in Oudtshoorn. "C.C." : Cape Colony, now the Cape Province .

2. St Jude's Anglican Church (consecrated 1863) where Pauline Smith was christened by Rev. Alfred Morris on 5 May, 1882.

3. John Pocock was editor, proprietor and founder (1879) of the *Oudtshoorn Courant.*

4. Mrs Tim Smith, sister-in-law of the late Dr Herbert Urmson Smith, father of Pauline. Dr Smith's brother ("Uncle Tim") practised law in Oudtshoorn.

5. The Anglo-Boer War had ended only two and a half years before P.S.'s visit.

6. Kitty le Roux was a sister of Mimi Bergh (née Le Roux) and it was the tragedy of her marriage which suggested the story "Anna's Marriage" in *The Little Karoo.*

7. A page was left open for idioms but nothing was recorded. The examples given by P.S. are obvious Afrikanerisms.

8. Six: the name given to one of the characters in *Platkops Children.* Identified as Colin Hicks, son of Dr Smith's dispensing chemist, Herbert George Hicks ("Six" would have been 2-3 years younger than P.S.).

9. Mrs Morris was the widow of Rev. Alfred Morris (see fn.2). Her daughters Florrie and Julia lived with her in Oudtshoorn.

10. Emma had worked for the Smith family, probably as nurse-maid.

11. Koos had been the driver of Dr Smith's horse-drawn cart when P.S. was a child.

12. Twin brother and sister of P.S. who both died in infancy. The baptismal entry reads: "Twins, John Urmson and Margaret Stewart, born 27.7.1886". P.S. inadvertently wrote "Dorothy" for "Margaret". Her sister Dorothy (Dolly) was born in 1884 and lived to a good old age. (See the poem "The comforting Ayah" and the story of "Jackie" in *Platkops Children.*)

13. The famous Cango Caves, discovered some 200 years ago, are in the foothills of the Swartberg mountains, north of Oudtshoorn.

14. Gideon Scheepers was a Boer Commandant who was sentenced to death and shot in Graaff-Reinet (not Grahamstown, as P.S. later records) in 1902, on a controversial murder charge.
    Paul Kruger, President of the Transvaal Republic (the "Z.A.R.") from 1883 to 1900, died in exile in Switzerland but was buried in Pretoria on 16.12.1904.

15. The Deas family were well-known in Oudtshoorn, originally as wagon-makers. Grace Deas is depicted in *Platkops Children* (Chapter XI,

"Concits an' Thin's"). Through her sister, Lilian Deas (Coaton), P.S. later became befriended with General J.C.Smuts, for his daughter became the wife of Jack Coaton, Lilian's son.

16. Mrs Mimi Bergh: her husband was a well-known ostrich farmer of Kruisrivier (see fn.6). P.S. was to stay with the Berghs during her 1913/14 visit.

17. Eddie Edmeades was an "ostrich feather baron". The Edmeades' home, "Pinehurst", built in 1911 during the boom years before the First World War, still exists as one of the former ostrich feather "palaces" of Oudtshoorn.

18. "Us, Six and Nickum D" is the first chapter of *Platkops Children* and was written while P.S. was still at boarding school. ("Us" were Pauline and her younger sister Dorothy, "Six" was Colin Hicks, and "Nickum D" is partly based on P.S.'s cousin Wilfred, son of Tim Smith, who later became Col.W.Smith of the King's Royal Rifle Corps, in World War I.) Six's father, trading as "Hicks and Company" went insolvent in April 1905; hence P.S.'s cryptic expressions of sympathy: later we hear of "Six" taking up transport riding.

19. George, Southern Cape, was known as "Georgetown" when it was founded in 1811, but by 1905 the name had been officially changed to "George". Named after George III, it became "Princestown" in P.S.'s stories.

20. Mr Krausz owned "Woodifield" forest estate (opposite the present "Saasveld" forestry station, near George). He was later to marry Esmé Dumbleton, sister of Laura and the other Dumbleton girls: Helen, Violet and Kathleen.

21. An elder brother, Charles Urmson Smith (b.1880), who died in infancy and was buried in George.

22. Archdeacon Peter Fogg. Pacaltsdorp was established as a Coloured mission station in 1813 by the Rev. Charles Pacalt.

23. Norris, son of Douglas Dumbleton, had been born in Kimberley during the siege (1899-1900), when the inhabitants suffered great hardships.

24. Fairy Knowe, near the Wilderness, (a seaside resort near George) was the home of the Dumbleton family. It is now a hotel.

25. *Cranford,* the Victorian classic by Mrs Gaskell, has as its main character the gentle spinster, Miss Matty, whose long-lost brother, Mr Peter, returns from the East so that they can spend their old age together.

26. In March 1901 a mounted squadron of the Oudtshoorn Volunteer Rifles under Capt. George Wallis, Acting O.C., lost four men at Vlakteplaas (8 miles east of De Rust) in a skirmish with Theron's commando, then raiding the South Western districts.

27. Alfred Lyttleton, Secretary of State for the Colonies.

28. Chair, usually made of yellow-wood, oak or stinkwood, with thin leather thongs ("riempies") interlaced to form a seat. Such chairs, now valued Africana, greatly interested P.S.

29. P.S.'s "hunt for Lazarus" is misleading: there was a subsequent court case in which two men were charged with the theft of valuable ostrich feathers from an Oudtshoorn buyer, Mr L.Lazarus.

30. The Rev.G.B.Anderson was in charge of the Mission Church and school at Pacaltsdorp.

31. Kruisrivier. A railway siding, but also the name of the ostrich farm belonging to Mr Bergh: this lay east of Oudtshoorn, near Vlakteplaas.

32. The short story "Ludovitje" (*The Little Karoo*) was based on Pieter. The story of his illness and death was told to Pauline Smith by Mimi, during her 1913/14 stay in South Africa.

33. The Swartberg mountain range which separates the Little Karoo from the Great Karoo, to the North.

34. The Outeniqua mountains lie to the south west of the Little Karoo plain. According to legend the name, that of a Hottentot tribe, means "the honey-laden men". P.S. in her writings refers to the mountains as the "Teniquotas"; the foothills received the (wrongly translated) name of "Patchwork Hills".

35. At this period the Cape Colony was governed by Britain. Many Cape Boers remained loyal to the British Crown during the Anglo-Boer War.

36. Mrs Piet le Roux, Mimi's mother. She and her late husband were the characters Oupa Carel and Ouma in the short story entitled "Oupa Carel's", in *Platkops Children*.

37. As children P.S. and her sister Dorothy had spent a few days at the farm and had slept in the feather-bed, so vast to them that they felt lost in it (see the story referred to in fn.36).

38. This was probably *Madame de Sévigné*, edited by Miss Thackeray (Mrs Richmond Ritchie). Published by Blackwood & Sons 1881.

39. F.Muller Rex, a journalist with the *Oudtshoorn Courant*, was elected President of the Debating and Literary Society, scheduled to meet twice monthly. P.S.'s account of the meeting should be compared with the report published in the *Oudtshoorn Courant* a few days later (see Appendix).

40. Thomas Pringle (1789-1834), settler-poet, journalist and fighter for Press freedom, spent only six years in South Africa but decisively influenced events here – both during his stay and later, when he played a leading rôle in the anti-slavery campaign. The poem cited by P.S. has not been identified, but there are lines similar to it in Pringle's *Afar in the Desert* and *Bechuana Boy*.

41. Olive Schreiner's first book, *The Story of an African Farm,* was published in 1883. By 1905 she was a well-known, and controversial, figure whose feminist views offset, in Afrikaner eyes, her pro-Boer stance and efforts to prevent the outbreak of war.

42. Cornelis Jacob Langenhoven, the celebrated Afrikaans poet and writer, was born near Oudtshoorn in 1873. In 1905 he was practising in the town as a barrister, but had begun writing.

43. Possibly Charles Wilhelm Thesen of the well-known Norwegian timber, shipping and trading family of Knysna. Thesen's fluency in English would account for Langenhoven's subsequent reference to him as an Englishman.

44. The grandstand at the race course. Horse-racing was a popular sport in Oudtshoorn and meetings were held every Wednesday afternoon.

45. "Mossies": common sparrows, but also South African slang, meaning "nothing in particular".

46. Fay White was evidently related to Mrs Ham and the Whites of Blanco, a hamlet near George, named after Henry Fancourt White.

47. Mrs Stegmann was the widow of Ds (the Rev.) G.W.Stegmann of the Dutch Reformed Church, Oudtshoorn. Her daughter Marie was a life-long friend of P.S. and well-known in Oudtshoorn.

48. Girls' school in Britain attended by P.S. and her sister Dorothy.

49. "Dooibank": the form and meaning of the word cannot be established from the text. (Possibly "dooitenk", i.e. "dew-tank": underground cement tanks into which dew which fell overnight was channelled.)

50. P.S.'s poor command of the language (officially Dutch; colloquially, Afrikaans) is evident from the passage which follows. Roughly translated, it reads: "What is your name?" – "Bart" "And what else?" – "Nothing" "Nothing? But you must have another name" – "No, my name is just Bart". "But what is your father's name?" – "Andries van Wyk" "Oh, then you are Bart van Wyk" – "No! I am not Bart van Wyk: I am just Bart!"

51. Shrubs which flourished along the banks of the Gamka River. They are in fact double oleanders, known locally as "selonsrose" from "Ceylon se rose" (Afr.) or "Ceylon roses".

52. Probably "twist tobacco" ("roltabak"; "roltwak") as against pipe tobacco. In the entry for 26th May (not included in this selection), P.S. records seeing "an old man winding 'twak' over a delightful old rimpje chair which made us very envious!"

53. "Mill River" is a farm in the Langkloof still owned by the Taute family, and features as the farm "Harmonie" in P.S.'s novel *The Beadle.* (P.S. often stayed with the Taute family on subsequent visits, and Mill River features prominently in the "Wagon Trip Diary" of 1934.)

54. P.S. was fascinated by the patchwork dresses worn by some of the Coloured women, and had collected patches or "lapjes" to make herself one. (See *Platkops Children,* "Katisje's Patchwork Dress".)

THE WAGON TRIP DIARY: AN INTRODUCTORY NOTE

In January 1934, Pauline Smith, accompanied by her two good friends Kathleen Taute and Ethel Morris (Mrs Hooper), went on an adventurous trip by mule-wagon, which lasted just over a week. Their starting point was the farm 'Mill River' in the Langkloof, which was the home of Kathleen Taute, and their route took them through the rest of the Langkloof to Avontuur, then down the treacherous Prince Alfred's Pass, on through the Knysna forest to Knysna and finally to George, and back via the Montagu Pass to 'Mill River'.

Pauline kept a day to day diary of the trip (presumably for the benefit of her sister Dorothy) but as writing was extremely difficult while journeying in the wagon this was only written up properly at Mill River on January 19th, 1934 — a few days after their return.

The original idea for the trip came from Babette Taute, Kathleen's niece. She had told Pauline how she had recently gone by mule-wagon to take a load of bedding and supplies to Plettenberg Bay (where the family had a holiday house), as there was not enough room in her father's Model T Ford for it. Pauline was fascinated, and when Ethel Morris came to stay with her at her home in Dorset (on her way back to South Africa from Shanghai where she had been teaching), she discussed the idea with her and asked her to suggest to Kathleen Taute that they go on a similar trip. She wrote to Kathleen too, asking her to make all the arrangements for the hiring of a tented wagon, the mules, a good driver and other details. This Kathleen did very efficiently.

In a hand-written account of the adventure, Kathleen Taute details the provisions which were packed in an old tin trunk (the *trommeltjie*) discovered in the loft of the farm-house. It easily held a six-dozen box of eggs, loaves of home-made bread, *mosbolletjies*, a tin of home-roasted coffee, and tea for Pauline who never drank coffee. They also had salted rib and dried sausage, potatoes, and butter, fat, jam, Golden Syrup, flour and baking powder, and of course kitchen utensils. A three-legged pot was slung beneath the wagon, and the *water-vaatjies* or water barrels hung from a railing. As for the sleeping arrangements, Pauline and Ethel shared the *wakatel* (a kind of hammock bed) which was slung under the tent, while Kathleen preferred to sleep on a stretcher underneath the wagon.

The driver in charge, young Martin van Rooyen, was very experienced but there were times when he delighted in pleasing himself about where to outspan, rather to the annoyance of Pauline. The Coloured driver, Koos Geduld, was expert with the long whip, which was never actually used on the mules but skilfully cracked over the span. Sometimes he used the short whip or *kerwats* while walking alongside the mules while Martin held the reins.

Kathleen and Pauline both wore *Voortrekker kappies* (sun-bonnets) specially made for the trip, and found them very comfortable, while Ethel, the youngest of the three, was content to go bare-headed. The wagon with its English-speaking women occupants caused some interest at the outspan places, and once while Pauline was alone some people came and asked who they were. According to Kathleen, Pauline said, 'My friends might not like me to tell you their names, but I don't mind telling you mine, it's Smith!'

One of the highlights of the trip was a visit to Miss Duthie, at Belvidere, near Knysna. Pauline's Oudtshoorn-born cousin Wilfred (Wilf) had been a colonel in a regiment of the King's Royal Rifle Corps when Rev. Alfred Duthie was appointed chaplain to the same company. In this diary we meet again some of the people mentioned in the previous journals of 1905 and 1913/14, such as Myra Eustace, Dr St Leger, Mrs Parsons (who owned and ran the George Hotel) and Dr Owen Snow. Pauline's great friend Kathleen Snow had died, and Dr Snow had married again. Many other old friends are referred to, showing that Pauline always maintained an interest in them.

When Pauline Smith embarked on the wagon trip she was already in her fifty-second year and often afflicted by headaches and severe neuralgia. Yet she entered into it with courage and enthusiasm. Ethel Hooper (Morris) has suggested that she wanted to experience what the Dutch farmers and their wives and families had gone through when they journeyed long distances by wagon in the past. Whether her purpose was to collect background material or to recreate the Voortrekker experience, she obviously enjoyed the adventure in spite of veld fires, flooding rains, recalcitrant drivers and ever-present headaches. Parts of the Diary (about 30%) which are of little interest, and unlikely to throw any new light on Pauline Smith or the persons, places and events she describes, have been deleted — such deletions are indicated in the usual way (. . .). Obvious errors in the text (a typescript) have been silently corrected. All editorial interpolations are in square brackets, and a marginal 'chronology' has been supplied. The map on pages 130—1 shows the route followed by Pauline Smith and her friends.

Sheila Scholten

[THE WAGON TRIP DIARY, 1934]

Mill River,
Long Kloof,
Jan 19th 1934

I can't write fully of our trip but must give you some notes on it. Kathie [Kathleen Taute] had found a Klaas Jonck willing to let us have a wagon and 8 mules, with a good coloured boy to look after them. He had to find a tent for the wagon, and also a 'white man' to take charge of the expedition. There was some difficulty about the latter, but eventually we heard that he was to be a nephew of Fred's wife, a young man of 21 called Martin van Rooyen. He was, we were told, going to bring his concertina — but he didn't. All Wednesday Mrs Taute was very busy baking bread and most bolletjes [must-buns] for us in the big oven. They don't ever use the big Dutch oven now and I was glad to see it in use again. The kitchen was full of stir and leaves and firewood and coloured girls tending the oven. Kathie had salted ribitjes [*ribbetjies*: spare ribs] for our trip, and roasted coffee. and on Thursday all our provisions were packed in a large tin trommeltje [small trunk] ready for the start. Mrs Taute was not at all encouraging, and Fred was frankly scornful, but Ethel [Morris] when she arrived had enough enthusiasm to support Kathie and me against all the forebodings of the family! . . . The wagon was to have come at 9, but on account of the rain did not come into sight until nearly 12, when we saw it in the distance coming along the brow of the hill from Jonck's. It looked really beautiful with its full white tent — so seldom seen now and Ethel and I were quite excited. Mrs Taute hurried up lunch, and Martin had it with us. A shy young man he seemed, and without his concertina. After lunch we packed up the wagon gear, mattress and bedding for the cartel [*katel*: bedstead, mounted in the wagon tent], mattress and stretcher *Departure* for Kathie, etc, climbed in after mournful goodbyes to Mrs *Friday,* Taute and set off. The rain was quite over now, but the bump- *5 Jan* ing of the farm road was a horrid revelation to us all!! Kathie and

128

I wore our kapjes and very comfortable we found them. The road was better when we got down to the river, and gradually we learned to find the best place on the cartel and on the boxes in front of the wagon, and found the bumps less trying. What surprised Ethel and me was the slow pace of the mules. Only when whipped up by Koos the coloured boy did they trot for a few minutes at a time. I liked watching Koos. He seemed really fond of the mules in spite of the awful noises he made in urging them on! When Martin drove, Koos, if not at the 'break' [brake] at the back, walked by the side of the team cracking his long whip at them, or dancing lightly up on his toes to touch up certain sluggards with his short stock or with a stone. He did this with a curious silent cunning which never failed to surprise the mules into sudden action — and incidentally to rattle us about like peas in a pan on the cartel. Our first stop was at Jonck's farm, to get our faikies [water-barrels]. Our first outspan was at Keurbooms River — the K.R. that afterwards flows in to Plettenberg Bay. We outspanned again on Gwarna Heights at 9 p.m. for supper — and a great scramble in the dark-ness that first supper was. We had no candles, and only one lantern which Koos needed for tending the mules. . . . It was bitterly cold, for we were high up and all through that outspan a jackal was screaming as I had never heard one scream before. It was a strange melancholy sound, very eerie in the stillness of those heights at night. The cold was so intense — or seemed so to me — that I slept in my great-coat with my head muffled up. Ethel and Kathie, very superior, undressed like Xtians. Ethel shared the cartel with me, and took up most of it, curled up like a contortionist — a habit, she says, born of sharing her bed at night with her two dogs! For some reason the men decided we must travel still further that night so inspanned again, and went on until two a.m. It was very pleasant jogging quietly on half asleep listening to the click of the stopper, the crunch of the wheels, and Koos's strange cries. But very cold, and I wondered what I should do if it got worse. We outspanned again at 2 at Avontuur Neck, made an early start from there and reached Avontuur soon after 7 on a lovely clear, but very

Saturday 6 Jan

129

KEY

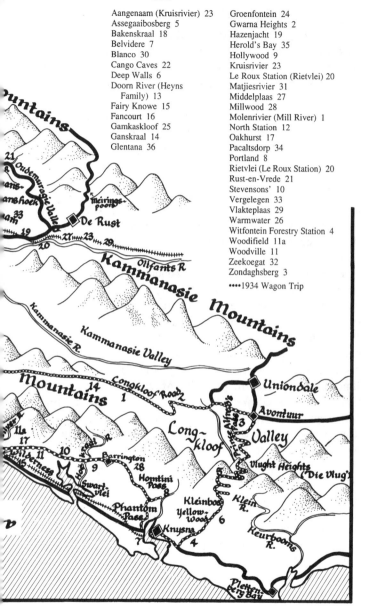

cold morning. At the shop I got a new torch, and two tickies [threepenny piece] candlesticks and candles — and 3 pairs of socks for a shilling — one pr for each of us as extras for warmth! All through this trip the changes in climate surprised me. I used to think one knew what to expect out here in the different seasons — but if one ever did one doesn't now. . . . All along the kloof harvesting was in progress — in stony uneven lands men were cutting with sickles, in others reapers were being used, and on some farms threshing was in progress. The stooks and ricks looked very untidy compared with the English ones — or clumsy rather. They stack the sheaves in stooks with the corn downwards, not up as with us — we stack ours in England to dry, here the sheaves must not get too dry or the corn is shaken out before it can be loaded on the wagons and threshed. This gives the little stooks a funny up-side-down appearance. (I put these things down as I want to remember them.)

From Avontuur the journey up Zondag's berg was very lovely in the clear morning air. Quite high up on the mountain sides here there is sufficient soil for grain and men were harvesting with sickles and machines. Ploughing was going on too where the reaping was over, and the lights on the mountains — always changing — and the yellow of the corn-lands with the dark rich brown of the ploughed lands was very beautiful. I sat for some time in front with Martin practising Afrikaans and got on better than I had expected. We outspanned on the Berg at 11 for breakfast, went on again to Vlught's poort, outspanning there at 2. The Vlught is a curious bit of country. We leave Long Kloof when we take Prince Alfred's Pass over Zondag Berg, and now the country changes, and though we are still high up, and constantly going up hill and down, all this journey along Vlught Heights overlooks a wide flat winding valley through which runs the Keurbooms river (from our outspan place on the heights we had looked west to see, most surprisingly, Diep River valley open to view between the mountains). Martin had amused himself making Ethel guess what the valley was — which she could not do. On Gwarna Heights she had pointed back to Mill River as the direction we must travel to get to Uniondale — a mistake

132

which delighted Martin and gave him a sense of superiority for all the rest of the journey. He had a very childish sense of humour and thereafter exercised it much on Ethel. But Ethel's complete lack of any sense of direction or locality was amazing to Kathie and me too — considering she spends her life teaching geography to the young! She never knew where she was or where she was going — but was supremely happy in the getting there whatever misadventure befell her on the way. She was the untidiest of us all, and the most adaptable. Her clothes were always all over the place — her pretty chinese lawn dresses as often as not draped the three-legged pot and the coffee kettles. Her dilapidated red-backed aluminium-bristled hair-brush was always tossing about the floor or cartel (which Kathie says is spelt katel) waiting for someone to sit or step upon. . . . In any crisis Ethel could just withdraw to the katel, curl herself up, and sleep. While we dressed or undressed, Kathie and I, Ethel would say Well I'll just have a sleep till you're ready — and *sleep*. We would wake her when we needed any of the articles she had commandeered for her comfort, and she would be wide awake, and perfectly happy and cheerful in an instant, and give us up our own belongings most graciously! She was really very good company, and never once through all the trip did we have any sort of disagreement. Kathie was boss as far as there *was* a boss, and had the management of the meals. I don't know how Ethel and I would have fared without her. Well, we would never have set off without her at all. She did all the catering, and pre-pared the meals which Koos, when he had got the fire going, cooked for us. We lived on baked potatoes, ribbetjies, coffee (tea for me), porridge, vet cook (lovely these were) roster cook [*roosterkoek*: griddle-cakes] or scones, and the bread and rusks made for us for the trek by Mrs Taute. Ethel and I were always hungry and desperate for our meals, and always getting into trouble with Kathie for making inroads on bread and rusks be-fore the meal proper began. Kathie's blunt commanding manner was a great contrast to Ethel's irresponsibility. . . . Kathie has very strongly the feeling of the Dutch that if coloured people are not kept strictly in their place life and work with them be-

133

comes impossible. Sometimes on this question I am reminded
of my talks in the old days with her father.* She has something
of his vigour of statement too. We used to have long discussions
sitting in front of the wagon, and I felt she has a much more
exact and masculine mind than either Ethel or I have. She
reads well too — grasping what she reads, refusing to accept
without understanding, and constantly surprising me by the
aptness of her quotations (I can never quote). . . . We had a
short outspan again at Asegai Bosch Berg, and then on through
the dark to Klein River, further than we meant to go but the
intervening outspan was occupied by other wagons and mules,
and ours could not be let loose there. We got to Klein River at
11, and tumbled into bed. . . .

Sunday
7 Jan
I woke very early and while the others still slept watched the
sunrise on the mountains. To the right was a narrow valley and
beyond it (this was looking back the way we had come) range
after range of mountains. The day was very clear, and very hot.
At 7 the rocks were scorching, and the ground hot to one's feet
through rubber soles. I had a bad headache, and could do little
[until] evening, yet in spite of it this was one of the days I liked
best, so lovely were the mountains around us, so peaceful the
little valley. . . . We had decided to rest here through the heat
of the day, and I was thankful because of my head. We lay in
such shade as we could get round the wagon, and were glad of
the little mountain breeze. Koos had a long way to go to get
the Vaatjies (that says Kathie is the proper way to spell the
water-barrels) filled, and the mules watered. Martin disappeared
to go keuring [*kuiering*: visiting] in the hills across the valley,
and we saw him no more till evening, when he returned with a
water-melon. . . . It was growing dusk when we saw him coming
through the scrub and bush, and by the time he reached us Koos
was inspanning and making ready to start under Kathie's very
severe and abrupt orders to do so. And only when we *had*
started were we told that Mr Jonck had stipulated that the
mules were not to travel on Sunday! By then however we were

* Thys Taute: see the *South African Journal* of 1913-14.

134

all determined that Martin should go on — and on we went, the
evening most perfect, the sky ablaze with stars (the waning moon
not yet risen), the world very still. . . . As we reached the forest
— the first or little forest [Kleinbos] — we forgot our scruples.
It was a wonderful experience — no light through the gloom of
trees but the wagon lantern, the narrow strip of stars overhead
above the road, and the amazing fire-flies sweeping down
through the trees towards us. . . . It grew very dark towards the
end of the trek and was still dark and moonless when at 11 we
got out of the forest on to Yster Neck, where we outspanned.
Here there was neither grazing nor water for the mules, and
they had to be tethered to the wagon for the night to keep them
from straying. There were mosquitoes about, and poor Straker
got badly bitten. We feared there might be a stampede, there
was so much stamping through the night, and that punishment
for travelling on Sunday was to overtake us here. But though I
did not get much sleep nothing un-toward happened, and early
next morning I lifted the wagon flap to watch the mists rising *Monday*
from the forests and slopes. The mules were let loose for a bit *8 Jan*
before we set off, which we did after early coffee at 6. We
journeyed for some time in the open with forested slopes all
around us, and then entered the Main forest, outspanning at
Deep Walls, near the big yellow-wood tree at 10 am for breakfast. Here there was a little slimy water in a pool for the mules
but none for us, and the forest road looked terribly dry and
dusty in spite of the trees. . . . We spent a long time under the
giant yellow-wood (we had been graciously allowed by Martin
to outspan here as *he* had never seen the tree and wished to do
so! Otherwise his perversity would surely have taken us past it!).
We went on again about 11:30, anxious now for good water
both for ourselves and for the mules, and to the great satisfaction of both Martin and Koos saw the little forest-train on its
way to Bracken Hill. All this day's journeying in the forest had
a lovely monotony — but it was monotony, for we saw no
flowers, no baboons, no elephants. Our one adventure was the
meeting of a rampaging bull, being driven by two men and a
boy. Its bellowing was so agonised that at first we thought it

135

must be a wounded elephant at least. Where it was going to, and what the men were going to do with it remained a mystery, but long after they passed us its bellowing echoed through the forest. . . . On we went into drier and drier country until suddenly, under a blue-gum plantation the wagon was halted, and down a short slope we saw the river again. This was Vitfontein, and we outspanned here at 3 and Kathie made scones for us and Koos baked potatoes in the ashes. As we were now nearing Knysna we all went down to the river to wash and tidy-up, Kathie and I discarding our kapjes and donning hats. After we set off we had lovely glimpses of the lagoons and Heads, but everything here too looked in need of rain. I found myself a little shy about riding down the Main Street, and got Martin to go by a side road which took us through to the other side of the town on the way to Salt River where we were to camp. I think I would have been less shy had our wagon been tidier, – but tidy with Ethel it could never be! Knysna has grown and looks much more flourishing. And the Regatta was to begin next day, so the place was busy – for Knysna. We were evidently taken for a water-melon wagon coming in for the regatta, as Martin was asked if we had melons for sale (another joke for Martin). The road out to Salt River was very dusty but Ethel knew the camping ground here and a camp for the mules as well. . . . We had supper round the wagon, and I went early to bed, while Ethel and Kathie entertained Mrs Maurice* and Bunny Newdigate who came down from Portland with butter and wine for Kathie, at the wagon. We had a rather public camp there, and Kathie slept on the wagon instead of on her stretcher.

Tuesday   We all breakfasted at the cottage with the Blakes, and after it
9 Jan   Ethel and I went in to Knysna on Sass's lorry while Kathie waited for the Newdigates who came down in their car and took her out to the Heads. . . . Went on down to the Thesen Office, where I hoped to find old Mr Charles Thesen[+] to whose

* (Née Newdigate) wife of Colonel Maurice of Portland.
+ Ship-owner and timber-merchant who played a dominant rôle in the development of Knysna.

136

daughter, Marie, Bill Coaton had written about my coming. Mr Charles, an old man of nearly 80 now, was not in the office but we saw his son Mr Harry. Mr Harry knew nothing about me, and was a little surprised, in a dignified sort of way, when he asked how we had come and I said by wagon. Where were staying? In a camp at Salt River. How had we come in to Knysna now, by car? No, on a lorry. He was a little pained! But recovered after 'phoning up to his father and returning to us with the news that the car was being sent down for us and Mr Charles would be pleased if we would take 11 o'clock tea with him. Presently the car arrived, driven by a married daughter at present on a visit there with her baby, who told us that Bill's Marie had gone off early that morning for a few days to the Wilderness. The Thesen house is right out of the town up on the hill, with most lovely views from its stoep. . . . I found the old gentleman's talk most interesting. . . . He and 7 or 9 brothers and sisters came out with their parents and an uncle (who then or later also had a family) from Norway in their own small sailing ship in the early seventies. The uncle was a sea-captain, and he and his brother, old Charles's father, owned the ship (I wish I could remember the name! I ought to have written all this down at the time, but writing was impossible in the wagon). They were bound for New Zealand but coming into Table Bay at a time of great distress (it must have been the sixties not the seventies I think) when Knysna was suffering from lack of provisions through a terrible drought, and provisions could only be taken there by sea as there were no roads, they were asked by the Government to take a cargo to Knysna before proceeding further. They were well paid for this (it meant the unloading of their own cargo for New Zealand first) and found it to their advantage to carry further freights to Knysna before going on to N.Z. In the end old Charles's father decided to give up N.Z. altogether and start trading in Knysna, where he had both the wood to deal in and the scenery he was at home in in Norway. Here the fjord was wider than in Norway, and the enclosing mountains not so high, and the climate entirely different. But it was as nearly Norway as one could expect — and home it

137

became. . . . The married daughter took us back to camp and we then joined the Blakes and Kathie for lunch at the cottage. After lunch Kathie and I packed up while Ethel bathed and presently we set off once more, bound for Portland where Mrs Maurice and Bunny Newdigate had asked us all to spend the night. We had got up to the top of Phantom Pass — the view back along the Knysna river to the Thesen farm in the valley is a lovely one — when Bunny appeared with the car and a small niece — come to pick us up for Portland, leaving the wagon to go on to the outspan at High-way (from where the Portland road branches off). The weather was a little uncertain now with threatening rain. (Newdigate?) Portland was the old Barrington homestead — a big square stone house with large rooms and long passages, all falling into decay and yet all having charm, and, amid much disorder, beautiful old bits of furniture, prints and paintings. Ethel and I had a big room to the north, and I thankfully accepted the hot bath in the bath-house in the garden suggested by Mrs Maurice. Many things reminded me of the old Oakhurst days — the big dining-room, the long table, the smaller table for the children, the general way of life. So much more English in its atmosphere than Mill River. . . .

Wed
10 Jan
. . . A lovely morning, and after baths and breakfast we wandered about the farm, watching the threshing (corn brought by various bywoners [tenant farmers; share croppers] and some coloured people to be threshed, the mill surrounded by men and women and boys: one old woman making coffee: verneukery [cheating] about the bags at times: all pleasant and patriarchal and Russian!). Mrs Maurice in corduroy divided skirts, and Bunny also. Mrs Maurice's thin legs, no longer young, bare, her white hair cut short, but lank and long: her English talk and English-country manner — all very interesting and part of the picture with the square stone house falling into decay, the forest and mountains, for setting and background. Mrs Maurice took us to the little church where Alfred Duthie used to come for service once a month. Then on in the car to see the cows dipped. A big herd of cows, and some lovely little Kerry calves. All this in sunshine — and then the decision to go down to Belvidere to see Miss

Duthie. . . . Bunny took us down in the car, going down not by the pass but by the lakes road which we found partly ablaze with veld fires. The smoke made driving rather difficult for her and disagreeable and on our return she took the Phantom pass road.

Belvidere. Somehow Belvidere struck me as colonial in the old American Virginian way. The house reminded me of old American and Anglo-Indian prints, and though it had no prosperous air — for no farm out here and no estate has that at present — it did not suggest the crumbling away of past values that Portland did. And it was all very much tidier and cared-for indoors, with a sort of faded charm which Miss Duthie herself has. (Mrs Maurice had said I reminded her of Miss Duthie but I felt robust and clumsy beside her.) She took us into the drawing-room for 11 o'clock tea — and sat and talked with me in a gentle tender way of her brother Alfred about whom she and Capt. Hart are compiling a memoir. . . . She spoke of Alfred's work in France and his admiration for Wilf [Pauline Smith's cousin]. And of the old days of the Rex's, showing me a little sharp knife set in part of the tusk of the elephant shot when the Duke of Cambridge came out in [1867]. Old prints she showed me too, and paintings of Duthie ancestors in Highland uniform. Presently 11 o'clock [tea] was brought in by Miss Armstrong, an elderly lady who was once her governess and had remained on in the family ever since as housekeeper. . . . [Then] into the room sailed two apparitions — one in sandals and shortish garments with on her head one of Woolworth's sixpenny straw hats tied under her chin with what seemed to me a bit of black elastic but which Ethel told me afterwards was a bit of narrow black velvet: and the other in flowing fluffy frilly mid-Victorian gown with a little hat over the brim and under the brim of which were arranged little bunches of curls — Miss Jessica Grove and the Baroness de Wagstaff [Olga Racster]. I felt as if I were suddenly back in a Marie Corelli novel! Miss Grove was so effusive, so impressive, so overwhelming. The Baroness so beaming and so much the literary celebrity. I was introduced as Miss Smith and it was only after they had said that they 'knew' Pauline Smith

139

that they tumbled to it that the P.S. they knew was in the room! Miss Grove claimed Uncle Tim and Aunt Maud then as among her dearest and most intimate friends! But Kathie's description of all this is best, for most of it happened to her while Miss Duthie was talking to me. The Baroness was very much the literary lady to Kathie in the true Corelli manner. They have a little house not far from the church and take paying guests. It was really a very odd Alice-in-wonderlandish tea-party, every one of the eight of us in the room a little odd!. . .

We had to go on in haste after this to catch up the wagon, going up the pass and overtaking it at the Homtini bridge a good way beyond Portland. The men had outspanned here at 12, and our next outspan was near Barrington at 4. It was a very hot journeying, as fires were raging on the mountains and in some of the forest-lands. We went on in the evening to Hollywood, the Gordon Robertsons's farm. A curious dreary looking house with a large square werf [farmyard] surrounded by pines in front of it. We camped out not far from the werf, then Kathie and I went to pay our respects to the Gordon Robertsons while Ethel cooked the supper. It was to be boiled rice done very specially by Ethel who was very important about it. . . . We were very hungry and on the strength of Ethel's promises of a really good meal had refused the Gordon Robertson's offer of provisions. The rice according to Kathie would take hours to cook in Ethel's patent, but Ethel herself was so hopeful that we consented to wait a little — waited half an hour and then as the wretched stuff was still quite hard fell upon whatever we could find! Ethel accused Koos of spoiling her steaming process by taking the water for her [his?] potatoes, but what actually happened inside that pot I never discovered. When last I saw the rice Ethel had it tied up in an enamel plate inside a handkerchief or towel. It was she who put the butter into a patent refrigerator made of her was-lapje [face-cloth] and hung it up from one of the beams of the wagon — with disastrous results on the following day. . . .

Thursday . . . This was our one really trying day, a day of intense heat,
11 Jan with enormous fires all round us. We learned later that the temp.

at Knysna was 113° and at George 109°. It was the worst day they had had along this coastal region for many years. The Homtini was impassable, the fire raging there on both sides of the road. Cars had to turn back there and we were thankful we had got the mules through the day before. Every little current of air was like a furnace blast. I had never been in any thing like it, and Kathie who has spent summers with Edie in Vryburg said she had never been through anything to equal it up there. I had waked with neuralgia, and through the heat this got steadily worse. Our first outspan was at Hoogekraal River about nine, where I lay under the shade of forest trees while Ethel and Kathie bathed and washed some of the household linen. This was about 9, the heat even then intense. We went on from there to Diep River (so many Diep rivers!) in heat getting steadily worse, my neuralgia doing the same, and outspanned here at 12, leaving the wagon on the road near a desolate looking two-roomed house, and taking our things down through a tangle of brushwood to the river to the shade of the bridge. Koos made the fire up at the wagon, and Kathie − the brick − managed to get us a meal of tea and baked potatoes (lovely potatoes we had on all this trip) brought down to the shade. . . . Below us children were driving cows and little calves into the river with much noise and laughter. But I was all alone and it was quite quiet when I saw my snake! It was the most beautiful snake I have ever seen and came all along the bend of the river close to the bank. What I noticed first was a sudden scurry of frogs jumping one after the other into the water with flat fat 'plomps'. I turned to look just as one beside me jumped − and there moving along the edge of the water more swiftly than I could ever have believed possible was a most lovely liquid green snake. The kind of green you can almost see through − the light green you get in streaks and patches sometimes in a darker green sea. The green almost of crème de menthe! It rested for a second just in front of me looking at the escaped frog, its forked black tongue out, its tiny black eyes fixed on the frog − then slithered off. I had never thought a snake could be so beautiful and marvellous as this. I suppose it was not poisonous. Somehow it was too beautiful to make one feel afraid, terrified as I am of snakes in general out here! This was the only beauty of this terrible day. We went on again, all nearly overcome, and me lying on the floor of the wagon to get away from the heat of the tent, at about 4:30, making for Stevenses, where we hoped to get rooms and a meal. But Stevenses no longer take in guests, and we had to go on to Leggat's farm in the hope that they might do so there. It was on this part of the journey I think that Ethel's patent refrigerator collapsed. The butter in its tin was now oil, and like golden syrup in colour and substance, when down it fell in its lapje and tin, pouring through the planks of the wagon floor on to the ground beneath. We reached Leggats at about 6:30 when the fire on the mountain opposite was really terrifying in the evening light. And all around were fires and alarms of fires. . . .

Friday   . . . This was a much happier day for us all. There were still
12 Jan   fires but the intense heat was over, and as we neared George little showers of rain fell from time to time. We left Leggats at 6, and made our first outspan at Silver River at 9 for breakfast, where Ethel and Kathie bathed while Koos prepared porridge, and Martin made his toilet and removed his little white beard. All along the road we had met many cars, and had many greetings from the less smart of them. We had also had some scowls from those who thought the swinging out of the mules when taking a corner was negligent driving on the wrong side of the road. . . . We made our second outspan near the Vintcent's farm of Peter Koen in threatening rain, Koos grilling salt ribbetjes for us while we wandered down to the river and tidied ourselves up for the entry into George. Rain was intermittent but becoming steadily heavier and nearer. I had hoped we might outspan on the Blanco side of George, but Martin proclaimed this impossible and declared the only possible place to be the open green or show-ground near the station. We had to pass this (it is on the Knysna side) to get to York St, where I was to be dropped to go and call on Myra Eustace, the Snows and Mrs Parsons [of the George Hotel], while the wagon was to go on to Hibernia St for Kathie's shopping, and as we did so saw that our fellow-campers there included an Algerian Mermaid and a Merry-go-

142

round — the beginning of the circus travelling-show due next week. We passed the old Schoemann house, the garden simply a mass of thousands of agapanthus blue under the old oaks. Very lovely. The old Edmeades-St Leger house opposite Myra's just the same, and Myra just the same too. She opened the door to me herself and again I felt how I should like a little house out here like hers! . . . On then to Mrs Parsons. And here I found supper in progress with a strong smell of fish which made me realize suddenly how hungry I really was! But Mrs Parsons came to me in the sitting-room, leaving the fish behind her and as she took some little time to grasp who I was, and having grasped it, made no enquiries after any of the family, I realized that as Myra had said the old Mrs Parsons was gone. . . . I went on from there thinking I must get on quickly from the Snows to the wagon to get a chop from Kathie who had promised us fresh chops from her friend the butcher in Hibernia St. Got to the Snows and after ringing several times was asked by a maid whom I wished to see. . . . At last Mrs Snow* appeared. Quite grey. A blank as to who I was, and her mind much occupied as it always is with other matters which she seems never able to come to any decision about. As she was puzzling over me Dr Snow appeared and cleared up the mystery for her and insisted that I must stay for supper. There wasn't much, he said, for they had just a few moments before arrived back from the Wilderness, and were having a light meal before a bridge-party, etc, etc. But would I stay? I must stay! It was their only chance of a talk — and before I could answer I was in Mrs Snow's room having a wash — which I was most thankful to get! And the supper was fish — soles brought up from the Wilderness, and most delicious to my hunger! They had a friend staying with them, in full evening dress and I was conscious of my wagon-dust, — but still more so when the bridge-party began to arrive, and thankful when one of them, Dr du Plessis, offered to take me down to the show-ground in his car. . . . He was gloomy about the rain, foreseeing a deluge after the long drought, and

* Dr Owen-Snow's second wife.

not at all sure that we'd get off before the flood began. He was
right. We had planned to start as early as we could next morning to get through if possible, but at about 9 the deluge began.
It rained in torrents. Martin and Koos had put up the buck-sail
and sheltered under that, and our tent was perfectly water-tight
so we were all quite dry and comfortable on the katel. But the
noise of the rain was really terrifying when we remembered
that we were on the wrong side of the mountain with Klaasie
Jonk's mules and that there might be wash-aways as bad, after
the long drought as those which had kept Aunt Jean and Julia
and me storm-bound in [George] for 10 days 20 years ago!
There was no cessation of the rain all night and next morning
Koos and Martin came out from under the buck-sail looking
wretched. Koos managed by breaking up part of a paraffin box
and using candle ends to make a fire (it took a long time) while
Martin went off to see the mules in their camp some distance
away. Kathie heroically cooked us a meal, wearing my torn black
mackintosh and the little knitted cap D. [her sister, Dorothy?]
had made for me, and we tried to make plans.

Saturday . . . The outlook got worse and worse as the morning advanced.
13 Jan. It was impossible to lift the end flaps of the tent as the rain beat
in and though the Snows had expressed great concern for our
welfare the night before, to Kathie's annoyance no one
appeared to ask how we fared though they could not, she
declared, imagine we had set off in this flood! I don't know
what sanitary arrangements the Algerian Mermaid and the
Merry-go-round folk had, but through the morning each of us
in turn went down through the pouring rain to make enquiries
at the station and visit the ladies' room. As we possessed only
one mackintosh and one umbrella between us this arrival at
intervals of a bedraggled female in torn black mackintosh, and
split black umbrella caused some interest to the station clerk,
who remarked to Ethel: What, are you back again? What do you
want to know now? In the end, after many consultations we
decided that for this day the wagon must be given up to Martin
and Koos so that they could have its shelter while Kathie and I
went to friends and Ethel went on to Brak River by train (she

144

was to have left us at Camfer by train).* It was then that Kathie and Koos got the fire going to grill chops, and we had a breakfast lunch. . . . After our meal Ethel in a great scramble packed up her belongings, and Koos carried her suit-case to the station, she following bare-foot through the rain with her rugs, once more in the mackintosh and under the torn umbrella. These were brought back to us by Koos, and from the station (where Ethel would have to wait several hours, writing letters, for her train) she presently sent us a taxi. Into this Kathie bundled with her belongings and her bedding, and I with my suit-cases and off we set, going first to Kathie's cousin Thelma. Here, in pouring rain, we stopped and Kathie in her kapje, and carrying her bedding, went down the garden path and knocked. Thelma opened the door to behold this vision out of the clouds! She knew nothing of our wagon-trip, and had no idea that Kathie was in George, and could not grasp what this apparition of her in soaking kapje with mattress and bedding could mean! But she had room for her, and took her in, and the taxi then took me on to Myra's. Myra grasped my predicament at once, and took me in bag and baggage. Her maid was out, and we made up a bed together and presently sat down to lunch! After which I went and lay down till tea-time, getting up every now and then to look out at the weather which showed no signs of improving. It did, however, lighten a little towards evening. . . . Myra spoke a great deal about Gordon Mills⁺ and the church trouble. Feeling seems to be *very* strong against Mrs Beale's 'Fanatic'. Myra said it was said he is so sure of winning his case that he has already chosen a portion of the Bishopscourt estate on which to build his house. . . . All this time we were going at intervals to the side stoep to watch the weather. The rain stopped for a little but did not clear, the mountains still enveloped in mist. . . . And to bed, with the roar of the waterfalls, and the rain and the fall of acorns on the roof to cheer us, we went.

* She had to return to her teaching post in Cape Town.
⁺ Involved in the Church of England in South Africa and the Church of the Province controversy, raging at the time; hence the further reference to Bishopscourt, residence of the Archbishop of Cape Town.

. . . This was a better day. Still soft rain at times, but every now and then a clearing and lifting of the clouds. The old woman who turned up to help in the kitchen, brought some kaatje pierings [gardenias]which Myra gave to take to little C.H.U.S.'s grave.* A surprise for little C.H.U.S. I thought after all these years! It was very peaceful round the little church, and I was glad to be there again. But I think the garden of remembrance, at the top of York St, a great mistake. The red stone is harsh and hot-looking and the whole thing so formal and out of keeping with the old natural free beauty of the wide grass-grown oak-lined George streets. . . . Earlier Kathie had called in her cousin's car — the cousins setting off to Long Kloof and willing to take us down to Mill River if we wished to abandon the wagon and let the men follow when they thought best. But this I felt very unwilling to do. For one thing Fred would have jeered at us so! And for another, as Kathie had said when we rejoined it after Portland, the wagon had somehow begun to be home to us! So we decided to remain, and when the cousins went off Kathie went for a time to the wagon and watched the merry-go-round and other folk coming to life. Whole families appearing from under the wagon tents under which they had been kept prisoners in the rain without any means of fire making or of getting hot food. One woman had a small infant, and one small child emerged in a marvellous pale blue satin dress with large hat, and white shoes and socks and sat in state on the wagon front. No sign of the Mermaid! But a small boy to ask for a cupful of salt for his Pa, and to ask if we had grapes to sell! All this time the weather was steadily improving, and back again Kathie presently came to tell us that in spite of the bar against Sunday travelling the men wanted to set off at mid-day and get over the mountains before night-fall! We decided to agree, and soon after 12 the wagon appeared and we set off. But what an empty tidy wagon it now was without Ethel! We could not have believed she took up so much room! The slow journey up the pass was lovely. Everywhere the sound

* Charles Herbert Urmson Smith, who died in infancy (see 1905 Diary).

146

of rushing water, in the little streams and the rivers and the
waterfalls. Sun began to shine as we got up a little way and the
air was so fresh after the rain. We outspanned about 3 and had
chops, a little way below the old toll-house . . . . On again, and at
the toll Koos got a little pepper without which it seemed impossible for Kathie to prepare meals. There were lovely patches
of watsonias here and there, and a few proteas, but very few
other flowers. We managed all the turns very comfortably in
spite of oncoming cars, and enjoyed all this part of the journey
very much. . . . We drove, unwillingly, past North station, and
some distance on outspanned for supper. It was now about
6:30 and a cold clear evening. We had thought we should spend
the night here — but no, the mules from here would surely run
home, said Martin, and we must go on. So on we went, and
down near Doorn River took in the darkness the wrong turning
— or rather missed the right one, and found ourselves suddenly
involved in a motor accident! At first Kathie and I thought we
were responsible for this, for it was impossible to see what had
happened in the darkness, and a policeman's inquiry of Koos
where was our lamp seemed to put us at once in the wrong.
(Koos replied that it *had* been lit but had 'just now' gone out!)
All this commotion threw Martin into a pitiful panic, (his
family are renowned for their timidity) and Kathie had to come
to Koos's aid to get the mules backed on to the right road, I
holding the torch for Martin at the wheels. . . . When we got on
to the Long Kloof road there seemed some uncertainty in
Martin's mind as to whether we should go on or wait for the
policeman to take us all to gaol — but Koos I think it was who
decided to ignore the policeman (his lantern was now lit) and on
we went. And on we did go, to Kathie's intense annoyance,
until 2 a.m.! We were really annoyed about this, which was
Martin's last spasm of perversity. At 2 a.m. we at last were
allowed an outspan, near an old coloured people's church. Kathie
had her stretcher put up, and I tumbled into bed in the katel . . . .
. . . A lovely clear morning, and for a time I watched the *Monday*
swallows and other birds flying in and out of the broken win- *15 Jan*
dows of the 'coloured church'. The mules were in the veld and

147

down by the river, but there was water available for us in a tank by the church. Kathie was not very well at first, but recovered as we went along and was soon herself again to my great relief! All our comfort depended upon her, and she was the only one who could ever stand up to Martin! We outspanned at Gans kraal for our mid-day meal, and lay under the shelter of a line of pear-trees. The light on the hills and mountains was marvellous, as I always find it here, and again I felt that the Long Kloof has a beauty that surpasses that of almost any other part of the country I know — though so few seem to see it! The colour of the hills is always changing, the ranges are always opening to reveal fresh ranges beyond. But I won't try to describe more now. We ended our last outspan by giving some of the remaining provisions to Koos who was delighted to get them, and delighted with his 5/- tip. When I gave it him he asked me to be sure to tell Dr Anderson that it was 'Koos' who had taken us safely round the mountain. I felt more than ever sorry that I did not know more Africaans so that I could have had more talk with him in spite of Kathie's scruples! For Martin I could feel no regrets! We trekked on again and got back to the farm about 4. Very sorry I was that it was all over, and realizing only next day how tired I was, and how full of bruises was my body!

PART 3
CHAPTERS FROM 'WINTER SACRAMENT'

'BACKGROUND TO PLATKOPS' AND *WINTER SACRAMENT:* TWO INTRODUCTORY NOTES

The typescript of the hitherto unpublished 'Background to Plat-kops' was the subject of correspondence, in the course of 1949, between Pauline Smith and Mr Justice B.A.Tindall, who was made a judge of the Supreme Court in Bloemfontein in the same year. It is clear, particularly from the pencilled comments P.S. added at the end of the typescript, that 'Background to Plat-kops' was intended as an introductory chapter to *Winter Sacrament* — her long-projected but never completed second novel. She is here doing, on broader historical as well as geographical scale, what Arnold Bennett had insisted she provide for her 'Little Karoo' stories: a descriptive setting, to acquaint the reader with 'the conditions of life in the place and time' of which she wrote. (*The Beadle,* it is worth noting, opens with a fairly detailed description of the Aangenaam Valley, its inhabitants, and the topography of the region.) After her long absence from South Africa, P.S. obviously felt uncertain about the spelling and accuracy of the Afrikaans place-names and terms she had used, and asked Justice Tindall to advise her. In a letter dated 18 August 1949 (now in the U.C.T. Library collection), Justice Tin-dall points out that he has little personal knowledge of the Little Karoo; however, he commends the general historical soundness of the 'Background' sketch and appends a list of emendations and explanations of terms incorrectly or inaccurately used in the text. 'Background to Platkops' should obviously be read in con-junction with the opening chapters of *Winter Sacrament,* which follow immediately after the first-named text.

E.P.

*   *   *   *

In July, 1953, less than six years before her death, Pauline Smith made one of her final recorded references to the novel that she had begun more than twenty-five years before and that

151

she would never finish. In a letter to her good friend, Frank Swinnerton, the British novelist and critic, she wrote that she hoped "to get on, *somehow*, I don't know quite how, with *Winter Sacrament*. It is growing in a curious way that is somehow beyond my control — or my strength". But later that month, in the pattern of hope followed closely by despair that was to become characteristic of her struggle to write the novel, she told him, "Since my illness my memory has at times, when I get tired, been a very *stupid* one — with now & then a glimpse of the people in *Winter Sacrament* which sends me to my desk with a spark of hope — But it all goes so terribly slowly in my present tiredness." Late in August, she wrote to another writer friend, the South African novelist Sarah Gertrude Millin: "I still hope somehow to get on with the book (a small one) I have wanted so long to finish — but you know Sarah dear I have *never* had your wonderful strength of will, & feel more than ever a broken reed shaken by the wind . . . ."

The conception of the novel, like all of her creative work, was rooted in her earliest and happiest years, those spent in the area of the Little Karoo, when she savoured her close ties with her father. Later, when she was writing the stories that would become *The Little Karoo* and when she was writing the novel, *The Beadle,* she was already thinking of the work that would, she hoped, become *Winter Sacrament.* As early as 1928, her friend, mentor, and business manager, Arnold Bennett, wrote to her publisher, Jonathan Cape, to discuss royalties for three new books to be written by Pauline Smith. Cape responded, "For the three books in addition to the one now under discussion, I will offer an advance of £300 for a novel, and £150 for a volume of short stories . . . ." The novel "now under discussion" was *Winter Sacrament.*

But in those early days, that was not the title she had in mind for the work. She had decided on *Green Were the Lands* (she would later, in 1939, comment on the similarity between her title and that of the recently published *How Green Was My Valley,* by Richard Llewellyn). But Bennett was not satisfied: "A title has been chosen for the novel." he wrote to Cape on the 14th of April, 1928, "but Miss Smith fully agrees that it will not do." In the end, she decided on *Winter Sacrament.*

In 1933, at least in part to gather material for the novel, Pauline Smith went to South Africa. It was her fourth return trip since leaving that country as a child. She planned to remain for a year, but stayed until 1936. When she arrived in Cape Town, she was reluctant to talk about her literary activity during the seven years since her last visit to South Africa (that was in 1926, at the height of her creative period when she had returned a literary celebrity). She hoped that this trip would do for her writing what an earlier trip, in 1913-1914, had done (that visit had been the inspiration for *The Beadle* and for a number of stories in *The Little Karoo*). During this 1933-1936 journey, she would prepare her book of children's stories, *Platkops Children,* for publication, and do germinal work on *Winter Sacrament.*

To gather material for the novel, she embarked on a journey by ox wagon down the Long Kloof in the Eastern Cape "to the Knysna forests where Shaw met with his accident & his black girl met her god . . .," a reference to George Bernard Shaw's *The Adventures of the Black Girl in her Search for God,* written in 1932. She told Millin, "I hope I am not rash to be setting out on this journey — but I've long wanted to do it, & the old friends at the farm I always go to in the Long Kloof [i.e. the farm of Thys Taute] have arranged it for me — to set out from there on the 5th [of January, 1934] . . . ." She would trek as they did long ago by covered wagon; such a trip would provide, she was convinced, the experience and the details that she required for descriptions in her nascent novel. Later, she would continue her research in a less rigorous way in the archives of Cape Town's libraries.

Smith would do little actual writing of *Winter Sacrament* during this stay in South Africa. Illness dominated her visit, as it was to dominate the remainder of her life. She wrote to Swinnerton of "this constant struggle against a sort of *niggling* ill-health which really affects my eyes & keeps me many days in darkness . . . ." In September, 1934, she wrote to Ethel Campbell (who constantly encouraged her to write), "I have *really* begun to work," but she was not working on *Winter Sacrament.* She was preparing the collection of childhood sketches that she had written for her sister years before — then, "*perhaps*," she said, she would begin the other. But the work was slow and, as always, tedious. She continued to spend days in darkness, and attacks of neuralgia regularly plagued her.

She returned to England in 1936 and, with a legacy willed to her by a friend, was able to rent a small attic in London. Here she hoped to be able to work on her novel without the difficulties of living with her sister, Dorothy Webster, in Dorset. But she did not write in her new home either: she was a "prisoner of my attic" and "caught cold in my throat and in this cold weather can't get rid of it." She moved back to Dorset.

In 1937, Smith and her sister went on a brief tour of South Africa. She told the *Cape Argus* that "she was here on a purely holiday visit, and had no intention of gathering material for another book on South African life in the Karoo." In 1938, back in her attic apartment in London and still suffering from ill-health, she told Ethel Campbell, "I'm getting on *very slowly* with my work." The winter of 1938-1939 was a very difficult one for her, and at the beginning of the new year it was clear that she would have to give up the London apartment. She wrote to Swinnerton, telling him that she had "nothing good of myself as a writer to report — The bitter winter used up all my physical energies & numbed all my mental ones — & everything I tried to do seemed so worthless that everything in turn was destroyed." It was not the first time that she had destroyed parts of *Winter Sacrament.*

She began the last two decades of her life in illness, sorrow, apprehension. And as she became progressively aware of the rapid narrowing of her life and her inability to escape that, she centred her attention on the minutiae of the immediate community of Dorset. The weather and its apparent effect on her health were to become routine excuses for her inability to create. She struggled with *Winter Sacrament,* but with little hope now of completing it, for that part of her that was discipline, Arnold Bennett, was gone, and thus her writing found-

154

ered. No one could replace Bennett — not Frank Swinnerton, not Sarah Gertrude Millin or Ethel Campbell; her relationship with him had been exceedingly complex, and went beyond the encouragement of a pupil by a teacher.

Her poor health persisted through the war years. In 1944, she "was most unexpectedly bitten in the face & above one eye by a friend's dog." She summed up the state of her health for Swinnerton: "I am never as strong as I sometimes *hope* I am — & never as ill as I sometimes *feel* I am — I vary too quickly I'm afraid between the ups & downs of depression . . . ." Later, in October, she told Swinnerton, "I have the unreasonable feeling that if only I could have a spot of South African warmth & sunshine I should be able to do all sorts of things which are beyond my power in the cold & damp of English winters — But in this I am almost certainly wrong! — And anyway it is impossible for me to return to S.A. just yet." When her financial ebb was at its lowest, Sarah Gertrude Millin began to send cheques to her. These were not good years.

Considering that her writing had hardly progressed at all during the period of the war, Pauline Smith wondered if she lacked her father's wisdom: "Is *that*, perhaps, why I can't write my novel? It is there in my thoughts day & night, yet I can't ease my mind of it — & feel always, with distress, that I am failing Arnold's faith in me."

1949, a good year for *Winter Sacrament*, was to be her last productive year. *The Little Karoo* was republished by Jonathan Cape that year, and there was some hope that *Platkops Children* would be filmed. She completed the introduction to her new novel, a chapter entitled "Background to Platkops", and in July she sent it to Swinnerton. "The kindness of your letter this morning," she wrote, "gives me courage to send you the enclosed — It is the beginning of the book that I have so long been anxious to write — *Winter Sacrament* — (the coming together of various simple people for the quarterly communion of their church in Platkops dorp) — But I am now so doubtful about ever achieving it that I wonder if I ought to offer this to Cape as an ending to the L.K., which would in some respects explain how the village & the district in the Little Karoo in which I spent my childhood remained for so long so isolated . . . ." Swinnerton found the chapter "beautiful"; however, he also insisted that the chapter should remain the introduction to *Winter Sacrament*, which she must get on with. She wrote, "And I will go on — though it will have to be very slowly, for I am really not very well at present — & at times a little frightened about the future . . . . And if I *can* achieve it I will, I feel, owe Winter Sacrament to your insistence!"

But *Winter Sacrament* was never to be. She could not bring herself to write, using first the war, then family obligations, and finally her own health and the weather as reasons for inactivity. What she did write, she destroyed. "The very very little that I've been able to put together," she had told Swinnerton in November, 1945, "has cost more blood toil & sweat than it can ever be worth — yet I just somehow go on, for I feel what I'm trying so hard to do is *worth* doing if I can ever achieve it — & that it is something that ought to be done for S. African people before my generation passes out of ken — I've just realised how *pompious* [taking a pronunciation from her childhood] that sounds & am horrified! For what I'm trying to do is as simple as all my S.A. stories are, & God only knows why it should cause me such labour & misery!"

So it was that, stricken by continuous illness and crippled by old age and a dimming memory, fearful of her financial state and ever more dependent on her sister towards whom she harboured decidedly ambivalent feelings, Pauline Smith stopped work on the novel. After 1955, her health declined rapidly. Her correspondence was also affected. "I have tried several times to write to you," she told Millin in July, "but so *stupid* were my efforts that I tore them up in despair." In the same month, she told Swinnerton, "I am *not* ill, only very very tired." In 1956, she complained of "the feebleness of my body!" and of being "a *very* shaky feeble 'old lady'." She was seventy-five years old in April.

In 1958, she was able to write to William Plomer, "I wish I were a stronger & a younger woman & a more *courageous* one

– But I am, you know, only a rather timid one who finds herself frightened at times by her seeming success." *Winter Sacrament* was no longer mentioned. In 1959, on the 29th of January, Pauline Smith died. Her sister told Millin, "She became quite incapable of making any effort latterly, but I always hoped that, when this trying winter was over, things would be easier for her . . . ."

Harold Scheub

Acknowledgements
Correspondence, Pauline Smith to Frank Swinnerton, Arnold Bennett to Jonathan Cape, Cape to Bennett – University of Cape Town Libraries, Manuscript Division.
Correspondence, Pauline Smith to Sarah Gertrude Millin, Dorothy Webster to Sarah Gertrude Millin – University of the Witwatersrand Libraries, Manuscripts Collection.
Correspondence, Pauline Smith to Ethel Campbell – Killie Campbell Museum, University of Natal.
Correspondence, Pauline Smith to William Plomer – Strange Collection, Johannesburg Public Library.

BACKGROUND TO PLATKOPS

Within the north-eastern boundary of the Platkops district in the Little Karoo, where the Aangenaam Hills sweeping north from the Teniquota mountains in abrupt bare ridges of red and yellow rock bring a strange fantastic alien beauty to the sombre foothills of the great Zwartkops range, lies a winding and fertile valley which takes its name from the river flowing through it. This river, the Ghamka, enters its valley by way of a narrow twelve-mile gorge which, in cleaving the mountains from south to north gives men here a natural, but difficult and at times impassable, corridor from the Little Karoo to the Great. As the river flows south-west its valley gradually widens and the foothills, losing height, sink at last to the level of the low flat-topped hillocks of the open Platkops plain. In the heart of this plain — across which far to the south rise the Aangenaam hills and the Teniquota mountains shutting the entire district off from the sea — lies Platkops dorp. And here, a mile beyond the old homestead of what had once been Platkops farm [Bakenskraal], the Ghamka joins the river Baaken [Olifants River] and is known as the Ghamka no more.

Throughout its length the Ghamka, fed by storm-freshet in the Great Karoo and by winter rainfall and snowfall in the Zwartkops mountains, is a treacherous river, dwindling quickly in times of drought to a single trickling thread in its sandy bed or to a chain of stagnant pools among its slaty rocks, and 'coming down' in wet weather in sudden swift and violent floods which frequently change its course. But the soil through which it flows in valley and plain is good, and though again and again the Ghamka has failed them both in drought and in flood, the Plat-kops men who farm here are proud of their inheritance and jealous for all those water-rights to which the passage of the river through their lands entitles them. They are proud also of the fact that it was on the banks of the Ghamka that, in the days of the Dutch East India Company, and in the year 1759, the first white men to settle in this region of the Colony of the Cape of Good Hope had made their homes.

In 1759 the plain between the Teniquota and the Zwartkops ranges formed part of the district of Swellendam by which, fifteen years earlier, the Company had enlarged its boundaries eastward from the Stellenbosch district to the Gamtoos river, and northwards from the Indian Ocean to the great Zwartkops range beyond which lay the waterless plateau of the Great Karoo. The new district had included thus both the grass-veld south of the Langeberg and Teniquota mountains and the wide dry stretch of open and broken country to the north of those ranges known as yet only to hunters and explorers and called by them the Little Karoo. Though this northern region, so difficult of access, came now within the jurisdiction of the Swellendam Landdrost and Heemraden it was at first only in the coastal belt, where Stellenbosch men had long been sending their cattle to graze and where protection and control by the Company could be more easily maintained, that settled farming was encouraged. And here grants of land were made by the Company to men and women bearing the names of Dutch-Calvinist officials of earlier generations who, when their term of service ended, had elected to remain in the Colony; and of French-Huguenot refugees to whom in the years of persecution the Netherlands government had offered asylum at the Cape. Among these trekkers came also little family groups of 'immigrants and orphans', brought out from time to time in the Company's ships for the Company's benefit as 'agriculturalists, vine-dressers, craftsmen, schoolmasters and sick-comforters'. And throughout the Colony it was such as these who were the begetters in time and circumstance of a new race for this new world — a race to be called 'the Cape Dutch' in the nineteenth century, 'Afrikaners' in the twentieth.

Here then between the mountains and the sea in the new Swellendam district these settlers cleared and ploughed the veld for their cornlands, planted their vineyards and orchards and, having at first no homes but their outspanned wagons, built in due course white-walled gabled houses in which to rear their many children. Here across the grass-veld in which they grazed their cattle went the rough wagon-tracks by which the produce of their lands was taken in comparative ease and safety to the

159

Company's stores at the Cape. Here in Swellendam village on the Breede river was the Drostdy [magistrate's office] from which the Swellendam Landdrost now ruled his district in the Company's name for the Company's profit. Here, with its Pastorie [parsonage] was the white-walled gabled church of the Reformed Faith to which men, women and children journeyed many days across the veld for Quarterly Sacrament or Yearly Thanksgiving. And here, as elsewhere throughout the Colony, arose from time to time independent, obstinate, righteous, difficult and adventurous men who in just or unjust resentment against official control, sought escape from it by the simple expedient of removing themselves, their wives and their children, their cattle and their slaves beyond the immediate reach of the Landdrost's authority.

Two such men had been the cousins Cornelis van Eeden and Stephanus Coetzee, whose trek from the Breede to the Ghamka after a quarrel with the Landdrost was but one of the many family migrations unrecorded in the history of the Colony yet having place there as surely as has the epic of the Great Trek by which all are overshadowed. Though always in time the Company overtook these wanderers and established again its authority over them — enlarging, if need be, its borders to do so — in each succeeding generation throughout its rule and, later, under the rule of the English, did men in grievance set off in search of the freedom which seemed forever to lie yet farther to the north. For Cornelis van Eeden and Stephanus Coetzee, however, the crossing of the Teniquota mountains into the plain beyond brought freedom enough. In this region of the Little Karoo, though still within the Company's borders, they were safe from swift or frequent interference by the Swellendam Landdrost. For here, north, south, east and west around their wide solitude, mountain ranges strong as the hills of the psalmist, rose like a rampart between them and the outside world — a rampart which, in the physical isolation it imposed upon them and in the Biblical sense of security it held for them, was long to influence the way of life and the trend of thought of all who came to dwell within it.

Here, then, the trek of the cousins had ended, and here in due course 'loan farms' on the Ghamka were granted by the overtaking Company to 'Cornelis van Eeden and Stephanus Coetzee, agriculturalists come lately over the mountains from the Breede River'. Cornelis, settling in the valley with his young wife Suzanne Arniel, had called his lands there Louvain after the province in France from which her people had come. Stephanus in the plain had named his farm Platkops, after the low flat-topped hills upon which his beacons were set.

So with these cousins was the white man's story of what was later to become the district of Platkops begun. And slowly through the closing years of the 18th century and the opening years of the 19th came other men and women over the mountains to add to its chapters. These later families settled not only on the Ghamka but among the foothills of the surrounding ranges, in valleys where the soil was good and where water could be led to their lands. But for all alike, wherever they made their homes, Platkops farm in the heart of the plain made their natural meeting-place and became in time the centre of their small universe. To rumours of the happenings in the distant world beyond their mountains these men and women paid little heed. Yet in those same years, through which they so peacefully ploughed their lands, planted their vineyards and read their Bibles, corruption was bringing the Dutch East India Company, with certain of the Colonists in open rebellion against it, at last to its downfall. While the Cape itself, becoming a pawn in the European revolutionary and Napoleonic wars, was captured by the British in 1795: given up by them, after the Treaty of Amiens, to the Batavian Republic in 1803: recaptured and occupied by the English, at war again, in 1806: and ceded finally to Britain by the Treaty of Paris in 1814.

These upheavals, taking place so far beyond their own horizon, had meant little to the few scattered families in the Platkops plain, but in 1811, under the rule of the occupying English, there had come a minor change which had touched them closely. This was a subdivision of the Swellendam district by which the narrow forested coastal belt immediately to the south of the Teniquotas and the Platkops plain immediately to the north of those mountains, were together proclaimed the new district of Princestown.

It was in the pleasant southern shade of the Teniquotas, and on the edge of the forest-country that the English built their court-house for the new district and planned their first village in the Colony of the Cape of Good Hope — a village of wide grass-bordered streets shaded by giant forest-trees, with low white-washed thatched houses standing back from the roadways in deep gardens watered by dark mountain streams. And here the first small company of Colonists from Britain — government officials and employees, artisans and tradesmen — was established as a small English community. Later — drawn by reports of mountain forests in which elephants were still to be hunted, and of heath-veld and grass-veld in which lesser game abounded and through which mountain streams broadened out into rivers, rivers became lakes, and lakes linked up with the sea — came English officers, garrisoned at the Cape or on leave there from the East, eager to purchase estates on which to spend their fur-lough or to which to retire with their families when their term of service ended. And on these estates in the wild green beauty of the forest-country they built their pleasant colonial homes, bringing to them their English servants and estate craftsmen, their English speech and outlook, their English culture and con-servatism, and the ordered leisurely ways of English country life.

For these English settlers in Princestown village and the sur-rounding forest-country, the dry bare plain to the north of the Teniquota mountains had no attraction whatever. Nor, over those difficult mountains, could they make easy contact with the slow-moving slow-thinking Cape-Dutch folk who dwelt there, whose speech to them was but a patois and in whose simple Biblical way of life they saw but the crudities of an isolated peasantry. Thus once again the barrier of their moun-tain ranges played its part in the lives of Platkops men, becoming a dividing line between two races of colonists — the English of Princestown, the Dutch of Platkops: each strong in its own tradi-tions and each by that very strength hampered in its understand-ing of the other.

162

While south of the Teniquotas a new way of life was thus beginning, north of the mountains the old went on with but little change. True, authority — and alien authority — was now much nearer to Platkops men than it had been in the days of the Swellendam Landdrost. But it was still authority based on Roman-Dutch law which the British had retained for the Colony, and it was still authority administered from the far side of their mountains. And though within a few years the English built a pass over the mountains by which it was possible, but not yet without danger, to take their produce to the Princestown market, it was Platkops farm which remained, and not Princestown which became, the centre of their small world. Here, in the heart of their plain for all who journeyed from east to west, from north to south over the mountains and home again, were outspan and meeting-place, welcome and rest, food and drink for man and beast. Here news was gathered and spread abroad, letters were left and called for, and the Government Gazette could be read. Here, for all who had corn to grind, was the only water-mill north of the Teniquotas. Here, built by the grandson of the first Stephan Coetzee, was the workshop of old Kramer the Hollander whose skill in the making and repairing of wagons was long the pride and boast of Platkops men. Here were the 'Hok' [lock-up] and the stocks in which evil-doers were held secure until they could be taken under escort over the mountains to Princestown gaol. Here, close to the giant fig-tree under which in earlier days the Swellendam pastor had held yearly service for those too old or infirm to make the long journey to the Breede, was the white-washed, mud-walled, mud-floored church to which from his new church and parsonage in Princestown village the Princestown Predikant now came four times a year to administer the Sacra-ment. Here, in short, at Platkops farm, were all the small begin-nings of village life. And here, when in a general scheme for the opening up of the Colony English engineers succeeded in building a safer and easier pass across the Teniquotas, was the site chosen by the government for a second township in the Princestown district to be known as Platkops dorp.

For all who, in earlier years, had come to it across the plain,

Platkops farm had had the simple beauty of a green oasis in a dry and thirsty land, with the distant mountains always in view. As a village it was, in sharp contrast to Princestown in its forest shade, little more than a makeshift, and for long its only beauty lay around the old homestead left standing among its vineyards and orange groves in the centre of what was to be, in time, the Hoog [High] Straat. On each side of this street — which was in fact but the deeply rutted track by which from north and south wagons had reached the homestead — the farm-lands had been divided into erven to be sold as building plots for the shops and houses of the new township. But the sale of these plots was slow, for there was little at first to tempt men to settle here. Not until, some years later, a further division of districts was made, and the plain between the Teniquotas and the Zwartberg range was proclaimed the new district of Platkops, did changes come. For now, over the mountains by the new pass, for the building of the new district's gaol and the making of the new district's roads, came Englishmen, Irishmen and Scotsmen engaged by the Government at the Cape as stone-dressers, masons, carpenters, wheelwrights, roadmen and smiths. And for the housing of these men and their families the village of Platkops, in a long straggle of mud-walled thatched cottages along the river bank, began to grow.

Towards the new-comers brought thus into their midst the Cape-Dutch in the Platkops plain had from the first a kindlier feeling than any which had been possible between them and the English settlers south of the Teniquotas. These men and women came among them not as members of a ruling or leisured class or as those in service to that class, but, for the most part, as immigrants of humble stock who had little to bring to their new country but sturdy independence and a determination to maintain it, skill in husbandry and craftsmanship, and, for some, bitter memories of the hungry forties and of hardship suffered through the loss of their commons by enclosure. Their outlook on life was thus one which the Cape-Dutch colonist by tradition and experience could understand, and between Dutch and Scotch there was, further, the bond of their Calvinistic Faith.

But it was, perhaps, to the calamity of a cycle of 'bad years' by which the newly-proclaimed district of Platkops was so quickly overtaken, that the friendship between the old settlers and the new owed most. In those disastrous years, in which drought and rinderpest, fire and flood brought ruin to many districts throughout the now English Colony of the Cape of Good Hope, far to the north, beyond the Orange River and the Vaal the Dutch of the Great and later Treks had succeeded at last in establishing and gaining recognition for Governments of their own. And up to their kinsmen in the new Republics went little companies of ruined and embittered men from the drought-stricken districts of the Cape. Even from the Platkops plain did several of the younger men set forth through the flood-wrecked Ghamka poort with the old hope of promised fortune to the north renewed. For those who remained, however, came fortune of another kind, for the continuing ordeal of suffering shared by all Platkops men alike within their mountain ranges drew Cape-Dutch and English, Irish and Scotch into the blessing of friendly fellowship which was to last long after the desperate need for it had passed — to last until the century drew to its close in the tragedy and bitterness of war against kin, war against friend.

As yet, however, this war of man's making lay in the distant future, while the calamities visited by God upon all His people alike in the Platkops district, belonged to the recent past and the still precarious present. For it was to a winter in the late 1860's — that decade of strangely varying fortune for the Colony of the Cape of Good Hope — and to a keen clear bright morning in June, that time and its seasons had now brought Platkops men.*

* The typescript is followed by a pencilled rephrasing of the closing lines and a note by the author. The first reads:

> and to the week of the Quarterly ['Winter', in another draft] Sacrament in Platkops dorp that time and its seasons had now brought Platkops men —

The author's note reads:

> Begin new chapter with description . . . [illegible] on that winter's morning and with description of Louvain in particular

A glance at the first section of *The Winter Sacrament* proper, will show how well P.S. effected the transition between a largely historical, semi-fictional 'introduction' and the opening chapter of her novel.

WINTER SACRAMENT

Journey to Platkops

I

In the crisp keen winter air of the Little Karoo on a bright early
morning in June an old man was journeying by ox-wagon across
the open veld of his farm in the Ghamka valley towards the
lately built Government Road which would take him to Platkops
dorp. He was Jan Cornelis van Eeden of Louvain, on his way to
Winter Sacrament, and with him on his wagon-box were his only
daughter Lijsbet Maria and his small orphaned grandchild Susannah. From other farms, far-lying among the Zwartkops foothills
and Rooi-kranz ridges, came other wagons, and as these too
lurched and lumbered across the veld towards the government
road Susannah, enchanted, saw their swaying white tents as
giant white butterflies, their long spans of oxen as giant brown
caterpillars. "Butterflies! Butterflies! Great white butterflies!"
she sang. And, like a bird whose swift brief ecstasy is spent in a
single burst of song, at once grew still.

Old Jan Cornelis, looking across the valley, could see neither
butterflies nor caterpillars, only the slowly-moving wagons of
distant neighbours – the Fouries of de Dam, the van Niekerks
of Vergelegen, Dirk Lategan of Doornkraal and, from that portion of his own farm of Louvain known as de Hoek, the widow
de Neysen and her son Matthys in their donkey-wagon – all
bent upon the same errand as himself. He was a short broadly-
built silent man whose secret grieving for the death of his wife
many years earlier had become with time a gentle melancholy
into which he had withdrawn for solace in all later sorrows. He
was a good farmer, but had never been a rich one, and was now,
like many another throughout the colony, a poor one. Of all the
children born to him only two had survived infancy – his daughter
Lijsbet Maria, the eldest of his family, and his son Arniel, by many
years the youngest. And Arniel had been swept to his death by
the Ghamka in flood three days after his young wife had died in

166

giving birth to their only child Susannah. To many in the valley Susannah was thus the child of tragedy and woe. She was, in fact, a happy child — friendly with all around her, black and white alike, and on terms of surprising intimacy also with the stern Calvinistic God of her race. To old Jan Cornelis in his secret grieving Arniel's Susannah had become a little singing-bird in a land where few birds sang. To her beloved Tan' Lijsbet she was, and had ever been, the most precious of many cares.

Lijsbet Maria van Eeden was a woman in her fifties whose care and concern for others was so spontaneous and enduring, so natural and unself-seeking that it was accepted as their right by all in the valley, herself among them. That she had never married was a fact which had long ago ceased to be a matter of comment in the district, and if she had ever loved who was there that now remembered it? She was a quiet woman, unhurried in all her ways and movements, and unhurried too in her speech, and wherever she went in time of need compassion and comfort went with her. All children loved her and to them, as to Susannah, her rather long, calm, plain face was beautiful. In this they were right, for though in truth not one of her features could have been called beautiful it was as if, unknown to herself, some hidden grace within her quiet heart gave a beauty of its own to all.

Having eased her heart of its delight in giant butterflies Susannah, drawing closer to her Oupa Jan, thrust a searching hand into the bulging side pocket of his winter jacket and looked out upon the early morning world. And in the keen sparkling air of that June morning how lovely to this small child was all her small world! How dark rose the mountains against the blue sky! How red rose the hills against the dark mountains and how white stood the homesteads against the red hills! How clear and full of what strange magic was every sound which broke the spacious stillness of the winter veld! The crunch of wagon-wheels on the rough road with its sharp ridges of iron-stone or slate: the soft plodding pad of the patient oxen: the long-drawn cries — Lipman! Borkman! Hartman! — of the old Hottentot Dias as he ran, leaping, by the side of the span, cracking his long bamboo whip: the occasional deep Borkum! Borkum! of watching baboons, suspi-

cious of man, keeping guard among the high kranzes: the long
deep boom of an ostrich, likened so easily by the fearful to the
roar of a lion: the sharp call of a bird, and, from the back of the
wagon where they sat looking out upon the way from which they
had come, the contented low singing of Tante Lijsbet's old ayah
Deena, and of Susannah's own meidje, Klein Sara — each and all
of these enchanting early morning journey-sounds 'made music'
for the small Susannah.

And music too they had made for old Jan Cornelis by her
side. For over seventy years had he been journeying up and down
the valley about the simple business of his life to such familiar
sounds among these familiar hills. And to such familiar sounds
but among hills that as yet were strange to them and forbidding
in the hidden dangers they might hold, had his grandparents Cornelis van Eeden and Suzanne Arniel, the first white folk to seek
a home here, come journeying up the valley more than a hundred
years earlier. With them on that trek from the Breede had come
their only son Johannes, then a boy of six, and, in particular
charge of Johannes, Suzanne's orphaned cousin, Lijsbet Naude,
the beloved 'Tante Bette' in his childhood of Johannes's own
son Jan Cornelis.

It was within a wide sweep of the Aangenaam hills that Cornelis van Eeden had made the last outspan of his trek from the
Breede and here that he had burned and cleared the veld for the
ploughing of his first lands on the Ghamka. When, in due course,
the Company overtook him these lands and the surrounding veld
were, after some argument, granted to him as a 'loan-farm' —
measured, as was the custom, for the setting up of his beacons,
by the riding of his horse at walking pace for half an hour in
each direction, north, south, east and west, from the central
point of his outspanned wagon. And in the shelter of the hills
which had first given shelter to his wagon he had built his homestead.

The homestead of Louvain — so named by Cornelis to please
his wife and her cousin whose people had come from that province in France — was a long, low, white-walled dwelling,
thatched roofed and dark shuttered, with the date 1761 and the

initials C.v E./S.A./J.v E./L.M.N. roughly cut in the beam above
the doorway. This rough carving was all its ornament, for Cornelis, whose only home had for so long been his wagon, had built
his house on lines as simple as were those of that wagon, and
with gable-ends as wide and rounded as the wide-curved frame
of his wagon-tent. But time had long since drawn his bare plain
homestead into the landscape, giving it an unexpected yet serene
and fitting beauty there against its wild background of towering
black mountain and vivid red hill. Time had made beautiful too
the orange groves and vineyards, and the wide straight avenue of
cypress trees and pears planted by Cornelis for his descendants.
But time which had multiplied his orange trees and vines had not
so generously multiplied his descendants and the three travellers
on the wagon-box were the last of the van Eedens now left in
the valley, while strangers to the district farmed those lands in
de Hoek from which Arniel had been swept to his death by the
Ghamka.

2

It was of these strangers to the valley, the swaying white tent of
whose donkey-wagon made one of Susannah's giant white butterflies, that Lijsbet Maria was thinking now. The lands from which
they came lay in a crook of the Aangenaam hills not easy of
direct access from the Louvain homestead, and here, nourished
by some particular virtue in the soil and watered by streams
from the hills and by sluits dug from the Ghamka River, the
best of all Louvain tobacco had long been grown. In charge of
these lands, and making his home in the small white-washed
dwelling-house built there by Cornelis for whichever of his children should inherit this portion of his farm, there had lived
throughout Arniel's boyhood the bywoner Hans Doppleman —
a bitter obstinate grumbling old man whose mind could hold
but one thought at a time and all else must give way to it. Up in
de Hoek that one thought had been the tobacco he grew on
part shares for the Oubaas of Louvain, and through all his years
of morose and seemingly resentful labour there, Hans Dopple-

man had served his master well. Only when Arniel reached manhood and, as the Kleinbaas of Louvain chose the lands in de Hoek and the small white dwelling there as the home to which he would bring his bride, had the bywoner's feelings for his tobacco turned suddenly to something like hatred. In bitterness and haste then had he left the farm and gone from the valley to his daughter Katrinka in Platkops dorp. And in bitterness and haste but surely, thought Lijsbet Maria, yes, surely in penitence also though never once was it spoken, had he come again to Louvain after Arniel's death to work, he said, the Kleinbaas's lands for the Oubaas for so long as the pain in his chest would let him. For three years, living alone in the small white house up in de Hoek, he had worked the lands and done all that the Oubaas had wished with them. And then on a day when the wind blew cold with the promise of winter rain for all the drought-parched valley, he had come suddenly to know, by the pain in his chest, that his end was near and that he must go now, and at once, to his daughter Katrinka in Platkops dorp, for with her would he die. And at once — yet, as was always his way, without seeming haste and with but little talk — the Oubaas himself had taken him there and made settlement with Katrinka for his care and comfort so long as he should live.

Yes, thought Lijsbet Maria, watching the wagons, yes, so it had been. And how mysterious, and yet how simple when one paused to look back upon them, were the ways of the Lord in His dealings with His people in their time of need! For it was in the market-place in Platkops dorp, where old Dias had gone to rest and feed his horses, that after leaving Katrinka the Oubaas had first seen the widow de Neysen and her sons — strangers, said Dias, come from beyond the Buitekant where drought had brought them close to ruin, and trekking now by donkey-wagon, with all the little that was left to them up to the Great Karoo where Mevrou had people of her own who might yet be able to help them. So, said Dias, their Hottentot voorloper [span-leader] had told him. But, asked Dias, with the drought still so bad in the Little Karoo, where surely the rain would come first, would a man that was wise go seeking for help in the Great Karoo where there was scarce a living thing left in the veld?

170

A man that was wise would not, the Oubaas had thought, but a man that was desperate might. And once again, without haste and with but little talk, he had set about to do that which it seemed right for him to do — that which, thought Lijsbet Maria, still watching the wagons, surely the Lord had meant him to do. Crossing the market-place to where they sat by their outspanned donkey-wagon he had given these strangers greeting and made himself known to them — Jan Cornelis van Eeden of Louvain in the Ghamka valley — and had learned in return that he spoke with the widow de Neysen and her sons Barend and Matthys, trekking, as Dias had said, from the ruin of their own district up to the Great Karoo where Mevrou had still, she thought, people of her own who might be able to help them.

So the widow had spoken, and the Oubaas had answered, "Mevrou! Up in the Great Karoo so bad still is the drought that scarce a man is left there that can now help another! But see how it is in our Platkops district! Up in the Ghamka valley already the wind blows cold with the coming of rain for winter-ploughing, and there I have lands that wait but for ploughing to be green when it comes to spring. A house I have also that stands empty beside them, for this day have I brought my by-woner Hans Doppleman in to the dorp to his daughter Katrinka to die. How will it be if Mevrou comes with her sons to work these lands and live in this house and afterwards goes — when the drought there has broken and so, then, it seems right to her — up to her people in the Great Karoo?"

And the widow, whose sons through all this talk had stood silent beside her, had answered slowly, "It shall be as Meneer says. For surely if Meneer has dealt kindly with his bywoner he will deal kindly also with me. And with my sons I will come."

Yes, thought Lijsbet Maria, yes, so had these strangers first come among them — and a stranger to all in the valley was the widow among them still. She was a tall, dark, silent and sorrow-ful woman who had answered but "Yes" and "No" and "I know not" to those who had first come to give her greeting — and from that day to this she had sought friendship with none. And a stranger too, to most, was her younger son Matthys. It was as if

171

Matthys, a quick-thinking, quick-moving silent man, had time
to give to little but the ploughing and planting of the lands in
de Hoek, and to the planning of new sluits by which water could
be led to them. Up in the morning and late into nightfall out in
the lands he would be, his dog always close by his heels, and
only with children and the Oubaas did it seem easy for him to
speak. But with Barend all was different. Barend de Neysen,
with his thin fair hair, his thin fair beard and his legs that seemed
always too long for the little red horse that he rode, was for ever
trippling up and down the valley, now here and now there, on
this errand or on that, making friends wherever he went with his
pleasant ways and his easy talk, that told, men said, so little of
himself and gathered of others so much . . . . But God forgive her,
thought Lijsbet Maria in sudden distress, was there then some
evil in herself that made her fear evil in Barend?

It was at this moment that, as suddenly, out of Jan Cornelis's
care-guarded jacket pocket came the cries of a vigorously protesting small black kitten — the starveling which, some weeks
earlier, Matthys de Neysen had found straying in the veld and
brought down to the homestead to be cared for by Susannah. In
an instant all was commotion and confusion. Before Lijsbet
Maria could give voice to her amazed "But what, then, Susannah!
But what, then, Oupa!" the kitten had freed itself and was leaping wildly about the wagon to the ancient cackling laughter of
old Dias and old Deena, to the triumphant shrieks of delight of
Klein Jafta and Klein Sara, and to the slow apologetic smile of
Jan Cornelis as he looked towards his daughter. The wagon was
halted and when at last the kitten was caught and handed over
to its small mistress with Klein Sara as joint custodian Susannah,
drawing close to Lijsbet Maria's side, looked up into the dear,
kind, plain, grave face above her and pleaded, "But how could I
leave him, Tan' Lijsbet? How could I leave my little black Boetie
that cried so hard to come to the Winter Sacrament?"

3

It was not on the driver's box, but behind it, within the shelter of the sail-tent that the widow de Neysen was journeying down the Ghamka valley in the donkey-wagon which had brought her and her sons to the Platkops district. Of her sons only Matthys, walking beside the wagon, was with her, for Barend had set off early on his little red horse to see to some business of his own in Platkops dorp before the church services there began. What this business was the widow did not know, nor did Matthys. There was, indeed, much that Hanna de Neysen did not know about her son Barend and much that she feared to learn. So it was, she thought, as one grew old — one closed one's heart against possible pain, and in closing it thus barred it also against possible happiness. Happiness? Happiness? But where, even in youth, had she found happiness? Had not bitterness been always her portion? Yes, surely it had! Surely it had . . . . But God forgive her that she should say it! Had not Roelof been a good husband to her and a good father to Barend and Matthys? And was there not in Matthys something of Roelof's own goodness? Yes. Yes, in Matthys she could see again his father Roelof, a good man. In Barend she saw only Roelof's brother Hendrick, a bad one.

She leaned forward a little to look out upon the son who reminded her of Roelof. He walked steadily by the side of the span, his dog close by his heels, his gaze going quickly from koppie to koppie, from this farm to that, from one group of travellers to another, but returning always to the wagon from Doornkraal — the wagon in which, with Dirk Lategan and his wife and their many small children there journeyed also, in charge of those children, Dirk's young cousin-in-law Antoinette Malherbe. Did Antoinette, she wondered, look as eagerly across the veld to the de Neysen wagon as Matthys looked towards Dirk Lategan's? She could not tell. Antoinette had little freedom in her cousin Marta's busy household. Yet there were days, she knew, when the young girl would come with some of the elder children down to that stretch of the river bed which marked the boundary between the Lategan lands of Doornkraal and the van

173

Eeden lands in de Kloof van Louvain. Here pig-lilies grew, and maidenhair fern, and here in the river bed were to be found the smooth, rounded, water-worn stones so eagerly sought by all farm children, black and white alike, for the long spans of oxen of their favourite play. But was it for long spans of oxen that Antoinette Malherbe came to the river bed? Was it for pig-lilies and maidenhair fern? Or was it perhaps to meet Matthys? Oh God, was her cry, if it be to meet Matthys let no evil out of the past, no evil held by the future, come between them . . . . For a moment, caught by her fear, she sat rigid — then bending forward again saw the flutter of a handkerchief from the Lategan wagon, and heard, in the double crack of his long bamboo whip, Matthys give answer to this secret greeting.

From the Louvain wagon-box Lijsbet Maria too had seen the flutter of Antoinette's handkerchief, and had heard, in the still, clear air, the double crack of Matthys' whip. And how swift and deeply moving, how right though how unreasoned was the happiness this secret greeting between young man and maiden brought her! It was as if the valley were suddenly enriched by something which though as fleeting as the moment in which it had passed was yet as eternal as time itself and brought youth again to her constant heart . . . . But it was of the present and not of the past that she must now think — of the present and the future for Matthys and Antoinette. Life for Antoinette could not be easy in the crowded Lategan household, for Marta was a quick-tempered and demanding woman who spared neither herself nor others in the carrying out of her many plans for the good, as it seemed to herself, of all around her. And Marta's was the only home Antoinette now had. But it must not be for ever Antoinette's only home. Antoinette must not be for ever dependent upon Marta for a home. Antoinette, if she wished it, must have a home of her own — a home with Matthys. And she, Lijsbet Maria, with the Oubaas's help, must do what she could for Antoinette and Matthys. Even for the most fortunate the path of love could be precarious — and in worldly goods and circumstance neither Antoinette nor Matthys could be counted among the fortunate. All their good fortune must come from the strength and steadfastness of their love — and she and the Oubaas must do what they could for that love . . . .

The slow steady progress of the oxen had brought the wagon now to the last bend in the road from which travellers journeying down the valley could look back upon the farm-lands and home-steads of Louvain. And here, as always, a halt was made by old Jafta so that his Oubaas and the Nooi [Mistress] could wave their last farewells to those left behind. For this ritual Jan Cor-nelis and Lijsbet Maria, with Susannah between them, went as always to the koppie crowned by a cluster of red rocks from which, more than a hundred years earlier, Cornelis van Eeden and his wife Suzanne had looked out across the veld to that sweep of the hills in which they had seen promise of shelter for a home. And how wise had been their choice, thought Lijsbet Maria. How well had Cornelis planned and planted his vineyards and lands, thought his grandson Jan Cornelis. And was there in all the world so lovely a farm, so lovely a homestead as Oupa's Louvain? asked Susannah eagerly of God. And was answered, to her complete satisfaction, that THERE WAS NOT.

For a few moments they stood thus together in that clear winter sunshine — the last, in three generations, of the van Eedens of Louvain. Then, as her elders turned to go back to the wagon, Susannah, as always, lingered alone to wave her special farewell to old Scots Carel — the ship's carpenter who long, long before she herself was born had come to Louvain to mend a wagon for Oupa Jan and had remained there ever since. An old, old man was Scots Carel now, who lived by himself in an outside room near the great wagon-house, and not once in all the years that he had lived at Louvain had he gone back to Platkops dorp even for a day. Was not this strange? asked Susannah, seriously, of God. And was it not strange how always when she asked him to come with them to Nachtmaal in Platkops dorp old Scots Carel got a sudden pain in his maag [stomach] which doubled him up and made him too ill to do so? That very morning the pain had come again and Tan' Lijsbet had called to her not to bother old Carel and make it worse. Yet there he was now, waving back to her, and standing up straight to show that his pain was gone. Was not this strange? asked Susannah urgently of God — but could not await His answer, for there, down by the wagon, was Tan' Lijsbet once again calling her . . . .

PART 4
PAULINE SMITH AND ARNOLD BENNETT

'WHY AND HOW I BECAME AN AUTHOR' AND
'A.B. . . . A *MINOR MARGINAL NOTE*'

The short autobiographical sketch, 'Why and How I Became an Author', exists in typescript and has only once before appeared in print (in *English Studies in Africa,* vol.6, 1963; with an introduction by Geoffrey Haresnape). It records with 'honest brevity' how after the death of her father, Pauline Smith came to recreate in semi-fictional form her childhood world of the Little Karoo and how a chance meeting with Arnold Bennett, already acclaimed as a novelist, set her on the road to authorship. Short as it is, 'Why and How' reveals the extreme modesty, amounting to self-deprecatory diffidence, of the author as well as her fine sense of humour. She took her work much more seriously than she took herself (a trait rather less evident in Arnold Bennett) and her sincerity of purpose is evident in the 'apologia' reprinted below, which in itself constitutes an admirable introduction to the poignant memoir, *A.B. '. . . a minor marginal note',* published by Jonathan Cape in 1933.

A.B. '. . . a minor marginal note' will come as a pleasant surprise to readers who tend to equate Pauline Smith with Oudtshoorn and the world of the Little Karoo. South African readers, in particular, are little aware of the overseas reputation these two novels, and the Arnold Bennett memoir, earned the author; and of her life in Britain and Europe almost nothing is known. Yet from her early 'teens P.S. was no more than a visitor — though a fairly regular one — to South Africa and the last twenty years of her life were spent in virtual seclusion in Dorset. Despite chronic ill-health and extreme shyness of disposition she became — thanks mainly to Arnold Bennett — a much more widely read, cultured and experienced traveller and observer of the European scene than her initial background and modest life-style would lead one to expect. The sophistication and wit she never could command in public — or even, to Bennett's exasperation, in conversation — found expression, sometimes in her notebooks and diaries, most notably in the 'A.B.' memoir. Here we have the assured

179

style and tone of a writer moving in circles very different from the world of *The Little Karoo*; a writer capable of viewing both her own apprenticeship and the 'master's' tutorship with ironic, but appreciative, detachment. Those readers who have regarded Bennett simply as a 'father-substitute' for an emotionally dependent spinster will be agreeably surprised by the maturity of her judgments, the frankness with which she discusses both their own relationship and A.B.'s personal as well as professional life, and the firmness with which she asserts her own integrity as an artist — a quality which Bennett, though he coaxed and cajoled her in every other way, came to respect and admire.

Apart from her own acknowledgements, Arnold Bennett's *Journals* and comments on her work in critical articles and reviews attest to the support and encouragement this endearingly egotistical 'professional author' constantly provided through the long years of her apprenticeship. His belief in her talent never faltered, and his delight in her success — which he gleefully attributed to his own sagacity — is memorably recorded in P.S.'s memoir. Without his persistence, and the professional pride he instilled in her, Pauline Smith may never have produced the two major volumes by which she is today known; it is owing to him, too, that we have this remarkable record of friendship between two such widely differing personalities. The high praise accorded the memoir on its appearance in 1933, is a tribute both to its subject and to the perspicacity, tact and sheer craftsmanship of its author. *A.B. '. . . a minor marginal note'* proved to be the last substantial production (*Platkops Children* was written much earlier, though it appeared only in 1935); as one of her finest, most readable prose writings, it not only merits reprinting, but fittingly concludes the present volume.

The text of the memoir as reproduced is that of the published volume; no editorial emendations or interpolations have been considered necessary. Some initial orientation may however prove helpful, as Pauline Smith is vague as to chronology and — as usual — reticent in matters of personal identification.

P.S. first met Arnold Bennett in Switzerland in the winter of

1908-9, and was invited to stay with him and his French wife, Marguerite ('M.'), at Fontainebleau the following autumn (1909). In the spring of 1910 she again joined the Bennetts on a visit to Florence, going by way of Paris and Switzerland. There she received news of her sister Dorothy's engagement to A.W.Webster, a close friend of A.B. However, P.S. herself became ill in Florence and had to be nursed in hospital, and it was the spring of 1913 before she again visited the Bennetts — this time at their new home, Comarques, in Essex. She spent another short holiday with them just before sailing for South Africa in the summer of the same year (this was her second return visit; the first was in 1905, when she met the author E.V.Lucas E.V.L.).

She returned to England the following summer, but saw little of the Bennetts during the War years of 1914-1918. Then came, in rapid succession, the sudden death of her brother-in-law, A.W. Webster, in 1919; the death of another mutual friend, E.A. Rickards, in 1920; and in 1921, Bennett's separation from his wife. These events did not disturb the tenor of their friendship, and in the following years it was Bennett's firm guidance that saw her successfully launched as an author. Nor was their relationship affected by A.B.'s subsequent liaison with Dorothy Cheston ('D.C.'), who bore him a daughter in 1926, and P.S. found herself as welcome a visitor at their home in Cadogan Square, as she had been at Comarques or the Bennetts' George Street flat. (A.B. and Marguerite were never divorced; in 1925 she published a generally laudatory biography, but Bennett was hurt by what he regarded as a breach of privacy.) Towards the end of 1930 the Bennetts moved again, to a flat in Chiltern Court: in the next year, the strain of overwork finally took its toll and A.B. succumbed to an attack of typhoid fever. He was sixty-four years old.

E.P.

WHY AND HOW I BECAME AN AUTHOR

To neither the 'Why' nor the 'How' is there any very definite or romantic answer, but I seem to have set about it, at a very early age, with prayer. The first of my prayers, however, was not for a pen but for 'a beard like my father and a tail like my dog Tycho'. The beard and the tail were never granted me. Yet it was with the same hopeful importunity that, a little later, I prayed: 'Give me an orphanage and make me an author'. The orphanage has never been achieved, and if at last I am an author it is author of so very little that the title now embarrasses me much as, in earlier days, the beard and the tail might have done.

Though I made my wishes known thus early and clearly to heaven I can remember no remarkable or precocious plunge into authorship in my childhood. It was in fact only slowly, through years of ill-health, that I came to write at all, and though ill-health may have made me a little more sensitive and impressionable than other robuster children it did not make me an imaginative genius. It did not even make me, so far as I can remember, particularly bookish, for books in quantity played no great part in the out-of-door life we led as children in our small Dutch village in the Little Karoo. But for that very reason, perhaps, such books as we did read made a tremendous impression upon me. Among these were 'Rab and his Friends', the tales of Mrs Ewing, 'Robinson Crusoe', and the amazing and terrifying 'Fairchild Family'. But the three which influenced me most deeply, though I was then too young to realize their beauty as literature, were the Old Testament, 'The Ancient Mariner', and 'The Vicar of Wakefield'. To these three books and to my father's insistence always that our use of the English language, both written and spoken, should be simple and direct, the 'author' in me owes much.

Much too, I owe, to the unconscious storing up in my memory, through those impressionable years, of all that was dear and familiar to me, as well as that which was mysterious and strange, in the small world — set in a wide sun-parched plain, bounded north, south, east and west by mountain ranges — which made my universe. In those unhustled days, when a visit to the nearest neighbouring village meant a day's journey by cart or a several days' journey by ox-wagon 'over the mountains', the Dutch farmers among whom my father's work as a doctor lay, still lived in a primitive simplicity close to their God. Among these people we had many friends and all their way of life, and their slow and brooding talk, which fell so naturally in translation into the English of the Old Testament, was full of interest to us. Often my father took us with him when he visited their farms, and these journeys with him across the wide empty veld: the long low white-washed homesteads we came to — some bare and treeless and poor as they were bare, some set in green lands in narrow fertile valleys among the mountain foot-hills: the mountains themselves, varying always in colour, over which, once a year, we travelled to the sea: the long quiet village, its streets lined with giant eucalyptus trees, poplars and willows, to which we returned from all our wanderings with such deep content — all these things were beautiful to me as a child. And when, at school in England, after my father's death, I did at last begin to write, it was to set down for my own comfort the memories of these happier days.

These sketches of a South African childhood were followed later by others of Scottish village life, but all I wrote (and it was little) was written slowly through years of ill-health. Authorship as a career, in spite of my earlier prayers, was something that I felt to be for ever beyond me. I knew no literary people, and had no guidance in my work whatever. My only asset, if asset it can be called, was patience. And with patience I began at last to write a novel.

I had written about a third of my novel when, in Switzerland, I met my first literary critic. With the severity of a school-master this famous man asked to see my work, and with the timidity of a school-girl I gave it up to him. A few days later I was asked to tea. And after tea I was told that anybody could have written my Scottish sketches (which had found publication in a north-country newspaper): that not everybody could have written the South African sketches (which had never been published): and that the novel was no good and that the 'artist' in me, having achieved the South African children sketches, must know as well as he did just how bad it was.

This 'damning' of my novel brought me an astonishing sense of relief, and established my faith in the critic's judgment as no praise would have done. I knew nothing about the undeveloped 'artist' within me but I did know that this adverse criticism of my novel was just and that in damning it the critic had done for me what I had not had the courage to do for myself. I destroyed those opening chapters and never afterwards regretted it. And I began to work, with a clearer purpose, for this self-appointed master.

Yet, as always, everything I did was done slowly and painfully, with many long breaks. A second novel, begun in France, was ended by illness in Italy, and all the little I had written despairingly destroyed. Still the 'master' insisted that I must write – and after a year spent among our old friends in the Little Karoo I turned again to the writing of South African sketches, dealing now not with children but with their elders.

From the first these short stories, written at long intervals, won the critic's praise, but their gloom and austerity, he declared, would make it almost impossible to place them with any ordinary English magazine, and they remained in my desk. There came at last, however, a moment when even he rebelled against the austerity of these Little Karoo tales, and the 'bare bones' of my next short story, he insisted, must be 'clothed'. This story had lain for long in my mind, and I set to work upon it now in the way he indicated. But the result filled me with so despairing a sense of failure that I sent him my manuscript only half-finished, asking if what I was doing was really worth while. Three days later we met, and with the air of a triumphant fellow-schoolboy-conspirator he returned my half-finished manuscript crying: 'Now you've done it! Now you've done it! And *I've* shown you *how* to do it!' Then he added sharply, the school-boy no longer but the school-master: 'And now you'll go home and finish it!'

I did finish it. And again the sense of failure oppressed me. Again, it seemed to me I failed to do justice to these people as I saw them — so fine in their simplicity and humility, so courageous in their poverty. But I satisfied my critic. 'God knows whom I'll get to publish this,' he said, after three words of praise, 'but it has got to be published.'

It was published — by Middleton Murry in the Adelphi, and it was called 'The Pain'.

And that is how and why, so far as I can judge, I became an author.

A. B. '... A MINOR MARGINAL NOTE'

Contents

IN EARLY FRIENDSHIP

Switzerland

It was in Switzerland that I first met Arnold Bennett — at an unpretentious hotel in the hills above Vevey, where my sister, my mother and I had gone to spend the winter months, and where later he came with his wife from Fontainebleau to write his novel *The Card.* Though *The Old Wives' Tale* had been published in the previous autumn his fame as a writer had not yet reached our small English community, and he came among us as a rather disturbing element with his French wife, his high-pitched voice and difficult stammer, his riding-breeches and black silk bow, and that ruthless Midlands down-rightness which, so alarming and discouraging to others, was in my own case to lead to the enduring friendship set down for remembrance here. At dinner on the night of their arrival the elegance of his wife, and the rather jaunty swagger with which, all through life, he sought to hide his own secret diffidence, caused much comment among his fellow-guests. And when, in the *salon* afterwards, he made a rather abrupt demand for information as to the meaning of a certain stamp on the newspapers provided by the hotel management, his manner was held by the lady questioned to be lacking in the deference naturally expected of a new-comer.

But almost from the first this new-comer interested my mother, who, as a Scotswoman, was perhaps a little outside the rather conventional English circle. Of his books she knew nothing, for she read few novels. But it happened that, as Jacob Tonson of *The New Age,* he was at that time engaged in some controversy with Claudius Clear of *The British Weekly.* My mother, the only other reader of *The British Weekly* in the hotel, and, as a Scotswoman, a less critical admirer of its Editor than he himself was, recognized in one of his remarks to her the Jacob Tonson of *The British Weekly* argument and hailed him by that name. This delighted him, as, I think, recognition of his work in any form and from any quarter always did. They fell into talk together, finding a further common interest in their appreciation of Trollope, and later, unknown to me, he learned from my mother that I too 'wrote a little'.

I did in fact, at long intervals, 'write a little', and had done so ever since leaving school. But the ill-health which had been my lot since childhood, and the shock of my father's sudden and early death, from which, though years had passed, I had never fully recovered, had made me in all things diffident and despondent. All my happiest memories and my most formative impressions were those of my South African childhood and my father's companionship. For the rest, none of the adventures of youth and none of its attributes, so wonderful to me in others, had ever been mine. In all our wanderings I had remained strangely inexperienced in life, and in literature I knew myself to be ill-read. Of all these shortcomings I was painfully aware, and in company the shyness and self-consciousness they caused me made me awkward and silent. Yet in spite of this, because I too wrote a little, A.B.'s interest in me as fellow-craftsman was at once aroused, and characteristically one evening he showed it. On that evening I had been called upon to make a fourth at bridge, but played so badly that the wrath of my partner descended loudly upon me for 'dreaming' the game away. A.B., sitting reading near by, heard the hubbub, and as it subsided pushed towards me with a smile a torn scrap of the margin of his newspaper on which he had written: '*I* know why you play badly. You are thinking of something you are trying to write.'

Such was his first greeting to me as a fellow-craftsman — and one of his first as a fellow-creature. Later he asked to see, and in spite of my alarmed protests insisted upon seeing, all the little I had written since leaving school. My 'all' was but a few sketches of Scottish village life: some children's stories which were in fact memories of my own South African childhood: and the opening chapters of my first attempt at a novel. These, in spite of my agitation, he carried off calmly under his arm, telling me firmly that as a would-be author it was my immediate duty to cease to be shy about my work and to realize that whatever its first or abiding inspiration might be, writing in its achievement was a 'job' to be frankly discussed and tackled like any other.

For some days after this I lived in secret agitation and suspense – and then came an invitation to tea with him and his wife in the quiet of their own rooms. After tea, while his wife sat and sewed, he lit a cigarette and told me bluntly that 'anybody' could have written the Scottish sketches (which had found publication): that not everybody could have written the children's stories (which had never been published): and that though if I finished my novel a publisher would probably be found for it, the artist in me (having achieved the children's stories) *must know just how bad the novel was.*

No one had ever before called me an 'artist', and though I could not believe myself to be one, there was indeed something within me which knew how bad my novel was and leapt to the justice of his verdict. His damning of those opening chapters gave me a confidence in his judgment which no praise could have won, and brought me so overwhelming a sense of relief and release that it was as if he had broken down for me an imprisoning wall and drawn me out into the open air. I destroyed my novel and never afterwards regretted it. And I made a friend whose honesty and sympathy, patience and understanding, were never to fail me.

Throughout the remainder of their stay (during which he finished *The Card* and pursued the art of water-colour painting – sitting down to this determinedly in riding-breeches and black bow on a camp stool in the snow) both he and his wife showed me much kindness. And in the following autumn I was asked to join them at their cottage at Fontainebleau. Here he was to write a new play – *The Honeymoon,* and I was to begin, he had decided, a new novel.

Fontainebleau

I knew little of France, and though the thought of the new novel which he believed, and I could not believe, that I was now ready to write filled me with alarm, everything else at Fontainebleau

191

was enchantment to me — the forest, the river, the little town, the sedate square little villa safe within its high garden walls. The autumn was a lovely one, slow and warm and golden. In the prim-bordered garden the beds were still gay with flowers which the *femme de ménage* arranged in curiously stiff but charming bouquets such as, but for the paper frill, English Judges still carry to ward off the plague. There was too in the garden a round thatched kiosk where lunch was sometimes served, and from which, by some device of his own of which A. was very proud, a bell could be rung in the kitchen. The little house indeed had various devices for its smooth and orderly running which he himself had planned and in which he took great pride. And he was masculinely convinced that none but himself could manage the stove in the hall, the *salamandre* in the *salon* and the geyser in the bathroom.

Through those pleasant early-autumn days nothing was allowed to interfere with the regular routine of his work, and so silent was the ordering of the household when, after his daily solitary promenade in the forest in search of ideas, A. shut himself into his study that I, on the floor above him, never moved except on tiptoe. Yet it was my careful tiptoeing downstairs one morning for a late bath which, to the alarm of us all, drew him out of the study before his appointed time. Pen in hand, mouth set firm and chin set hard he came — to save his geyser from the dangerous manipulations of an incompetent guest.

In the lovely golden afternoons when his work for the day was done he would sometimes join his wife and me, with John the dog, in walks in the forest — marching stiffly ahead of us when we lingered to gather the deadly-looking gaily-coloured mushrooms which later, in her tiny white-scrubbed kitchen, M. turned into wonderful dishes whose sauce for me was the fear of instant death. We walked, too, sometimes, along the lazy river bank, and sometimes made short expeditions to little neighbouring towns and villages. Occasionally, but very rarely, a visitor called — the most frequent being a young man, employed I think in a chemist's shop, for whose intelligence A. had much respect. Occasionally, too, for the good of my soul and my

French, I would be sent out alone to do some household shopping, or to purchase for A. vast numbers of the five-centime stamps which at that time he obstinately insisted upon using for the postage of all his correspondence.

As quiet and uneventful as our days were the evenings spent round the *salamandre* with the aloofly beautiful cat and the dog John — M. busy with her sewing, making and remaking her beautiful dresses: A. by some tremendous and fatiguing mastery of his stammer reading aloud to us, or, sternly ignoring my misery, insisting that I should read aloud some of my own 'stuff' to him. But quiet as these evenings were they were for me the gateway to a new world of literature and art. Until now, in the varying yet narrow circumstances of my life, this world had been beyond my reach. Such taste and feeling as I had for English letters had come not from intelligence but from the deep impression made upon me in my South African childhood by the beauty and simplicity of the Old Testament stories (whose country and people were so like my own): by the spell cast upon me by *The Ancient Mariner* read aloud to me one Sunday morning when all the rest of the world was at church: and by my accidental discovery of *The Vicar of Wakefield*. Later at school in England had come a wider acquaintance with English classics, and a deeper appreciation of my father's insistence upon a just use of words, but no change in the 'set' which my mind had taken in childhood. And after leaving school a fatherless wandering life had made my reading so haphazard that much of the best in modern literature was still unknown to me. But here now, in this quiet room, by one of the moderns himself, was the world of modern literature, in France and Russia as well as in England, revealed to me.

And revelation indeed it was. If in Switzerland A. had broken down for me an imprisoning wall, here I was drawn to a hilltop where keen airs blew through new worlds of thought that were mine for the taking. Books were heaped upon me, books were free to me. And as in my own work he would, with a phrase or a word, clear away a difficulty so completely that it afterwards seemed strange that it could ever have existed in my mind, so, with a word, would he reveal beauty to me in the work of others where never before would I have seen it. To the end this was so. To the end the discovery of beauty in any form was adventure to him — and adventure to be eagerly shared. In later years I never went with him to any play or art collection without being in this same way enriched either by the downright Five-Towns common sense of his criticism, or by the companionship — I know no other way of expressing it — into which one was drawn by his own response to beauty when he found it.

These evenings which I have called uneventful, and which were in fact to influence all the rest of my life, had at times their moments of alarm, for A. had determined that under his direction I should acquire not only the art of novel-writing but that also of carrying on a conversation. In the first art his labours met with some reward, for the early chapters of my novel pleased him. But in the second I remained so hopeless a failure that he was driven at times from a ruthless severity of rebuke to the helplessness of laughter. It was laughter that overcame him at the close of a day which had brought us the only important visitor of the season — an American whose mysterious calling took him on intimate business to all the courts of Europe. With this visitor, whose talk to me was amazing, we lunched, sat for some time over coffee in the *salon,* and drove for some hours in the forest. After his departure we retired early to our own rooms and it was then that A., in the methodical act of spreading out his trousers to press beneath his mattress, suddenly disappeared from M.'s view with those garments gasping 'That girl! That . . . girl! One whole day with X. and not . . . one word to him!'

If X's visit was one of the outstanding events of those quiet weeks the arrival of a travelling circus was another. I had seen no circus since my childhood in South Africa, and was thrilled, like a child again, when A. announced that if we were good he would take us to this one. Good we may have been — taken we certainly were: walking through the lamp-lit star-lit streets to the tent and being shown there, as the élite of a small country audience, to the only baize-covered seats it boasted. Before these seats all the important events took place, and to us, as to royalty,

194

after each event the circus-master made his deepest bow. How good or how bad the performance was I was incapable of judging. Here for me — in the sawdust of the ring and the naphtha flares, in the trotting ponies and their gaily spangled riders, in the painted clown and acrobats — was romance as long ago I had seen it with the eyes of a child in a small Dutch dorp in the Little Karoo. And romance, as A. himself has so often revealed it in unexpected quarters, was to meet us on our way home. Walking silent through the silent streets we came suddenly upon a streak of light shining across the pavement at our feet. It rose from the open grille of a cellar, and into this cellar we peered. Below us, intent upon his work, and silent as we ourselves were, stood a dark-bearded hairy middle-aged man, stripped to the waist, mixing dough in the large wooden trough of an underground bakery — an 'underdog' of industry brought for an instant thus vividly into our ken.

It was romance, too, perhaps, as the artist in him saw it in every relationship of husband and wife, and in every aspect of domesticity, that lay for A. in those big and little Anglo-French difficulties and differences of opinion which arose from time to time between him and M. But this was romance as I myself came but slowly to perceive it. A's seeming harshness in dispute I could understand, for I had learned in childhood from a stern and silent English parent to appreciate the justice which governs severity as I felt it to govern A's Five-Towns bluntness of statement. I could appreciate also that exercise of self-control in argument which A., handicapped by his stammer and dependent always upon the patience and goodwill of his listener for a hearing, had learned in so hard a school. But the sudden Latin tempests by which M., in unrestrained complaint of her 'so difficult English husband', was swept through argument and protest into a vehemence that gave no pause for reason were new and strange to me, and to my inexperienced ears made straight for disaster. Strange and bewildering to me, too, after their first swift unreasoning uprising, was the sudden cessation of these storms in a calm of that frankly-calculating self-preserving hard common sense which also, and so surprisingly, is part of the inheritance

195

of her race. But from storm and calm alike relief and returning warmth and light came always at last with a single revealing phrase – *mais il-y-a des moments!* And in that reassuring phrase, holding both concession and acceptance, I felt there lay the key to their romance in domesticity.

Paris

Though his play had been finished and read aloud to us it was not until winter was upon us that we left the villa – locking up the book-cases and rolling back the carpets one evening before going to bed, and walking down the garden-path early next morning to the waiting cab in falling snow. All through the previous night owls had hooted drearily round the house, filling me with unreasonable sadness and foreboding, and when, at the Paris hotel in which we were to spend a week before crossing to England, I received news of my sister's illness, reason forsook me completely. I must, I announced, set out at once for London, where she lay ill.

In this crisis of my anxiety and distress A. took a characteristic stand. My anxiety, he declared, was natural but completely lacking in common sense. My sister was not dangerously ill, and she was, moreover, in excellent hands. My hurrying over to her would be a touching sentimental gesture, perhaps, but it could, in the circumstances, be nothing more. It might, in fact, be something less – a confounded nuisance to others. On the other hand, in Paris there was much that I ought to see, and here, with them, was my opportunity of seeing it. In short, if I left them and went I would be making, he was convinced, a grave mistake.

Having said this much in those abrupt curt sentences which, with the pauses of his stammer, gave weight to his utterances, he left me free to come to my own decision – withdrawing as it were from my unspoken mental conflict yet watching it to the end with that strange mixture of sympathetic understanding and almost ruthless detachment which gave his friendship, his genius, and his whole outlook upon life each their peculiar value.

196

He was, in fact, one of those rare beings who not only recognizes but respects the right of another to hold his own opinion and to make his own mistakes. He watched me, without further comment or attempt at dissuasion, make one of mine now. I decided to set off at once for London — and found when I arrived there that I would have done better had I remained in Paris. This he, too, learned — but his only references to the episode were those which came in later years, in moments when, as it seemed to him, common sense was again about to desert me. Then he would say with a smile, and that familiar wave of the arm which could be either welcome or farewell: 'Yes, well! But I seem to remember . . . a very . . . emotional . . . flight from Paris!' At the time, however, he said nothing. Having made my mistake it was now, in his view, 'up to me' to make the best of its consequences. So, in the conduct of his own affairs, would he make the best of any failure of his own. Never did he seek for sympathy in the result of a mistake of his own making, or, however disastrous, shirk its fullest responsibilities. Unavailing regret was a weakness to which in his way through life he gave but little of his time.

Journeying

In spite of the instability of my common sense which my flight from Paris had disclosed, I was asked in the following spring to join A. and M. again and go with them, by way of Switzerland, to Florence. We met in Paris, and about our hotel there hung a disturbing odour of river-mud and disinfectant — the result of recent floods. Much of the country through which next day we travelled was still under water, but in spite of the devastation which made M. cry from time to time '*la pauvre France*!' and in spite of the shock of discovery in the train that A. had had the forethought to get down early enough to breakfast at the hotel before starting, which we had not, our journey was a happy one. Throughout the day, indeed, A. gave much thought to food — a subject which he was convinced neither his wife nor I understood, and proof of which lay for him in M.'s purchase of two

197

lunch-baskets for the three of us instead of one each. There was, he said firmly, to be no division of two into three so far as he was concerned. M. and I might share one basket if we pleased. The other was to be his entirely. And his entirely, to the last scrap of cheese and the last crumb of roll most carefully guarded, it was. At Dijon, however, he suddenly relented, hopped out of the carriage on to the platform and returned, triumphant and beaming, with three apple tartlets and two large oranges which we were graciously permitted to share. Later, for our entertainment and his own amusement he juggled with our empty wine-bottles and tumblers like a happy dexterous schoolboy.

In Switzerland we went again to the hotel in which he had written *The Card,* and after spending a week there in lovely warm and sunny weather, went on to Milan. (All this expedition had been planned with careful economy: we travelled second class, went to inexpensive hotels, and A. kept accurate account of every penny spent.) It was on this stage of our journey that there came to me, though I did not recognize it as such, the first warning, in acute neuralgia, of approaching illness. In our hotel at Milan my little 3 franc 50 room lay up in the roof under the tiles and was reached by way of the laundry. Here, on the night of our arrival, M. found me in great pain and cried in concern and exasperation: 'My poor P.! You look like an old woman of eighty!' Next day, however, I had sufficiently recovered to go with them both to the Brera where A. wished particularly to see Tintoretto's 'Finding of St. Mark', and where, with that stiff swing of the body and upward jerk of the head which marked both his audacities and his diffidence, he announced that the time had now come for him to turn his attention to the production of paintings in the style of the old masters. (He had, in the past year, determinedly progressed with his water-colours.)

On the following day, in weather turned suddenly bitterly cold, with falling snow, we set out for Florence. Our carriage was not heated and when, to gain warmth, I rolled myself up in my rug on the seat opposite him like a cocoon, A., watching me over his glasses remarked: 'Yes, well! You may have been an old lady of eighty two days ago . . . you're a child of three now!'

198

Safe and warm in my rug I found this cold day's journeying strangely beautiful, with its snow-storms sweeping across the Lombardy plains, and later breaking, with fleeting sunshine, against the Tuscan hills where almond trees were already in blossom. It was late night and still bitterly cold when we reached Florence and drove through its wind-swept streets to our *pension* on the Lung Arno.

Florence

None of my memories of Florence are so happy as those of the little villa at Fontainebleau. Our small and inexpensive *pension,* so full, it seemed, of old maids, was almost aggressively English, and in this atmosphere A., deep now in the creation of *Clayhanger,* was ill at ease and found little relaxation from his work. The writing of *Clayhanger* was not the 'lark' which both *The Card* and *The Honeymoon* had been to him, and his persistent, solitary search for ideas and inspiration for it in the pursuit of beauty through the Florentine galleries, palaces, churches and museums was, perhaps, more physically exhausting to him than any of us, himself included, at the time realized. There were days when exhaustion kept him in bed – in a small room looking out across the Arno to San Miniato – and days of gloom in which M. and I both shared. We all suffered, I think, from the treacherous winds of the treacherous Florentine spring, and in our too-English *pension* M. had no natural outlet for her energies. She could not here make beautiful dresses, or go hunting for mushrooms and concoct wonderful dishes. If she had not here the difficulties of domesticity she had not, either, its reliefs and rewards, and when A. encouraged her to seek occupation in the writing of short stories she threw herself vehemently into this new form of creation and fought fiercely against any criticism. Her stories – written in French, for her use of English remained always 'broken' and full of surprises – were as good, she held, as her dresses and her mushrooms had been. She knew it! There was, in particular, a story about a cat. Three-fourths of this had pleased A., but the last fourth must, he said, be rewritten: it was not good. For days the discussion about the cat continued – A. refusing to call good what he held to be bad, M. refusing to believe bad what she *knew* to be *parfait* and crying vehemently that what with A.'s not seeing how good all her cat was, and insisting upon opening her bedroom window at night, life in this so-extraordinarily English *pension* was full of difficulties for a Frenchwoman.

It was full of difficulties, too, for me. The cold winds had quickly affected my weak throat, and against the depression of oncoming illness my work made no real progress. Everything I tried to write here was futile – and well and bitterly I knew it. Yet A.'s belief in me as 'artist' persisted. However bad those chapters which I read to him so fearfully might be his patience as my 'master' never failed. However harsh his criticism might sound I knew its justice and valued it even when it drove me into still deeper despair. It was in one of these despairing moments that I asked him if I had not better give up writing altogether, for I could not, it seemed to me, with all my work as bad as it now appeared, have any talent deserving of his interest. This drew from him a sharp, amazed: 'Do you think I'd be . . . such a damn fool . . . as to waste all this time upon you if I didn't *know* . . . the stuff's in you?' And to the end he stuck to his belief in me, crying again and again in later years with that same amazement at my despondency: 'But if *I* believe in you why can't you believe in yourself?'

But if my failure in my work on my novel neither exhausted his patience nor shook his confidence in the 'artist' in me, my failure as a conversationalist was less easily borne. For this failure I may have been as greatly at fault as he held that I was, but to my natural habit of silence was added a weakness of throat and a lowness of voice which made talking, at the best of times, an effort to me – and these were not the best of times. Illness was upon me, and upon him was the creative strain of one of his greatest novels. Having written 'so many thousand words' of *Clayhanger* he would come down from his room to meals in need of mental relaxation and entertainment, and with a master's right, as it seemed to him, to demand, or at least expect it of his chosen pupil in the art of conversation. Yet invariably his pupil failed him. In the obstinate, expectant, and more and more gloomy silences which he himself maintained while awaiting my next remarks a paralysis of nervousness and distress would seize me – which pressure under the table from the concerned and exasperated M. only increased. In the horror as of a nightmare I would watch his head sink slowly on to his upraised hand, elbowed on the table, and await his deep, protesting groan. How our friendship survived those meals – so vexing to him, so exasperating to M., so painful to me – I don't know. But it did survive, though to the end of it, in any company, he would suddenly pause in his own talk to break into my silences with a rebuking and embarrassing: 'Yes, well . . . but we will now await . . . a remark from P.'

Because it was in the galleries and museums, and wandering through the streets of the city that A. now took his daily walks alone in search of ideas for his novel we did little sight-seeing in his company. In the midst of all the beauty Florence offered us, each of us was indeed, at that time, strangely solitary in the pursuit of it, and often in later years, when his guidance and companionship had come to mean so much to me, I regretted the missed opportunities of these Florentine days. Yet at the time I came more and more frequently, as spring advanced, to fail even in such adventures as it was planned for me to share, through recurring indisposition affecting my throat. It was on the eve of such a failure, when a visit to the opera had been arranged, that E.A. Rickards, of whose genius A. had so high an opinion, arrived from Carrara where he had been to see the quarrying of some of the marble to be used in one of his buildings. A few days previously had come the news of the engagement of my sister to Alex Webster, an old friend both of A. and Rickards. In Rickards's talk of Webster, with whom at one time he had shared rooms, and whom I had not yet met: in his talk of his experiences at Carrara: and in his unexpected and enchanting retelling of the story of Columbine and Harlequin my silences for once passed unnoticed. Next day, the day of the opera, speech was still more difficult for me, and my throat seriously worse. The doctor hurriedly sent for called my trouble 'squinanzia' – and my ticket for the opera fell to E.A.R., whom I was not to meet again for several years.

From this attack of quinsy I made a slow and melancholy recovery, oppressed by the sense of failure not only in my work and in the art of conversation, but in life generally, and becoming again, to M.'s concern, the neuralgic old woman of eighty of the Milan hotel. Plans were now being made for our return to Paris where A., whose time-tables were always strictly adhered to, had made an appointment for a certain date, and the fear that I might add to the complications of their arrangements by not being able to travel before that date added to my many anxieties. As it happened none of us was to reach Paris by that date. Before our seats were booked my convalescence ended abruptly and dangerously in that malady of the ear whose warnings I had failed to recognize. I found myself suddenly, uncomprehendingly, back in the care of the doctor, in the care of nurses and specialist, and of M. herself. My sister was cabled for and I was moved to the Casa di Cura of the Blue Nuns.

It was in my large, bare, pleasant room there, overlooking a courtyard gay with late spring flowers and loud with the song of nightingales that, later, A. came to bid me good-bye before setting off on his delayed return to France. Though the danger of the last few days had passed I was still too seriously ill to be called upon to practise the art of conversation and, as often happened with him, concern made his own hesitant remarks abrupt and harsh. The last of these, in benediction and farewell, came from the doorway. Having marched stiffly across the wide polished floor he turned there to give me the familiar salute of the up-raised hand and to say, in the high strained voice of his solicitude: 'Yes! Well . . . see that you don't . . . make a fool of yourself . . .' and was gone.

My illness in Italy led, in its after effects, to a narrowing of my
life – and the despairing abandonment of my novel – at a time
when the success of *Clayhanger,* confirming the reputation
which *The Old Wives' Tale* had won for him, carried A. and M.
definitely into the larger world of fame and wealth. Though I
was asked in the spring of the following year, in spite of the
remembered anxieties and distresses of our Florentine adventure,
to join them abroad again, I was not well enough to do so, and
saw them only when they came to England. Here, when we met,
though I was doing no work that merited it, A. still greeted me
always as a fellow-artist, and here M. remained when he went
over to America. His visit to the States, the publication of *Hilda
Lessways,* the marriage of my sister to his old friend A.W., the
gift to me by him and M., at the time of that marriage, of the
beautifully bound manuscript of *The Card* – to show, his inscrip-
tion said, that *some* novels do get finished some time – the First
Night of *Milestones* (which he and M. did not see, being then in
the south of France), and later the transplanting of his home
from Fontainebleau to an old Georgian house, Comarques, in
Essex, are the events which stand out most clearly in my memories of that time. Others there are of less significance, perhaps,
yet clear and vivid too – such as his coming down with A.W. to
our little house in Middlesex, turning out all our music there,
calling in vain for some one to come and play duets with him,
and settling down with a wave of the hand, to play alone: of my
going with M. to his room, in some club I think, overlooking the
Embankment, and being shown from his window there not only
the 'romance' of the river, but the 'romance' of the gliding humdrum trams below us.

It was I think in the spring of the year in which they settled
in Essex that I first visited them at Comarques, but later in the
summer they took me down there again, to spend a few days
with them before I sailed for South Africa. This was my happiest
visit to the beautiful old Georgian house which was now their
home, and we were at ease there as we had never been in Flo-

rence. M. had now plenty of scope for her activities, and for A. the place had still the charm of fresh adventure, achievement, possession and promise, and if he did not now, as at Fontaine-bleau, attend to the heating apparatus himself, its efficient working by others was a matter of sharp concern and intense satisfaction to him. He happened, too, at the time, to be taking something of a holiday, for his yacht *Velsa* was lying off Brightling-sea, and it had been arranged that E.V.L. should come down to join him in short cruises from there. And the weather was lovely.

It was E.V.L. who, on the evening of his arrival, persuaded us all to play croquet. The evening was a perfect one, and the garden, with its shaded lawns, full of the peace and beauty of that slowly-waning English-summer light I would so soon be losing for the swift South African nightfall. M. and E.V.L. were partners, A. and I. I played as I always did — with strokes of surprising brilliance which made A. swing his mallet aloft in triumph, followed by spells of such hopeless incompetence that only his calm and unreproachful patience and his Five Towns determination not to be beaten saved us from defeat. The game, which with less brilliance and less incompetence on my part might have been the short one for which we had time, went wildly, patiently, doggedly on its way into the gathering twilight, with the enthusiast E.V.L. going before and hanging his handkerchief, as guidance through the gloom, over each hoop in turn. Only when the handkerchief began to fail us did our play, with A.'s caustic refusal of E.V.L.'s gently murmured request for a stable-lantern, come to its inconclusive end.

It may have been on the following evening that, after dinner, E.V.L. produced a play he was then writing and had brought down with him for A. to read. A. insisted that it should be read aloud by E.V.L. himself, and that I, as fellow-artist, and in spite of the fact that I knew nothing of the technique of the theatre, should make one of his audience of two. The reading took place in the deep window of the 'Little' drawing-room, where there was a large round table upon which E.V.L. could spread out his manuscript — for spread like a tablecloth it had to be. So far as we could judge he had written the first drafts of his acts on ordi-

204

nary pages of note-paper, and to accommodate his later additions and amendments had pinned each of these pages on to a separate and very much larger sheet, such as is used for the lining of shelves and drawers. On to these his script had overflowed from its centre source in thin long streams of amendment, and large round lakes of encircling additions. And as these streams and lakes lay in all directions around the original draft, and as the size of the shelving-paper made it necessary for the MS. to be kept flat, E.V.L.'s reading of his play was given in a leisurely but impressive perambulation round the table.

THROUGH CHANGE

Camarques in War

Into none of my later memories of Comarques does there come
again the tranquillity and charm of those lovely summer days,
or the sense of ease in friendship that was born of them. When
next I went down to stay there, after my return from Africa, all
was changed, and the peace of the old Georgian house and its
garden, and of the little village beyond its gates, had fled with
the peace of the world. Everywhere about us and upon us now
was the stir and strain, the upheaval and confusion of the business of war — training-camps surrounded us, troops were quar-
tered in the village, officers were billeted in the house, horses
filled the stables. And with this strange new ruthless activity,
enthralling all that lovely countryside, went a social activity of
tennis-parties and regimental sports in the summer, of dances
and entertainments for the men in the winter, into which, with
the management of a club for the troops in the village M. threw
herself with all the old vehemence and enthusiasm with which,
in Florence, she had written and defended her short story about
the cat. She learned now to ride, to dance a little, to drive a
small car, and, with no sense of music whatever, to sing in her
peculiar, attractive 'Eengleesh' strange little songs of her own
composition at entertainments for the men — and to sing them
with complete assurance. And all the while, with an ardour that
was at times delightful in its simplicity, and at others embarrassing in its French vehemence, she kept a keen, but not unprejudiced outlook for the work of spies in the daily happenings
around her.

In this changing world in which for M. as for many others a
sense of proportion was becoming more and more difficult to
maintain, A., not yet called to the Ministry of Information,
remains in my memories of him almost obstinately his ordinary,
everyday, well-balanced self. Upheld by his blunt Five Towns
grit and sincerity against both the assaults of war and its feverish

social activities he makes, against the background of those first three years of upheaval, a sturdy yet somewhat withdrawn and solitary figure, doggedly pursuing his own set course in the midst of those whom the call to arms had brought so strangely as guests to his house. Through all the alarms and gaieties which swept M. off her feet he stuck calmly to his regular routine of work, to his appointed hours of repose. Though he did play tennis he had not yet begun to dance and took little part in those social events of the now military neighbourhood which M. found more and more absorbing. His interest in every phase of the life around him, and in the men and women, young and old who played a part in it, was the interest of a detached observer, almost of an outsider, with a note-book. Yet behind this detachment lay the quick sympathy and understanding, the rare patience and tolerance which came increasingly to be, throughout the years, his gifts to those around him.

Though most of my memories of these later days at Comarques are curiously war-hazy and dateless, varying only with changing seasons and alarms of raids, several there are which stand out more clearly than the rest. One of these is of a bright May morning when M., not yet dressed, came up to my room with the early post and news that a short article of hers, written from a Frenchwoman's point of view, had been accepted by a woman's magazine. Her excitement was intense — had she not always said that A. was wrong and she was right about that short story in Florence? — and so swift was her vision that it was as if in those brief moments she saw the whole world of literature opening to her, and made me see it so too. Her enthusiasm delayed her dressing, and it happened later that A. coming in to the diningroom for breakfast found me there alone. He gave me a curt greeting and asked if I had heard the news. I answered that I had, for M. had come up herself to my room with the editor's letter to read to me. He stopped short, looked at me blankly, then jerked out: 'But haven't you heard . . . the *Lusitania*'s . . . been sunk?' And I remember still the sharp high note of his amazement: the sudden silence of the room: the clear bright air of the May morning as we looked out upon it through the many-paned windows: and through all my dismay my strange feeling of guilt that I had not heard his news before.

Another of my memories of that time has nothing to war-date it, but again it is spring, and again we are in the dining-room — at lunch with many others. Though by now I had written a story of the Little Karoo, which had definitely strengthened his belief in me as an 'artist' I was as far from the mastery of the art of conversation as ever, and on this day had earned his rebuke for my silence when some turn in the general conversation made him suddenly announce that if I would agree to it, he would, on the understanding that I conversed, arrange a lunch for me in town with any writer that I cared to name — but that he well knew that I would not accept his offer. I did accept it — on the spur of the moment and as much to my own surprise as to his and to the surprise of those around us. And 'George Bourne', author of *The Bettesworth Book* was the writer whom I named. Out at once, lest I should repent of my temerity, came his note-book, and to that lunch, shortly after my return home, I went. But of my talk on that day I remember not one single word: it is George Bourne's, of country fairs he had known in his youth, that lingers still in my memory.

It was on one of my visits to Comarques at this time that I again met E.A.Rickards, now married and accompanied by his young wife. Though illness had swept me so suddenly out of his ken in Florence he greeted me here as an old friend, plunging at once into talk and giving, as always, strangely vivid expression to all his moody passionate, quivering reactions to life. All that he said, full as it was of the egoism of his genius, interested me intensely, but I made too good a listener for A., determined as ever that my voice, too, should be heard at his board practising the art of conversation. After our first meal together he ruth-lessly parted us, and thereafter we sat at opposite and far sides of the table with A. as master and host between us.

Throughout this visit we suffered much from raids, but none of our experiences on the previous night was so shattering, so amazing, so strangely and diabolically beautiful as those recounted by Rickards at breakfast on the following morning. To A., who

208

met all these visitations with Five Towns common sense, Rickards's tortured, sensitive response to them was always, in the sincerity of its egoism, the response of true genius, and he greeted it with respect. To those, however, whose egotism on any subject lacked the inspiration he found in all Rickards's talk he could be more severe – as happened one evening when, from M.'s small flat in town we dined in Soho with a lady of some importance who declared too emphatically that she never tolerated snobs among her acquaintance or her friends. Snobs were in fact swept so majestically out of her circle that A. broke into her talk at last with a dry: 'Yes . . . well . . . it seems to me *you* . . . must spend most of your evenings . . . *alone.*'

George Street

Through the later phase of the war we did not often meet, for I was living now in Dorset and seldom free to leave home. Thus it is that of his work at the Ministry of Information, so full of interest to him at the time, I know little. But at the close of the first year of peace another short story I had written pleased him and brought me up to town to see him. It had been arranged that I should spend the week-end with my sister and brother-in-law, his old friend Webster, and lunch with A. and M. on the Monday at the flat in George Street which, though M. still had her smaller flat and Comarques had not yet been given up, was now to be their principal home. But I did not go to George Street on the Monday, for on that day after an illness of forty-eight hours my brother-in-law died.

Though at the time I scarcely realized it, my brother-in-law's death, ending for A. as for me a friendship that had meant much to each of us, strengthened in our sense of common loss the surviving bond between us, and it was at this time that the tone of his letters to me changed to a deeper note. But family circumstances and my own ill-health kept me almost wholly in Dorset and only when flying visits took me up to town did we meet. On one of these visits I failed to report myself to A., as he had come now to expect, and he wrote asking why I had refrained from doing so. I answered, truly, that from both his accounts and M.'s of the busy social life they now were leading my only chance of seeing him had seemed to be at breakfast – an hour I had not liked to suggest, but now would, for our next meeting. By return of post came a note of two sentences asking me to come and breakfast with him. And this, on my next visit to town, I did, spending a night at the George Street flat with them both to achieve it. It was in talk at this breakfast that A. realized suddenly my need of books and my difficulty in getting them in our Dorset village. And with the curt 'That must be seen to' which heralded so often his prompt and practical help to others as well as to myself, he rose from the table, disappeared into his study and returned with an armful of volumes – the first of a regular supply posted to me at home and abroad which ended only with his death.

This brief visit to the flat, with its one quiet evening – the last, it proved, that I was to share with them both – and its friendly family breakfast for three next morning, was happier than any I had spent at Comarques in the crowded war-years. Yet in spite of its peace for me there came from M. at its close, as I bade her good-bye, the old impetuous complaint of the Frenchwoman married to the 'so difficult' Englishman who would never understand her as one of her own race would surely understand her – complaint through which I waited in vain for the once reassuring *mais il-y-a des moments* of romance in domesticity, and which, without this relief, hung ominous as a storm-bearing cloud in what had seemed to me so fair and serene and prosperous a sky.

It was earlier in this same year, 1920, that I had come once again into touch with E.A.Rickards, whose short term of war-service had ended tragically in a hospital for consumptives. In the sanatorium near Bournemouth to which he was eventually sent I was able on A.'s behalf to visit him, and to the end the brooding, wilful, sensitive egoism of his talk was full of interest to me. But the end came quickly, and following so soon on the death of his old friend Webster made for A. the second of three definite breaks with the past in three succeeding years. The third and last came towards the close of 1921 with his separation from M. Of the causes which led to this, and made it at last for him inevitable, A. seldom afterwards spoke, and never with bitterness or reproach. In this crisis of his life, as perhaps in others, the hesitancy of his speech which compelled him always to weigh his words stood him in good stead, and if much was spoken at this time which in justice must afterwards have been regretted it was not spoken by him.

IN LATER YEARS

The Man

At the time of his separation from M. I had feared, as one of its
almost inevitable consequences, the gradual loss of A.'s friendship through the natural drifting apart of our lives. But my fears
were to have no justification in fact, for though I had, and could
have, no place in his world, nor he in mine, our friendship, with
its roots in both, was like some tree of quiet steady growth
whose shade and shelter, for me at least, increased with every
year. The fact that our worlds lay apart was accepted by us both.
Mine could only have been boring to him. His sounded often
alarming to me – and he liked, I think, to make it sound so. He
liked to impress me, even through my fears, with its gaiety and
riches, its wit if not its wisdom, its rush and glamour and importance, as he himself, sometimes perhaps against his better
judgment, was so eagerly impressed. But though his delight and
my fears came so often into our letters – always was my anxious
'May you be as wise as you think you are' met by a dogged asser-
tion of wisdom in his conduct of life – never was our friendship
shaken. His response to the glamour of wealth, as to the romance
of the big hotel and the successful business, was, indeed, strangely
like the innocent unenvious wonder of a child whose memories
of starved unlovely days made this new world in which he had
now an established place a fairy-tale of his own planning at last
come true.

It was, I think, the fairy-tale-telling child in him that made
him delight in playing the part of the 'card' as he played it to the
end. To be known by his up-standing tuft of hair: to be famed
for his fob and the cut of his clothes – which, however elegant,
he wore always a little stiffly: to have his assured place in a First
Night audience, though he slept through many a First Night
(Why, he demanded of me once, when by some chance I had
attended a first night in other company than his, Why was I in
one of the front rows of the stalls and he somewhere behind IN

A DRAUGHT?) : to be in the know as to the best-but-not-yet-famous restaurants in Soho — these were among those lighter vanities which endeared him as another Denry to his friends, and of which he himself would at times take stock with humorous detachment. Humour played indeed a deeper part in his life than many realized, and typical of that humour was his quick, detached turning of it against himself when occasion arose — as when, hearing someone accused of a too great liking for publicity he smiled, pointed first to his topknot and then to his fob, and so took his place beside the damned.

But deeper than any vanity, and any humorous appreciation of it, was his feeling for beauty in whatever form it revealed itself to his vision: deeper than any vanity was his response to what he held to be 'fine stuff' in literature, music and art: deeper than any delight he might take in his playing of the part of the card was the integrity upon which his real success in life was built — his fearless common sense: his blunt, courageous honesty in the stating, accepting and facing of facts: his unaffected indifference to what might be said or thought of him, as artist and man, so long as his own conscience and purpose were clear. And with these things went the rare understanding of and patience with the difficulties and failings of others (of all faults the superiority of 'spiritual pride' was to him the least easily forgivable) which won him the loyalty of those who served him: an abrupt yet humorous and protective courtesy of tenderness towards the very young and the very old (he was 'Uncle' to many of the young who had no claim to call him so, and to the old he showed always something of that deference which had made him write daily to his mother through all her later years) and a readiness to help promptly and practically any whose deserving need was brought to his notice. No appeal for help that seemed to him justified was ever made to him in vain, and to none, whatever the result, did his help bring the after-grudge of the giver.

This was the A. of the later years of our friendship whom I came so much better to know when I found that, whatever might be the changes in his way of life, I was expected to report myself to him when any of my rare exoduses from Dorset

213

brought me up to town. At first the prospect of dining with him or drinking China tea with him alone filled me with alarm, for the art of conversation was not yet mine. But that fear passed after the first of our quiet evenings together – evenings that were to be spread through all the remaining years of his life – when, as we drove through streets whose brilliant changing lights he called upon me eagerly to note, I asked despairingly, with the memory of my long silences grown suddenly heavy upon me, if I had bored him, and was answered as the very young might have been answered by him: 'That is a question that should not have been asked . . . a question that should not . . . have come into your mind.'

And with that question unasked – though not always, alas, wholly absent from my mind – our friendship pursued its course, A. making it his habit to keep free for me an afternoon or evening, and sometimes, but more rarely, a morning whenever I came to town: writing to me regularly of the social and literary worlds in which I myself had no place: and coming into Poole harbour to see me when cruising in the *Marie Marguerite*.

The Master

Whenever and wherever we met it was always my work that was A.'s first subject of concern – though 'work' seemed to me too big a word to use for the little it was ever in my power to produce. Every short story I wrote was written not in the joy of creation but in the pain of it, through a misery of diffidence and despair and indifferent health which only his belief in me and his dogged persistence gave me courage to overcome. I wrote with little hope of publication for we both believed that no editor (A. had approached several) would accept short stories so uniformly tragic as those of the Little Karoo – and I knew that I could write no others until my mind was relieved of its burden of these. So, at intervals, had most of the Little Karoo tales been written, sent each of them in turn to him for criticism or approval, rewarded each in turn with the three words most precious

214

to me: 'It's fine stuff' – and returned to their drawer in my desk. But with the seventh came a change.

This seventh tale, *The Miller,* was in his opinion one of the best things I had done – but it was, he held, only a sketch, and in reading it he had suddenly perceived, comprehended, and understood what was the matter with all my stuff from the public point of view. I took for granted throughout, it seemed, a complete knowledge on the part of the reader of the conditions of life in the place and time of which I wrote, and while I had a strange and little-known state of society to deal with, I gave no explanations, and did not exploit the quality of rareness and remoteness in the material with which I dealt. From the British public's point of view my stuff was simply suspended in the air. There was no path up to it and no key to its enigmas. I gave it no point on the earth's surface, and who, in my lack of thought for my public, was even to guess that my scene was laid in South Africa? Geographically, sociologically, climatically, ethnologically this ought to be explained and set forth, and I could read either some Zola or Chapter 1 of *The Old Wives' Tale* for an example of what he meant . . . . Yes, this was what was the matter with me, and though it was curious to him that he had never thought of this criticism before, now that he *had* thought of it he realized, he said, how clever he was, if slow in the uptake!

With my next short story, which had lain for long in my mind, I tried to do as A. had suggested, but, half-way through it, was so oppressed by a sense of failure that I sent my half-finished manuscript up to him in despair. A few days later I came myself to town and dined with him alone one evening as usual. After dinner, in his study, he produced my MS., his verdict upon which I had not dared to ask, and circling round the table like an excited schoolboy, waving the manuscript above his head, stammered triumphantly: '*Now* you've done it! Now . . . you've done it. . . . And *I* . . . have shown you . . . *how to do it!*' His delight and satisfaction, and my own relief, brought me suddenly close to tears – and as suddenly his mood changed. 'Now,' he said firmly, '*you go home and finish it.*'

215

I went home, and through one of the long spells of neuralgia to which my illness in Italy had left me subject, and in much heaviness of spirit, I managed slowly to finish the short story called *The Pain*. It was summer-time, and before I had had time to make a fair copy (I had used my typewriter, not my pen, in the writing of it) a wire came from A. saying that he was bringing his yacht into Poole Harbour and would expect to see me there. I went down to him, taking my MS. with me for him to read at leisure. He put aside the manuscript, decided suddenly that a two or three days' cruise to the Isle of Wight and Southampton would do my neuralgia good, sent me home by car with a fellow-guest to break this news to my family and collect some clothes – and before noon next day we had set sail from Poole and run aground on a sandbank.

Though this short cruise, and his own pleasure in it as owner of the lovely *Marie Marguerite,* delighted me it did not cure my neuralgia, and it was through a cloud of pain, at breakfast in Southampton Water on my last morning, that I heard his curt emphatic verdict on my eighth short story: 'Believe me, the thing is fine! God knows whom I'll get . . . to publish it . . . but it's damn well got . . . to be published . . . .' Later, as we drove in a dilapidated musty-smelling four-wheeler to the station for my train he asked abruptly if I had a second copy. I told him that I had not. He swung round upon me in amazement and cried, with something like anger, 'But, good God! I've *posted* it!' And I was instructed there and then to make carbon copies in duplicate of whatever I wrote in future.

It was to Middleton Murry that A. had posted my MS.– and by Murry, in a quick and generous appreciation which meant much to me and which gave great satisfaction to A., it was accepted and published almost immediately in *The Adelphi.*

The Pain aroused Murry's interest in my earlier tales of the Little Karoo, and drew them from my desk – some to find publication in *The Adelphi,* all to be published later in book form by Jonathan Cape. Convinced that I knew nothing whatever about business matters A. acted for me in all these transactions, and in every other connected with my work, as self-appointed

literary agent – a part which, like that of the 'card', I think it
amused him to play, and which, through all its minute and
troublesome details, he played for me to the end. He liked particularly, I think, to impress upon me the commercial value of
my work, and to draft letters on my behalf which, calm and
clear and precise as they were in their statement of terms, could
never have been so unwillingly accepted by publishers and editors
as they were by me. Sometimes alarmed protests on my part
would cause delay and draw from him a cold and patient rebuke.
Was he or was I in charge of these affairs? Was he or was I the
experienced author, the successful business man? Did I mean to
let my stuff go for less than it was worth, and if so why? Why
should I propose making gifts to those whose legitimate purpose
it was to make money out of me? Did I imagine that publishers
were fools? Or editors philanthropists? Then he could assure me
from long experience that they were neither. Business for them
was business, and so, he was determined, it should be for me.

So, patient and unyielding, would run his argument until he
had gained his way, but only on questions of business did he
ever thus ruthlessly impose his will upon mine. (Ruthless, however, on this point he was, even to the extent on one occasion
of a bombardment by telephone and wire against some contemplated step on my part whose foolishness, he later declared with
coldness and severity, had cost him a full day's work.) For the
rest I was free, after the resolving of any difficulty I took to him,
to follow my own course in that clarity of vision which a word,
a phrase, a few curt sentences of suggestion or criticism from
him, always restored to me. In life I had neither his courage nor
his honesty in the stating and facing and accepting of facts, but
in my work I could set down nothing which I did not 'see', or,
often painfully, feel and know to be true. I could not *make*
situations to suit the needs of a story as a story – all I could do
was to describe, often after a long waiting, that slow development in the lives of my characters which lay outside my will.
This he understood, and when, as in the case of *The Father* –
the last short story I wrote before his death – a scene he thought
necessary was impossible to me because I could neither see it nor

217

feel it grow, he accepted, though he still regretted, my inability to write it. My slowness, my long spells of illness or indolence or both, my despair and despondency, my failure, in spite of all his efforts, to learn the art of compassing an article or story within a given number of words — these things must all have been trying to him, yet his faith in me persisted, and his patience, as master, never failed.

It was after Murry's publication of *The Pain*, and in the yacht once again, that A. made me sketch for him the plot of the novel which he held it was now my duty to write — and which he believed, though I did not, that I was now competent to write. Like all those of the Little Karoo series this tale had lain for long in my mind, but with each attempt to write it as a short story I had found it getting too big for me. This admission pleased A., for it was, he declared, proof that I had a novel 'in me' — and so far as it went this was good. But the rest, it seemed from his manner as I sketched my plot and characters for him, was not so good. Point by point, sitting undisturbed in the gay 'Lovat Fraser' saloon of the gently swaying *Marie Marguerite*, we went through the story of *The Beadle* as I saw it — and with every point he tussled, refusing to pass on to the next till he had this clear. This almost harsh insistence upon clarity of detail, this sharp questioning of every statement I made about my people as I saw them, filled me with apprehension of doom. From the way he tugged at them, shook them, worried them in his determination to try their truth and their strength I felt that all my characters to him were suspect and my projected novel worthless. The swaying of the yacht became almost unbearable to me, the silence of the gay saloon, when my voice and courage failed and I could tell him no more, damning and intolerable . . . . And presently, unbelievably, bringing me close to tears as his reception of the half-finished *Pain* had done, the silence was broken by painful difficult speech in the high-pitched voice — 'I wish to God . . . I had thought . . . of this myself!'

In spite of A.'s confidence in me I found the writing of my novel a slow and painful business. Never, it seemed to me, did what I wrote do justice to my people as I saw them, and never,

218

in spite of A.'s satisfaction with each portion in turn, would I be able to bring the whole to completion. Even his amazed and oft-repeated 'But if *I* believe in you why can't you believe in yourself?' could not rid me of my sense of failure and foreboding. Ill-health may have added to my diffidence, for my work was frequently stopped by illness, and once again throat trouble drove me into hospital and was followed by a slow and despondent convalescence. These breaks were accepted by A. with infinite patience – but never were they allowed to shake his determination that my book, at whatever cost to myself, should be finished. When I was advised by a too kindly and anxious doctor that my work must be stopped or its 'hold' upon me would kill me, A. told me bluntly that my novel had got to be finished even if it killed me – adding tersely for my comfort that it would not kill me. He was right, and I knew it, and his bluntness roused me to laughter. Somehow, in pain and misery, my novel was finished, and the news, as he had commanded, wired at last to him in Paris. His reception of that news roused me once again to laughter. He was damned, he announced, if he did not now take a holiday to recover from my labours.

It was immediately after the publication of *The Beadle* that I sailed again for South Africa. On my return, a year later, I wrote very slowly, and through much unreasonable misery, the long short-story called *Desolation*. This brought from A. not the three words of praise I had hoped for, by letter, but a telegram of two words only. Of all I had written *Desolation* I think moved him most.

Later, knowing nothing of the technique of the theatre, and at times appalled by my own presumption, I wrote, because I had always *seen* it so, a one-act play called *The Last Voyage*. I was at work on this when I was asked to come up to town to meet my American publisher and A.'s old friend George H. Doran. Before this meeting with Doran there came the usual investigation by A. as to the progress of my work – and I found myself, with A. clutching my manuscript, involved in a wandering discussion of my plot and characters which landed us now in the Strand, now in the Adelphi Arches, and finally in a mysterious dark archway peopled by mysterious foreign-looking men, each carrying a small despatch case or a brown paper parcel – some of the 'under-dogs' who were presently to serve us as waiters in the great hotel above.

The Last Voyage, though he found it dramatic, did not satisfy A. as my short stories did, and it was another short story, *The Father,* that we next discussed together – this time in a bitter wind and brilliant sunshine on the terrace overlooking the tennis-courts at Monte Carlo. Here we had met for lunch – he and D. from Antibes, I from Alassio – and here when *The Father* was disposed of he grumbled much at the damnable Riviera climate.

Such was the unfailing interest, persistence, patience, common sense and guidance to which, with his belief in me as 'artist' I owe whatever is of worth in the little I have written.

The Professional Author

Of his own work it was not easy for A. to speak, and only rarely when we met did I learn from him in talk more than the general scheme of any novel he was writing or its progress in the number of words achieved in a stated time. (With the 'Books and Persons' articles of later years it was different, and in these one often found repeated, unhampered by his stammer, the curt emphatic pronouncements of earlier discussions. It was perhaps a sense of escape from his handicap that gave these articles so personal and often dogmatic a vigour. One might or might not agree with him, but here, to take them or leave them, in full and uninterrupted expression were his views on books and persons.) But occasionally, with his novels, came moments when he sought, in spite of the effort it cost him, to give something more than bare outline or numbering of words – and in one of these, on the first evening I dined with him alone, he told me abruptly and painfully of the 'servant girl' who was to be the heroine of the novel he was then planning – *Riceyman Steps.* On that evening, after dropping me in Baker Street, he went himself to Clerkenwell to see the meeting-place of Elsie and Joe by night, and many months later it so happened that I was on board the yacht with him and his secretary, storm-bound in Poole harbour, when the galley-proofs of *Riceyman Steps* were sent down to him. These he brought me, and all through a wild grey day I read them, sitting wrapped up in rugs in the deck-house while A. paused from time to time in his own reading to ask diffidently from his corner 'You like it? You . . . like it?'

I did like it, and in his relief that I did, as in his anxiety that I should, was that complete and unaffected modesty about his greatest books which was so unexpected and yet so fundamental a part of his character. The honest card and craftsman in him might swagger a little at times both in life and in literature − the genius never did. He was, I think, proud of the craftsman, but always a little shy, a little uncertain about the genius. It was indeed almost as if he himself, quick as he was to recognize and appreciate the genius of others, never knew how great, at its best, was his own or wherein it lay − just as he seemed never to realize, and never did admit, that his fine and conscientious workmanship did not justify some of those lighter tales and novels which he so doggedly upheld or explained as 'larks'. Once from such a novel I withheld the welcome he had looked for and then, seeing his sudden school-boyish dejection, cried impulsively, 'But I do like it, you know! I do like it'. His answering smile brought relief to us both. 'No, you don't,' he said firmly. 'No, you don't. But I'm hanged . . . if I can see . . . *why!*'

I do not think he ever 'saw why' about that particular book or any other that disappointed me, yet, though his talk about his work remained always difficult to him, he came, as time went on, to write more and more freely of it in those weekly letters which, wherever he might be, it had become his habit to send me. These letters by his own wish were always destroyed, and their destruction − hard as I myself found it, so full of enduring interest did they seem to me − gave him in many matters a freedom of expression, impossible to him in speech, which he valued. In this way, through the last year of his life, I was kept in touch with his work on *Imperial Palace* − the theme of which, when first he told me of it, had caused me some misgiving and regret.

221

With the 'romance' it held for him a luxury hotel had seemed to me a subject which might carry him too easily into his impressionable second best. Yet anxious as I was I had to admit that my fears were founded partly upon prejudice. Because in my own work my most deeply-felt interest lay with the poor and the narrowing circumstances of their lives I was apt to be less than just to the rich. A. with unprejudiced eye saw the difficulties and generosities, the humanity in weakness and in strength, of both. His concern, like his justice, was even, not passionate or partisan, while the genius of his vision was that of clear sight, following with sympathy and understanding the working of the mind and the heart, rather than that of insight, sharing painfully in the turmoil of the soul. And when at last *Imp. Pal.,* as he called it, came down to me I acknowledged myself beaten by that genius. Here was no 'lark' but something which seemed to me as true to its time and circumstances in one phase of English life as was *Clayhanger* to the time and circumstance of another. Here was a world which I had no desire to share and of whose worth and importance compared with the worlds of *The Old Wives' Tale* and *Clayhanger* and *Riceyman Steps* I remained still sociologically and artistically doubtful, made enthralling to me by his own sanity and reason in dealing with it, his wisdom that was so much more than worldly though it might be less than spiritual, and his tolerance which came neither from indifference nor from weakness but from that wide understanding of human nature which 'marched' with his own sturdily surviving nonconformist conscience and refrained from judgment.

A.'s letter of relief when he learned that against my expectation and inclination I 'liked' *Imp. Pal.* and ranked it high among his books, touched me much and gave me measure once again of the diffidence which lay so close beneath the pose of the 'card' and the pride-in-skill of the craftsman. With it, but in a curious detachment from it, went the sturdy independence and integrity and the practical common sense by which he was more generally known, and which gave to his genius its particular place in the world of English literature. Yet this place in his own eyes was never more, and never less, than that of the 'professional author'.

Whatever claims he might make with generous enthusiasm for
others, for himself his most emphatic claim was the right to be
regarded as, first and foremost, a 'professional author' who knew
his job. So, in emphasis of this fact, would he sometimes sign
himself – 'A.B. professional author' – and so, I think, would
he wish to be judged. Writing was for him above all else the 'job'
at which he made his living, and to the best of his ability and
the satisfaction of his urgent conscience he fulfilled his job. For
the rest, inspiration when it came to him came not from some
divine afflatus lifting him above his fellow-men, but from that
human and humane comprehension of their ways of thought
and action in the humdrum romance of everyday life which kept
him always one of themselves – a little wiser, perhaps; more
patient and more kindly, detached and yet concerned, cocksure
and yet diffident – a man from the North touched surely with
the greatness of genius yet determined to hold his Five Towns
own against its dangerous uncertainties.

AT '75' AND '97'

Cadogan Square

When A. gave up the George Street flat, at the end of 1922, reports of the size and importance of the house he had taken in Cadogan Square, and particularly of its bemirrored doors, made me feel I should never have courage to visit him there. My fears, however, were tackled promptly by A. himself. I was mistaken, he announced, in thinking the house too large for him, for he had sublet the top floor as a four-roomed flat to his secretary and her mother. Two other rooms, his secretary's office and his own study, were, I must remember 'business' rooms – and that disposed of six rooms in the new house. Moreover in spite of the size which to me seemed so alarming he had found it impossible to find place in the rest of the house for all the furniture he had had in the flat and some of it was now stored in the basement. Moreover again the new house cost less to keep up than the flat had done. Having thus satisfactorily to himself disposed of my doubts for me, he added with disarming self-gratulation that '75' was 'rather a noble thing in houses', and he hoped I would like it.

I found to my surprise that I did like it – chiefly for the friendliness and quiet of the smaller drawing-room at the back of the house and the study above it, and for the mulberry tree which grew in the terraced garden, also at the back, and was reached through his secretary's office. The Victorian dining-room, familiar to me at the flat, delighted me too, its centrepiece of wax-and-feather flowers on the mahogany dining-table taking me back to an old toll-house on the Outeniqua mountains known to me in childhood. Here on our journeys over the mountains to the sea we had always outspanned for a meal, and while the meal was preparing had sat in the *voorhuis* where one of the chief ornaments had been just such a bouquet under a glass shade, on a bracket on the wall. On the opposite wall hung the crude and much more exciting picture of a race being run on a bright green race-course. But as our ayahs had taught us that horse-racing was a sin, and that to look at this picture would surely bring us within danger of hell-fire it was with our Christian backs set firmly to the race-course that we sat, gazing at the feather-flowers. And in something of that old childish habit I think I must from the first have turned my back on the mirrored doors at '75'. At any rate I ceased almost at once to be aware of them, and found, as all through our friendship I found, that much which had alarmed me by report had little or no significance when we met, and that those evidences of wealth which I had pictured as embarrassing to my lack of it slipped quickly into the background for us both after A.'s first delighted school-boyish display of them. 'Noble' though it was in the way of houses, what mattered to me most at '75' was the welcome given me by the faithful Fred when he opened the front door: by A.'s secretary, Miss Nerney, when I reached her book-lined office looking out upon the mulberry tree: by A. himself when I went up to his quiet study: and later, when D.C. had joined him, by the added welcome of their little daughter Virginia in her bright gay nursery at the top of the house.

It was in the spring of the year following his separation from M. that, at the Repertory Theatre at Liverpool A. had come to know Dorothy Cheston, then taking part in one of his plays there, and the friendship to which this meeting led influenced all the rest of his life. Though between him and M. there had been no divorce, time for A. had proved the breach to be final — a view of the case made for him the more emphatic by the publication of M.'s book in 1925. Thereafter his life was more and more closely linked with D.C.'s, and with the birth of their daughter in 1926, '75' became their joint home. This meant for A. the companionship of a young and beautiful woman whose keenly artistic but wayward mind never ceased to interest and surprise him. It meant also a big readjustment in the scheme of his life, and the acceptance by his friends of a situation whose difficulties and responsibilities he himself never sought to evade. Work still remained for him what it had always been — his first thought. But close upon that first thought came always now a second – 'Yes, well . . . but I've got to look after Dorothy and the infant!'

Into the larger social life of the literary world and that of the theatre, which both before and after D. joined him A. led at '75', and of which each week he found time to write to me, I myself was never drawn. Only rarely on one of my rare visits to town did I make one of his guests at the smaller dinner-parties given to his more intimate friends, and even these had their alarms for me – moments of embarrassment when he declared that though none present might have heard of me I '*could write*', and pauses in which he called for and awaited the 'next remark from P.' But on all my flying visits – spent, some of them, with his sister Tertia, in whose young daughters I had found in infancy and childhood that strange unity of Five Towns determination of character with the rounded beauty of Donatello's children which I was to see repeated again in his own Virginia – A. planned for me some quiet expedition with him to a picture-gallery, an exhibition of modern painters, a play, or a wandering in regions all unknown to me that evolved itself as we went along. (It was, I think, on the first afternoon that I had tea with him at '75' that we went exploring the narrow streets and slums which lie within a stone's throw of that noble thing in houses. They would, he said, surprise me. And they did.)

In this way, after that enquiry into the work I had done, was doing, or, too often, alas! had failed to do, which he held it his first duty to make, I went with him to South Kensington – to see, on our first visit, Bicci di Lorenzo's terra-cotta Virgin and Child: to the Tate to see the Blakes and the French collection: to Dulwich Art Gallery – on a lovely summer afternoon which made our drive there enchanting – to see the Poussins: and to Burlington House, to the Italian Exhibition, to see under his guidance much that I had failed to see in the difficult days and wasted opportunities of our Florentine spring. (At the time of the Italian Exhibition I was on my way to the South of France, and it was ten o'clock in the morning that, watch in hand, he met me on the steps of Burlington House.) And it was on expe-

226

ditions such as these — when A., overcoming his stammer with
a sweep of the arm, a jerk of the head, a shrug, a smile or a single
revealing word, made known to me what he wished me to see
— that I came to realize the companionship born of his eagerness
to share with others all that he himself found most beautiful
and satisfying in art.

Expeditions of another kind were those made from the yacht.
Though the long South African voyage was misery to me I loved
the short cruises into which I was sometimes drawn by A. as
one of his guests on board the *Marie Marguerite* — sailing always
within sight or scent of land from port to port, from bay to bay,
along the English coast. How full of romance, seen from the
yacht, seemed all the summer shore: how romantic, from land,
the dark blue yacht serene on a lighter sea, or bounding from
wave to wave of sullen grey! This was 'voyaging' as I could best
appreciate it, but never was I allowed to do so in idleness and
content. Even on board the yacht 'work' came first in A.'s scheme
of things and always I was expected to report on the progress of
mine, and never until his conscience was clear of his did A. himself join in the holiday activities of his guests.

   It was after his work for the day was done that we drove
together one afternoon from St. Peter Port in search of those
more adventurous members of his party who had set out earlier
on foot to bathe in a distant cove. Our crossing from Falmouth
to Guernsey two days before had been so stormy that all the
guests on board, and several of the crew, Fred as steward among
them, had been laid low, and upon A. himself, who, grimly, had
not succumbed, had fallen the care of the victims. For twenty-
eight hours that tempestuous crossing had lasted, and through
all its miseries there had loomed from time to time the stern
apparition of A., clad in thick Jaeger garments, bearing in a soup-
tureen the mess of shredded wheat which he insisted, regardless
of protest or consequence, should be eaten while he waited. But
the distresses of the storm now were over and the succeeding
calm full of an enchantment which, for me, embraced even the
patriotic old Guernseyman whose carriage A. had hailed on the

227

quay-side, and whose tongue as we drove never ceased to sing the praises of his island and its bailiff. Every few yards did the old man slow down to point out to us some natural beauty of the island, some further evidence of the bailiff's power and wealth. A. bore this quavering song of praise and consequent slow progress with great patience until for the third or fourth time we were halted in front of a vast expanse of glass-housing and called upon to admire it as yet another manifestation of the bailiff's interest in the tomato-growing industry. But A. had had enough now both of tomato-houses and the bailiff and into the old man's talk he broke with a ruthless: 'Yes, yes, but you drive on! There's nothing more I want to hear about the bailiff . . . I know . . . all about him . . . I'm . . . *his cousin!*' After which surprising statement the old man, reduced to suspicious or respectful silence, drove steadily on, sitting sideways on his box, keeping as far as possible one eye on his horses, the other on the bailiff's cousin.

It was after the birth of his daughter that A. gave up the *Marie Marguerite.* He could not, he said, afford two luxuries, and of the two the bright gay nursery at the top of the house came first. Here it was that on all my visits to town now I went to call upon that most Bennetty of Bennetts — the small, determined, Five-Towns-Donatello Virginia. Sometimes A. himself would join us, and in any opposition of will in which, on the nursery floor, Bennett met Bennett, I saw in him again, as long ago I had seen it, that Victorian severity founded upon justice which I had known in my own childhood. Upon obedience, in spite of the trend of modern nursery-philosophy, he insisted — and with infinite patience and no loss of dignity to either, from his strong-willed small daughter he won it. The doings of 'the infant' came frequently into his letters (to which sometimes were added strange hieroglyphics of her own) and, like the various activities and theatre ventures of her mother, were reported by him always with a curious tender and benevolent detachment and a mellowing irony which was directed partly against himself. It was, indeed, a mellowing of all 'the Five Towns man' in him which friendship throughout these later years revealed — a mellowing due to that last 'romance in domesticity' of which, in spite of all its difficulties and complications, in spite of the sacrifices of time and habit it involved, and the additional cares and anxieties it brought him, he himself said emphatically, 'I would not have missed it for anything.'

Chiltern Court

When A. wrote telling me of the contemplated move, at the close of his lease, from '75' to a flat in Chiltern Court, and gave me, proudly, the exact measurement, in feet, of the corridor I should find there, my first thought was one of unreasonable regret for the loss of the mulberry tree on the terrace reached through Miss Nerney's office — a regret which bore no weight with A. whatever. I regretted too, more reasonably perhaps, the loss to him of the quiet of Cadogan Square, but was assured that the noise of Baker Street did not trouble him in the least — and remembering how calmly he would work through the hum of an electric engine on board the *Marie Marguerite* which drove me nearly to distraction I had to admit that this might well be so. Yet in spite of his patient assurances and in spite of his enthusiasm for the new steel book-shelves and the modern furniture he had chosen for his study, my anxiety persisted, and was, indeed, as time went on, increased by a note of strain which seemed to me to run through all the determined satisfaction of his letters.

In November the move to '97' was made — and reluctantly from A. came the admission that even with all Miss Nerney's help the sorting out and arranging of many thousands of books on his new steel shelves had somewhat overstrained him. Still, the job was now done, and he would expect me up to see the result and report on my work before he and D. left for France, which they were to do immediately after Christmas when her work at the Fortune Theatre would cease.

A week before Christmas I went up and down for two nights

only. On the first of these I was one of A.'s guests at a small dinner-party at the new flat, and it was across the lighted candles of what I had been delighted to find was still a Victorian dining-table, that, in a pause in the conversation of George Doran, Robert and Sylvia Lynd, and G.B.Stern there came from A., in the unbroken habit of over twenty years, a call for 'the next remark from P.' On the following evening, D. having had to set off earlier for the theatre, we dined alone, and after dinner I was taken by A. down all the impressive length of the corridor to view on the return journey every room which opened off it. The tour ended in that strange modern beauty of his study of which he had written so proudly, and here, in the surroundings still unfamiliar to me, began the familiar, patient, determined, reveal-ing inquiry into the progress of my work – the sketching for him of its next 'book'. I was, he decided, to report to him again in February, when a visit to town would make another break for me in the English winter I dreaded, and when the Persian Exhi-bition could be visited. In spite of his obvious tiredness – about which, he insisted, I was over-anxious – nothing was forgotten, nothing was omitted.

To this last talk there came an unexpected ending, when Fred, much troubled, brought word that a young poet had called with a most urgent request that A. should see him. I rose to leave, but was stopped by both A. and the young man – whose urgent errand was to beg A. to use his 'influence' to stop if possible the lying gossip appearing in the Press concerning a well-known com-poser whose tragic death had occurred a few days earlier. The young man's loyalty to his friend and his fierce resentment against the Press were like a wind that swept around us in that unfamiliar book-lined room, and only when its bitterness was spent did A. himself speak out. He had, he said, no such 'influence' as the young man wished him to exert, nor did he think that any action now could benefit his friend. The man was dead. What was said of him could matter nothing to him now. His friends knew the truth – was not that enough? As for the gossip – ignore it. Such stuff as that was 'news' in the Press to-day, but forgotten by the public to-morrow . . . .

He spoke in that curious detachment which had made him always indifferent to personal gossip about himself — a detachment difficult for youth or poet to accept, but now, it seemed to me, increasingly marked in him by fatigue. For a little while the talk went on, and when all had been said that it seemed in his power to say — though what relief and to what resolve it brought the young man I could not tell — the three of us left the flat together: the poet making his way down Baker Street, A. walking with me to my hotel through the peaceful gloom of Dorset Square, and there taking leave of me. Next day I returned to Dorset; a week later A. and D. were in France.

On Christmas day I received from him as usual a package of books — and found among them, for the second year in succession, a copy of Bertrand Russell's *Outline of Philosophy*. Pleased as I had been to get my first copy I hoped he did not mean to make a habit of giving me one yearly, and told him so, begging him to send me rather, for the following year, *The Clayhanger Family* in one volume which I had seen on one of his new steel bookshelves. My anxiety to break him of 'the Russell habit' amused him, but through all his letters from France — Jo Davidson the American sculptor was doing a bust of him at the time — ran the note of fatigue.

In England the winter I had dreaded was cold and gloomy, and, like the bad workman I was, I complained bitterly to him of the lack of sun as cause of my idleness. But for idleness he would accept no excuse, and dealt firmly with me for mine. My work at whatever cost to myself must proceed. As for the weather — I must light a fire and a lamp and forget it.

The letter bringing me this advice reached me on a day when from my desk I could see the mists sweeping in swift grey clouds across our Dorset moors towards the sea, with now and then a sudden lifting that revealed the rich dark brown of winter heather, the lighter brown and gold of thick coarse grass. In spite of its gloom the day was full of beauty for me, and of a strange sense of peace and fulfilment enveloping not only the moors beyond my window but the long years of friendship which lay behind that rebuke to idleness awaiting answer on my desk. So deeply and so strangely did this sense of fulfilment move me, so clearly was the moment impressed upon my mind as marking for ever for me the realization of something beautiful and complete, that when at last I took up my pen and wrote: 'I am rebuked about the weather – but no heat of fire and no light of lamp bring me such warmth and radiance as do your letters, and after twenty-two years of friendship I say it,' it was as if I did so both for remembrance and in farewell.

Immediately on his return from France A. sent me, as proof that 'the Russell habit' had been broken, his copy of *The Clayhanger Family* signed 'A.B. professional author'. Several letters followed, each in turn increasing my anxiety, for the chill he had caught in France seemed now to have become a recurring form of influenza which his fatigue made it difficult for him to resist. Still, he hoped, he wrote, to be well enough to see me when I came up to town, as he expected me to do on the date we had arranged. On that date I went, as had been arranged, to his sister Tertia at Putney, and learned there that his illness had now been diagnosed as typhoid.

Though my errand to town now was vain, to the flat I went before returning to Dorset, and through all the changes and strangeness which illness had brought there found my welcome from Fred and Miss Nerney, from D. and Virginia the same. With Virginia, so that others might be free, I played until her bedtime. At the far end of the drawing-room, which was now half nursery, stood her dolls' house, and attached to it was a small post-office. We played at posts, Virginia dictating the letters I must write for her. The chief of these was to myself, about 'a cake with cangles on it' for her next birthday. Five 'cangles' it must have – one pink, one red, one yellow and one blue, and the last one black. I protested against the black. No little girl I knew, I said, had ever chosen black – but this one had, and black, most strangely and against all argument, her fifth 'cangle' had to be.

Through the latter days of February and the long weeks of March A.'s illness took its course, news of its varying progress coming to me regularly from Miss Nerney, from Tertia and from

232

D. As spring advanced I went when the weather was fine enough across the moors to a sheltered farm for violets grown there, and sent them up by post. 'How did she know it was my birthday?' he would ask, but the birthdays they marked for him now were not those which carried him on into old age, but back into youth and to childhood. When death came to him as it came at last, and as on that day of mist across the moors I had known that soon it must — it came not to the 'professional author' or 'the card' — but to the school-boy from the Five Towns whose fairy tale was told.